LOST HART

THE HARTY BOYS, BOOK 2

WHITLEY COX

ISBN: 978-1-989081-43-3

For Danielle Young.
You helped me sort this one out.
Without our Zoom and wine brainstorming
Lost Hart would probably still be sitting 30% done and haunting my
dreams.
This ones for you, girl!
Thank you!

CHAPTER ONE

SHITTY WEATHER, cold temperatures and a delayed flight couldn't keep him from smiling as Chase Hart stepped off the plane at Victoria International Airport.

Finally, at long last, he was home.

It'd be a few months yet before it was so fucking hot here that his nuts clung to his thigh. He would take the reprieve in stride. He never did like sticky nuts. Which was another reason he was glad to be done with Georgia.

Too fucking hot.

"Brother," Chase greeted Heath as he shook his youngest brother's hand in front of Victoria International Airport.

Heath, as always, was all grins, his shaggy blond hair appearing extra beachy and unkempt since the last time Chase saw him six month ago. "How was the flight?"

Slinging his bag over his shoulder, Chase followed Heath into the parking lot, where Heath's big black Chevy truck, a nearly identical model to Chase's, sat way at the back. "Turbulence over the strait. Had to circle six times, wind was so nasty."

"Ah, yeah, that's right. They can only land in one direction on this runway. I forgot about that." Heath clicked the fob on his truck. "What do you think of my new rims?" He bobbed his brows before heading to the driver's side.

"Way too fucking shiny," Chase said, climbing into the cab of the truck at the same time as Heath. "You don't need duallies or studded tires in Victoria. We don't get that much snow, and you're not hauling heavy shit."

Heath flashed a smile that always made women at the bar sigh. "Yeah, but isn't a man's truck a direct reflection of his cock?"

"No. A man's truck is an overcompensation for his cock."

Heath started up the engine and let it rumble for a moment. "I don't think that's right. I think a man's truck is a direct reflection, because we all know I'm overcompensating for nothing. I'm the biggest of the four of us."

"Just drive, dumbass."

"You missed me."

"Not likely."

"So how was babysitting duty anyway?"

"Stupid." Glancing out the window at the drizzly, cold February weather in Victoria, Chase rolled his eyes. He'd been hired to protect a wealthy politician's college-age daughter down in Georgia. The girl was receiving death and kidnapping threats, and her father was sparing no expense to protect his little girl.

Chase would have much rather been on the intel duty than the babysitting duty, where he was forced to share a three-bedroom apartment with Charlene and her roommate Bobby-June. But he jumped at the mission before he knew the details. At the time, back in September, he'd just needed to get away.

"Did you get *up close and personal* with the woman you were supposed to be protecting?" He didn't need to see Heath to know the man was bobbing his blond brows again.

"No. Farnsworth Price is one right-wing nutjob, but he loves his daughter fiercely. I don't think he'd be too happy to know I was banging her. Plus, her roommate is more than her roommate." He glanced back at his brother and wasn't disappointed with Heath's reaction.

"Is that so? Does Daddy dearest know about that?"

Scoffing, Chase shook his head. "Not sure he'd have paid for my services, along with a team of investigators, if he did. Guy is as white and straight as a Q-tip. Kind of looks like one, too. Would probably set fire to a rainbow in the sky if he could."

Heath made a noise in his throat and hit the Patricia Bay Highway. "Ignorant fucker. Did you guys at least catch whoever was threatening her?"

He nodded. "Wouldn't have returned home if they hadn't. More nutjobs. A few students who knew about Charlene and Bobby-June being *more* than roommates. Thought their relationship was sinful and disgusting. Thought her sexual orientation would hurt her father's run for president in the next election and figured threatening her and then eventually her death would get him sympathy votes. They called themselves The Pure Way."

"Holy shit. A big organization then?"

"About six kids. Caught them all. Just in time, too. They were planning to take Charlene and Bobby-June out over spring break. Make it look like an accident. Plans were all there on their computers and through emails."

Kids were too stupid to know not to leave a paper trail. Once it hit the internet, in an email or private message, it was there forever. The same with text messages.

Only Chase hadn't been the one to uncover all that stuff, even though that was his specialty. He had been on shadow duty and forced to just make sure Charlene didn't get hurt or kidnapped.

Heath raked his fingers through his shoulder-length tresses. "Jesus. So I'm guessing the girls' relationship is out now, then? How'd Daddy dearest take it?"

"Team kept it hush-hush. Told Farnsworth the plot was just to get him more votes, didn't tell him it was also because Charlene is gay. She begged us not to tell him. She and Bobby-June are switching schools, too. Both got into Columbia—need to get away from Daddy and the backward thinkers. Farnsworth still just thinks they're BFFs."

Heath took the off-ramp off the highway to head toward their mother's house, which was where Chase's truck was parked. "Score another one for the rainbow, I guess. Though the idea of having to hide who you love from your parents just sounds so fucked up to me. You'd think he'd love his daughter no matter what and who she loves wouldn't change that."

"You'd think." Chase pulled his wool cap out of his coat pocket and yanked it over his bald head. He chose to be bald—kind of. Unlike Heath and their eldest brother Brock, who had inherited their late father's thick hair, Chase and the other middle brother, Rex, inherited their maternal grandfather's thin hair and that horrific *M* growth pattern. Some guys could pull off the *M*, but Chase knew early on he couldn't. So he shaved it all off by the time he was twenty-five and hadn't grown it back since. Rex followed suit a few years later.

Saved money on haircuts and shampoo. But on days like today, it tended to get a little chilly, particularly around his ears, so that's why he had a wool cap collection fit for a king.

"Mom's sure missed you these last few months," Heath said, taking the back roads to get to their mother's house. "Been way less of a wreck since the last time you were gone for five months though. At least this time she could talk to you."

Scratching the back of his neck, Chase glanced back out the window. Yeah, the last time he'd been gone for *six* months, and it hadn't been by choice. He'd been in prison, and it'd fucked him up something fierce. He also hated being reminded of that time in his life. He had enough triggers and reminders already; he didn't need his big-mouth baby brother bringing it up, too.

But he also knew this was Heath's way of getting through his own issues with what had happened to Chase. Heath still felt responsible, even though he wasn't, and he also felt like they should have busted Chase out of there sooner.

That would have been nice. Yeah, he might not have the after-effects he did now, but what was done was done. At least he was still alive and in one piece, as his mother liked to remind him. Well, mostly one piece.

They pulled into their mother's driveway, his truck parked to the side, all black and shiny.

"Took the liberty of putting your winter tires on for you last weekend," Heath said, turning off the ignition.

Chase grunted a thank you and opened the cab door.

He was barely up the walkway to the front door when it flew open and just over three feet of strawberry-blond hair, blue gumboots, camo pants and a black shirt came barreling out toward his shins. "Chase!" Connor screamed. "You're back! You're back!" Connor flung himself at Chase, apparently not giving two shits that the ground was wet and mucky, forcing Chase to lunge forward in order to save the kid from eating concrete.

"Jeez, kiddo, watch yourself."

But Connor wasn't listening. He was wrapping his arms tightly around Chase's neck and rattling off information and news Chase couldn't make heads or tails of. Apparently, he was going to get a recap of the last five months in under five seconds.

Adjusting his bag on his shoulder, he propped Connor on his hip and headed inside, where his mother was standing in the foyer teary-eyed.

Chase fought the urge to roll his eyes. For a tough-cookie, single-mom sex therapist not even five feet tall, Joy Hart could bust out the tears at the drop of a hat.

"Don't even think about it," she said when Chase stepped inside and toed off his shoes.

"Don't even think about what?"

"Rolling those green eyes at me. I can happy cry when I see my children if I want to."

"Wasn't planning on it," he said, fighting a grin.

Just as he was about to remove his jacket a big, muscly beast on four legs came barreling into the foyer and shoved its nose into Chase's crotch.

"Did you get a dog?" he asked his mother, trying to push the Pitbull away before it decided to render him a eunuch.

"Diesel is Uncle Rex's puppy," Connor said. "He's the best dog in the whole wide world and I love him."

Heath stepped into the foyer, too, and shut the door behind him. "We raided a puppy mill few months back. They were breading them for fighting. Rex found little D here chained up and in rough shape." Diesel diverted his attention from Chase's crotch to Heath's, but Heath took it in stride and scratched behind the dog's floppy ears. "But he's in tiptop shape now, aren't you, buddy?" He took one look at Connor before glancing at his mother. "Baby here, too?"

Chase's mother shook her head, but not a silver strand of hair from her tight bun drifted out of place. "Stacey had to take her to the doctor for a checkup, so Connor and I have been baking cookies."

Chase's body stiffened at the mention of Stacey. He needed to get the hell out of there before she returned to pick up Connor.

Heath shucked his shoes quickly. "Ooh, cookies."

"Ginger snaps," Connor said with pride. "But Nana Joy says they don't *snap* because cookies that snap aren't as good as cookies that *mush*."

Nana Joy? When did Connor start calling his mother Nana Joy? And why?

The reason hit him like an anvil to the chest. He was calling her Nana Joy because she probably *was* his Nana now. Stacey was still with Rex, no doubt, and Joy had stepped in as a grandmother—something she was born to be. His chest hurt at the thought of Rex with Stacey, but he pushed it aside as best he could and focused on the little boy in his arms and his mother.

"Nana Joy is rarely ever wrong." Heath grinned and pushed past Chase to head to the kitchen. "Are any ready yet?" Diesel followed Heath.

"Yes, but they're cooling," Joy called after him with a warning in her tone. "I'm sending most of those home with Connor. Don't you inhale them all, you bottomless pit!"

"But I'm your baby boy," Heath called back.

"You're my baby boy bottomless pit. With two hollow legs and no self-control."

Connor still hadn't let go of Chase. He clung to him like a baby monkey, his little fingers gripping tightly into the back of Chase's neck.

"I think somebody missed you," Joy said as Chase, still balancing Connor and his bag, bent down to wrap one arm around his mother.

"We talked at least once a week on the phone," he said, knowing what she meant but feeling the need to tease her anyway.

She pressed a kiss to his cheek. "Phone calls and video chats are nothing like having you home in the flesh. I want to have a big dinner. Rex will be home next Friday night, which is why I have Diesel. Then I'll have everyone back in one town, safe and within driving distance like they should be. Let's do it on the Saturday. Brock, Krista, the kids, Rex, you and Heath."

Chase's spine straightened and he felt his face harden at the mention of Rex. Over the last five months, he'd spoken with his mother, Brock and Heath, but he'd deliberately avoided Rex and his calls. Not after his brother betrayed him the way he did.

Knock, knock.

Oh shit.

Diesel barked and came barreling out of the kitchen for the front door.

Chase's mother called his name and stopped and stood at her side, anxiously awaiting some kind of reward. She reached into her pocket and handed him a treat, which he gobbled up, sat back down on his butt and waited for more. The dog's whole body wiggled with the wag of his tail and he whimpered softly.

The door opened behind them, forcing him to step deeper into the house. His mother stepped forward to help open the door, where Stacey, looking more beautiful than ever, was wedging herself inside along with the bucket car seat carrying a much bigger, much more alert-looking Thea.

She stopped abruptly and nearly dropped the car seat when she saw him, her mouth opening to form a little O. "Chase."

He nodded. "Stacey. Hello."

She put the car seat down, stepped into his space and wrapped her arms around him. It was awkward, what with Connor still in his arms, but she didn't seem to care. "I'm so glad you're back and safe. We've all really missed you. It's been ..." Those last couple of words seemed to be choked out. "A long time."

A squawk from the car seat had Chase's mother pushing past them and pulling out a rosy-cheeked Thea. She planted a kiss on the baby's head. "Hello, my darling. And are we healthy as a horse? What's the verdict on this perfect angel?"

"Healthy as a horse," Stacey confirmed after breaking her embrace with Chase. "She's gained like four and half pounds in the last month and a bit. It's insane. Now that she's on solids, she's just packing on the weight."

"We made cookies, Mama," Connor said, Chase's neck still in the kid's death grip. "But Uncle Heath might be eating them all."

"I've only had two," Heath called from the kitchen. "Burnt my tongue."

"Serves you right," Joy replied. "Such a buffoon," she murmured with a headshake and a smile.

Organically, they all drifted into the living room. Connor finally slid down from Chase's arms, but he wouldn't leave his side. "I want to hear *all* about your job, Chase. Did you have to shoot anyone? Did you get kidnapped? Did you have to punch a guy in the face?"

"Leave Chase be, honey," Stacey said, dropping the diaper bag backpack she'd been wearing next to the couch. "Give him a chance to breathe."

Connor's nose wrinkled. "He is breathing. He's always breathing. He'd die if he stopped."

Chase snorted. He'd missed this kid, too. Connor was a fun, cheeky, smart little kid, and in the few months Chase had been hired to protect Stacey and her children, he'd grown to really care for Connor. And Thea.

And Stacey.

Chase's mother plopped Thea down on her bum on the carpet, and she instantly fell to a crawling position. "Oh, she wants to crawl so badly, doesn't she?" his mother said, staring down at Thea with so much love in her eyes. "I remember the determination and such intense focus. We dismiss it now as adults, but wiring the brain and limbs to work as one takes a lot of energy. You can practically see her synapses connecting and neurons firing."

"She's certainly getting impatient with her lack of mobility," Stacey said, taking a seat on the couch. "I've known since day one this was going to be my challenging child."

Chase's mother clapped her hands together. "Before I forget, I want to have a dinner next Saturday night now that Chase is home. Rex will be back next Friday, so I'll invite everyone. Can you guys come, too?"

Chase squeezed his eyes shut, praying that Stacey turned his mother down. The last thing he needed was his brother's relationship flaunted in front of him for hours over the dinner table. His brother's relationship with the woman Chase had fallen in love with.

"I think we can make it," Stacey said. "Can I bring anything?"

"Your spinach and artichoke dip," Heath said, wandering in from the kitchen. "You know I could drink that stuff straight." He had what appeared to be a giant sandwich in one hand and a tall glass of milk in the other.

Everyone, including Thea, seemed to be giving him the same look.

"What?" he finally asked. "I'm hungry. It's not like I'm eating all the cookies. I *do* listen." He sat down in one of the reclining chairs, set his milk on the side table and dove into his sandwich.

"Over thirty years old and you're still raiding your mama's fridge," Chase said with a headshake, doing his damnedest to keep his gaze from drifting back over to Stacey on the couch.

"You can raid my fridge until you're ninety," their mother cut in. "That's what a mother's house and fridge are for." She glared at Heath. "Though would it kill you to use a napkin? Or maybe offer to make the rest of us lunch?"

Chewing, Heath lifted his sandwich toward all of them. "Anybody want a bite?"

CHAPTER TWO

SHE KNEW when she finally saw him again, she'd feel a series of different things, one of them being relief, another being anger, and the final, the most predominant—love. God, how she loved this man. Five months apart had not diminished her feelings for Chase one bit, and yet the way he was looking at her, with hurt and confusion in his eyes, said he didn't feel the same way.

Had he moved on while he was away?

She'd heard through the grapevine that Chase was a bodyguard for a young woman in college. He'd probably become more than her bodyguard.

Just like he had for Stacey ... for one night.

She thought it would be more than just that one night. Thought that night was the start of something real, something possibly permanent.

But he'd clearly had other ideas.

He gave her a bit of comfort, a few orgasms, and then he was gone. On to his next damsel in distress, one with less baggage, no doubt, and probably a body *not* destroyed by having children.

He was trying hard not to look at her, she could tell, but as he played with Connor—who was currently trying to climb up Chase's legs while Chase held his hands—he would sneak glances at her.

And each glance gutted her more.

But she'd done nothing wrong.

They'd done nothing wrong.

After a scary day involving Connor falling on the playground and needing to be rushed to the hospital for stitches, she'd turned to Chase that night.

Not that their days and weeks hadn't been riddled with stolen glances and a sense of companionship she hadn't even felt with her late husband. Which was why she'd hoped, nay, *thought* that Chase felt something more, too. That the heated looks of longing and the connection she felt growing weren't entirely one-sided or manifested by her exhausted, hormonal, lonely mom-brain.

Up until their night together, they'd only kissed—once. It happened after they'd been approached by a Petralia stooge in a parking lot. Nothing happened—because Chase was there and in full-on protector mode—but it'd rattled Stacey nonetheless.

He'd been patient and kind with her frazzled nerves. Taking her in his arms, shushing her, he even kissed the top of her head. Something that normally wouldn't have sent butterflies into a frenzy in her belly but did anyway. Because she was falling for him, lonely, and hoped she was becoming more than just a job.

And then, later that night, with the kids asleep, as they washed and dried dishes in the kitchen like your average domestic couple in the suburbs, their hands touched, he pulled her in, and he kissed her.

And it wasn't just a sweet peck.

Oh no.

Chase Hart knew how to kiss, and he knew how to kiss well.

There was tongue. There was passion. There was an iron bar poking her in the hip in under seven seconds.

And she certainly hadn't pushed him away.

No.

She had mom-brain, but she wasn't insane.

A widow, a new mother and angry at the world for the shit her family was having to go through, she lunged at the blissful sensation of being wanted. Of being desired and considered sexy. She wanted to cling to the feeling of hope he instilled inside of her heart, that this, too, shall pass, that she was more than just a widow or a mom. She was a woman. A woman worth love and the desire of a good man.

Chase filled her heart with hope, the idea that the future might not be as bleak as it seemed and that good things and good men were not out of her grasp like she thought they were.

So feeling like they were finally on the same page, she grappled at him, pulled him down to her, wrapped her arms around his neck and pressed her aching, milk-filled breasts against his chest.

But he broke the kiss after a moment. A moment much too short, in her opinion. She'd reached for the hem of his shirt, wanting to see and feel more of him, and instead, he pushed her away, both of them left panting and flushed.

She hadn't been able to control where her eyes went, and of course, they drifted down to those gray sweatpants and the stiff snake hidden inside.

He claimed it was because he was on the job that they couldn't go further, that it wouldn't be right. But perhaps he didn't want to go further because in truth he wasn't attracted to her.

And why would he be?

She was damaged goods.

Her husband was dead—not that she missed him. And she had two children, one of whom wasn't even a year old and still used her body like a vending machine.

She ran and did workouts in her living room when she had time, but that fupa, or whatever you wanted to call the pouch of fat below her belly button after giving birth, hung on for dear life, no matter how many crunches she did.

A man like Chase, virile and chiseled like a Greek statue, didn't want somebody like her. Not when he could have any woman he wanted.

But then why, when they finally had that magical night together where they did a hell of a lot more than just kiss, did he make her feel like he was attracted to her? He'd been receptive to her advances.

Hell, he'd been more than receptive. Chase had made love to her like no man ever had. He'd been gentle but demanding, generous but also greedy. He was greedy for her. For her body. He'd taken her three times in the span of a few hours, bringing her to climax over and over again. She didn't think he'd left an inch of her untouched or unsatisfied by the time she fell asleep.

But when she woke up the next morning, with glorious aches in her muscles and body parts long neglected, he was gone. And not just gone from her bed or her room.

He was *gone* gone.

"Oh my God!" Joy cried, bringing Stacey back to reality. "Look at Thea!"

Stacey pulled her gaze away from Chase and her wayward thoughts to find Thea up on all fours and slowly crawling toward Chase. "Oh my God!"

"Look at that. She's a mover now. No turning back," Heath said, licking mustard off his thumb.

Diesel got up from where he'd been staring at Heath's sandwich, to investigate the excitement. He sniffed a few times at Thea's ear, making the baby smile and close her eyes. The closed eyes had her wobbling, even in the crawl position, but she caught her balance by leaning against Diesel's leg.

Only, when the dog sneezed it shook his body, and Thea's too. The baby giggled, let go and fell on to her belly.

But she wasn't discouraged and in less than ten seconds, she was back up

Diesel wandered back over to stare at Heath and his meal.

"Good job, little one," Joy cooed, getting down to Thea's level. "Look at you go. You see your big brother playing and you want to play, too. Monkey see, monkey do. I remember that well with my boys." She glanced at Chase. "Brock would do something and you'd have to do it, too, even if you got bruised and bloody in the process."

Thea placed her chubby little hand on Chase's socked foot, scooted forward more and started to pull herself up to standing.

"Careful of your sister, Connor," Joy said. "She's right below you."

Connor, who was now hanging upside down off Chase, his legs over the man's big shoulders, glanced down at his sister. "Hi, baby. You want up, too?"

Gently, because for his size, Chase could be extremely gentle, he put Connor down on the floor just as Thea, with her wobbly legs, used his pant leg to pull herself up to standing.

"She's never done this before," Stacey said. "And she normally plays strange with people."

"Probably remembers Chase from when she was a fresh little squish," Joy said, welcoming Connor into her lap.

With a grunt and more wobbling, Thea gingerly removed one hand from his pant leg and lifted it into the air.

"She wants up," Connor said. "I know what my sister wants because I just turned four. I'm a big kid now."

"You certainly are, sweetheart," Joy said, brushing Connor's hair off his forehead and kissing his crown.

Stacey was grateful for the woman holding Connor. Joy Hart had embraced Stacey like a daughter, welcoming her and the kids into her home and life like she was family. She offered to watch the kids constantly, baked for them, baked with them and always had a treat or surprise for Connor. She had grandchildren of her own,

Brock's kids, Zoe and Zane, but she said she had room in her heart for more than just two grandkids and wanted Connor and Thea to think of her as Nana Joy.

Chase bent down and scooped up Thea, plopping her on his hip and kissing her on the cheek. "Hey, baby girl. You've changed since I last saw you. You'll be driving a car before we know it."

"Me first, though," Connor said. "Because I'm older. And I don't want a car. I want a truck like you, Chase."

"Cookies should be cooled off and ready to put into a container to take home," Joy said, gently encouraging Connor to stand up with a soft pat to his butt. "Help me?" She reached for Connor's hand, and he took it with a smile.

"Can I take out a cookie to give to Uncle Heath? One that won't burn his tongue," Connor asked.

"Uncle Heath has had enough cookies," Joy said from the kitchen.

"Let Uncle Heath be the judge of that," Heath said, his voice booming around the living room.

Chase's gaze fell to Stacey, and his nostrils flared. She could feel her cheeks getting warmer by the second, and it wasn't because the fireplace was on next to her.

Joy's house was always warm and cozy. And on this particularly chilly day, the warmth from the hearth was welcome. Winter seemed to be hanging on with both hands, refusing to let go, even though that groundhog most certainly hadn't seen his shadow.

But it was more than just the toasty house that had her temperature spiking; it was the way the man with the black wool cap and forest-green eyes was looking at her. Like he'd seen her naked, tasted her body and wanted to do it again and again and again—but wouldn't. But couldn't.

Why couldn't he? He'd returned to her house once more after leaving the morning after they slept together. Rex was over helping her with something. Chase took one look at them, turned around and left again. Then she heard he took a job in Georgia, and that was the last she saw of him.

Heath's eyes darted back and forth between them. "Well, this is awkward," he said, not quite under his breath.

Stacey couldn't agree more. But it wasn't her who was making it awkward. It was Chase.

She'd done nothing wrong. At least, that's what her friend Emma kept telling her. Stacey had done nothing wrong. It was Chase who needed to sort his shit out. If a one-night stand was all he wanted, then he should have been clear about that and not worshipped her body like it was a damn temple, leading her to believe he planned to return with more offerings and a promise to convert.

Chase grunted and looked away, taking Thea over to the mirror slightly down the hallway and making faces at her in it.

A moment later, Connor came bouncing out of the kitchen with a big tin of cookies. He sidled up next to Heath and did a crappy job of trying to sneak the container open so Heath could grab one. For the sake of the four-year-old with the enormous heart, they all pretended not to look, and Heath went in like a covert operative and grabbed one.

Connor put his finger over his lips and went *shh.*

Heath's smile was sweet, and he nodded, hiding the cookie behind his hand as he took a bite, much to the elation of Stacey's little boy.

She wasn't just grateful for Joy. She was grateful for the whole Hart family.

Clearing his throat, Chase drew her attention away from Heath and Connor. He was handing Thea over to Joy, but Thea didn't seem to be keen on the pass-off. She reached for Chase again.

Weird.

Her daughter normally played strange with people she didn't

know, and for all intents and purposes, she didn't know Chase. *Neither do you, clearly.* She pushed down the growl.

Not right now.

He'd been gone for five months.

The last time Thea saw him, she'd been just shy of three months old.

Surely, Thea didn't still remember Chase, did she?

"You leaving?" Joy asked her son, bobbing her body up and down to keep Thea from fussing.

Chase nodded and headed toward the door. "Gotta get home and unpack. Check in with Brock."

Joy's disappointment filled the room.

Recognizing the growing signs of frustration and hunger in her nine-month-old, Stacey stood up and took Thea from Joy so Joy could follow Chase to the door.

He barely gave her a glance but made sure to give a smile and a wave to Connor and Heath before retreating behind the wall that divided the living room and foyer.

She heard whispering but couldn't make out anything specific, and within moments, the door opened, a gust of cool air whooshed around the corner into the living room, and she saw him stalking out to his truck through the big bay window.

"Gonna head out, too," Heath said, extracting himself from his chair, chewing what appeared to be another cookie. He ruffled Connor's hair just as Joy came back around the corner wringing her fingers, looking frustrated. Heath bent down and planted a kiss on his mother's cheek. "Thanks for lunch, Mama."

She swatted him playfully on the shoulder. "Did you at least do your dishes?"

"Always." He grinned, ruffling Connor's hair as he passed by. "I'll see you Saturday for dinner." He focused on Stacey for a moment. "Don't forget that artichoke dip."

She saluted him and nodded. Though with the frosty welcome

and goodbye from Chase, her heart really wasn't in the mood or into the idea of a big, noisy Hart family dinner.

She wasn't a Hart, and although they'd all embraced her with open arms, now that Chase was home, she felt a lot less welcome, a lot less like she belonged.

Joy saw her youngest but also largest son to the door as well, returning less than a minute later. "That boy," she said with a head-shake. "Now he's off to the gym."

Stacey snorted. "Has to keep that svelte figure somehow." Thea was now aggressively tugging at the front of Stacey's sweater, so settling into the cushions on the couch, she brought out her breast, and the baby latched on immediately. Thea, no longer a newborn by any stretch of the imagination, began to kick her feet wildly until Stacey had to hold on to them with one hand and give her daughter a stern look. Thea smiled around the nipple like it was all a game.

Joy brought out a bin of blocks from the bookcase in the corner, and Connor immediately began to build "the biggest castle in the world," as he put it.

Diesel was in front of the fire on his dog bed snoring. For a Pitbull not even a year old, he was actually very chill. His puppy-mode was insane, but it didn't last as long as some dogs. And he was so good with all the kids.

"Ask it," Joy said, taking a seat in the chair Heath had vacated.

Stacey's brow scrunched. "Ask what?"

"Whatever's got you making that face."

She was making a face?

She must have been. She was certainly thinking a lot of things and had even more questions.

"What is up with Chase?" she finally asked on a deep exhale. "I can't figure him out."

Joy's expression turned sad. "Hard for anybody else to when the man can't figure himself out."

"What happened to him? Why is he so ..."

"Lost?"

Yeah, that was probably as accurate a word as any. As much as he was kind and fierce, strong and protective, he also did seem like a bit of a lost soul. Searching for meaning, never certain in his decisions or his worth. She wasn't sure what actions of his made her think that, but the moment Joy said it, said the word *lost*, it all clicked. Chase was lost.

When they'd made love all those months ago, she thought for the first time since they met that she finally saw certainty in his eyes. Finally saw past the gruff, tough, bald, behemoth alpha exterior and deeper into who Chase Hart really was. Which was a kind, patient, generous man not only she but also her children were falling in love with.

And then he disappeared without a word, and she was the one left feeling uncertain and unsure ... lost.

Shrugging, she kindly swatted Thea's roaming hand away from her other breast. If her child had it her way, she'd be nursing on one side and fiddling with the nipple on the other—no freaking way! "Yeah, lost is a good word. What happened to him for him to be like this? Was it a mission?"

Joy's eyes closed slowly, and she pressed her lips together. Her petite frame seemed to heave as she inhaled deeply through her nose and opened her eyes. "Yes. But it's not my story to tell. I don't want to betray his trust. I don't know what happened between the two of you, but I know that when he was helping you with the kids, I hadn't seen him that happy, that *unlost* in a long time. And then ..."

"And then he left."

Joy nodded and blew out her breath. "And then he left."

"Did he ever say what prompted him to leave?" Was it her? Was it the sex? Was she too clingy? His abrupt departure had seriously messed with her already fragile self-esteem, and even after five months, she was still struggling with it.

Her parents' lack of ability to be parents to her had messed with her head big time. She knew she had abandonment issues. That was a no-brainer that didn't require a therapist once a week. Add in her late husband and everything he'd put her through, and then Chase—yeah, Stacey had some *feelings* about people leaving her, whether it be with warning or not.

Joy's head shook softly. "My boys aren't big talkers, if you haven't noticed. Heath's probably the chattiest of them all, and even he's got tight lips. I mean, I'm a therapist and pretty much demanded my kids talk to me, but they're also boys—*men*, so that's a hurdle of its own. They give me what they can. If I push too hard, then I'll get even less from them. It's a fine line to walk."

Joy knew more than what she was saying, though. Chase might not be a big talker, but he'd said enough to his mother that she knew the main reason for his *lostness*. Right now, it was *she* who was being the one with tight lips.

Joy cleared her throat. "Brock's better now that he has Krista. She's a cop and understands some of what he's gone through more than most women could. I just wish the rest of my sons could find love like Brock has. A soft place to land when the days and memories get impossible to carry alone."

Her gaze turned gentle, wistful.

"That's what I was for my Zane all those years ago. His soft place. He said even though I'm small, he never felt more protected than when he was wrapped up in my arms." A tear slid down her cheek, and she wiped it away with haste, smiling through the burgeoning emotions until a chuckle forced its way out. "Man's been gone nearly thirty years, and I still get all weepy thinking about him."

"A sign of true love right there," Stacey said softly, feeling her own emotions clawing their way up her throat. She'd always been a hopeless romantic—until Ted, her husband, ruined that part of her by lying to her from day one. She thought romance and love might still exist for her when she felt the tendrils of attraction begin to wrap around her last year with Chase. But he'd snapped those strands pretty damn quickly when he left.

Now, she really believed that the only true loves in her life were between her and her children. The rest could come and go— just like the men in her life—but the love that would stick, the love that would grow and never die, was the love she had for Connor and Thea. And even though she did love Chase and probably always would, she needed to put that pipe dream to rest and focus on her future, which was giving her two kids the best damn life possible.

CHAPTER THREE

IT MADE Chase's decision to visit his brother Brock a hell of a lot easier knowing he wouldn't run into Rex. Brock's office was in his basement, and there was always one brother or another hanging around, playing with the kids, helping Brock with paperwork, or eating Krista's delicious cooking.

But the knowledge that Rex was off on a job lifted the anxiety in Chase more than he would ever admit.

He'd popped home briefly and tossed on a load of laundry before climbing into his truck and texting Brock that he was on his way over.

Brock texted back immediately to say Krista was setting a place for him at the table and she wouldn't take *no* for an answer. The clock on the dash of his truck said it was four o'clock, and as if on cue, his stomach rumbled.

Chase hadn't eaten anything since the Atlanta airport, where he'd grabbed a sandwich from the restaurant across from his gate around six thirty in the morning. Add in the time difference, and his body was probably beginning to eat itself from the inside out.

It'd been good to see his mother, and he wished he could have stayed longer, but being in a room with Stacey was taking its toll on him. Add in her two adorable children, whom he'd come to love like they were his own, and it was like pulling his heart out and setting it on fire right in the middle of his mother's living room.

Parking downtown in Victoria was a premium, and his condo building charged monthly for parking stalls, so rather than fork over cash just to keep his truck in one place for five months, he parked it at his mother's.

Victoria was a beautiful city and there was nowhere he'd rather live, but he needed to get the fuck out of the downtown core. He wanted to be out in the country, with acreage, maybe get a cow or a horse, some chickens and a pond with ducks.

A lot of work for a single man, but the city life was not for him.

He needed his space.

He needed his privacy.

He needed to know that when he woke up in the middle of the night, he wasn't going to wake his next-door neighbors with his screaming and get a warning letter under his door the next morning.

Which had been the case when he first bought the condo he was in now.

The only plus side to where he lived was the view and openness of his loft. He couldn't do the cramped little bedrooms of the other units he'd looked at. Standing in those rooms with the Realtor, he'd already started to feel the walls closing in around him, so the open-concept loft it was. He wasn't in the penthouse, but the fourteenth floor still offered him a nice view of the harbor and the Johnson Street bridge.

Brock and Krista lived off in the boonies—sort of. Although in a subdivision with other houses around them, they were a ways out of town, surrounded by trees and land and the wild. Brock and Chase would often go running through the trails around his brother's house or do a couple of loops around Thetis Lake before jumping in to cool off.

It was already getting dark out by the time he approached his brother's house. The lights were on inside, smoke rose from the chimney, and both Brock and Krista's vehicles were parked in the driveway.

All four Hart brothers had big black Chevy trucks. The only difference between them was that Heath insisted upon having dual tires in the rear. Brock's was also the newest but only by a couple of years.

Krista—who had also named their security company, Harty Boys—often referred to them as "The Black Truck Brigade."

He parked on the street and was just slamming his truck door when the front door opened with its usual creak and a blast of light illuminated the front yard. "Uncle Chase?"

Unable to hide the smile from his face at hearing that high-pitched little voice, he made sure to bring the teddy bear he'd bought for Zoe out from behind his back when he made his way around his truck.

Her eyes, even from a distance, were glowing emeralds, and her smile melted his damn heart to goo. She bounced on the front steps, her red curls jostling.

"Don't you dare go out in your sock-feet, young lady," he heard Krista say from inside the house.

Zoe nervously glanced back inside. "I'm not, Mama. I'm just waitin'." She turned back to Chase. "Hurry up, or I'll get in trouble 'cause I got my feet wet on the grass runnin' to hug you." Oh, this three-year-old was going to give his brother gray hairs in no time. Another reason Chase was glad he was bald.

She was the spitting image of her mother not only in her looks but in personality, too. Kicked ass and took names wherever she went—and that included the playground.

Brock loved it. Called her his little ginger beast.

He was already teaching her hand-to-hand combat in his home gym, teaching her how to defend herself.

You'd never know by looking at her now that Zoe's entrance into the world had been a rough one. Born premature, barely viable because Krista had been attacked and beaten during her pregnancy, Zoe was as strong as she was feisty and ran circles around her parents with all her energy. It was almost like she came into the world fighting to stay alive and just kept fighting now that she was healthy and totally on course for her age.

He reached the stoop, and just like Connor had, she launched herself into Chase's arms, peppering his face with kisses as her little hands squeezed his cheeks until he had fish lips. "Too long, Uncle Chase. Too long. You're not allowed to go away for that long again. Too *too* long."

He squeezed her back. "I'm sorry, Zo-zo. I promise I won't leave you for that long again."

She reared back and gave him her deadliest Krista face. "You promise?"

"Didn't I just say that I did?"

Her lips twisted, and she spied the teddy bear. "Is that for me?"

"Would you like it?"

She nodded. "Where'd you get it?"

"Well, I was working in a state called Georgia—"

"Then I will name her *Georgia.*"

A strong gust of icy wind hit them both, and he felt her shiver. If she wasn't in long sleeves and pants, he was sure she'd be covered in goosebumps. "Let's get in the house before we freeze."

With Zoe still clinging into him like a baby koala, he held on tight, ascended the steps and entered his brother's home. Much like their mother's house, it was warm and inviting. A far cry from his cold, sterile, barely-has-anything-in-it loft. He would have stuff when he had the space. Right now, stuff just closed him in and added to the claustrophobia.

A baby's warble upstairs made him grin as he toed off his shoes.

"How's your brother doing?" he asked Zoe, not bothering to put her down while climbing the stairs from the foyer to the rest of the house.

"Puts everything in his mouth. Just started walking last week, has bruises everywhere because he's such a klutz." She rolled her eyes and shook her head like Zane was just one big nuisance and she didn't love him more than anything in the entire world.

Chuckling, he turned his attention to where his brother lay on the floor, propped up on his elbow, while Zane climbed all over Brock as if he were some kind of playground contraption.

"Welcome home," Brock said with a nod.

"Thanks." He set Zoe down on the ground, and she slid to the floor on her knees beside her dad, showing him her teddy bear.

"Did you thank your uncle?" Brock asked his daughter while twirling one of her red ringlets around his finger.

Zoe glanced up at him. "Thank you, Uncle Chase. I love my new teddy bear."

"You're welcome, Zo-Zo," he said, feeling the ache of how long he'd been away from his family in his chest to the point where some might think they were having a heart attack.

"Got one for Zane, too?" Brock asked with a playful brow lift.

Chase cleared his throat and nodded. He did indeed. The little boy's teddy bear hung out of the back pocket of his jeans, and Chase pulled the toy out from behind him. Earning a set of surprised wide eyes from Zoe, like he'd pulled a rabbit out of a hat or something. Bending down, he offered it to Zane. The little guy—also a ginger—snatched it and immediately stuck the bear's foot into his mouth and started to suck on it.

"Hope those are new and not something you found lying about," Brock said with a snort, yanking the bear from Zane's mouth, which only caused the little guy to grunt and furrow his brows in frustration at his father.

"Toy store in Atlanta."

"There he is," Krista sang, coming up behind him and resting a hand on his shoulder to encourage him to turn around. "You're a sight for sore eyes. Give me a hug."

He had no choice. She was already going in for one. Not that he would have balked at a hug. He loved his sister-in-law. Finally, someone who gave Brock a run for his money, didn't put up with his shit and loved him as hard as he needed to be loved.

"Sorry I missed Zane's birthday," he said as Krista squeezed him tight.

"Your gift of a strider bike with flames on it and a matching helmet was much appreciated," she said, laughing as they pulled apart. "He's still a little young for it, but he likes to straddle it and make engine noises."

She released him, and he straightened up to his full height, inhaling deeply and being hit with the scent of sautéed mushrooms and onions.

His stomach rumbled so loudly, Krista's blue eyes shot to his abdomen and she reached out and patted it. "Gotcha covered, big fella. Making your favorite meatballs with mushroom and onion gravy, mashed potatoes and steamed broccoli."

His stomach rumbled again, prompting Krista to laugh.

Zane had climbed off his father and toddled awkwardly over to Chase.

Would the little guy remember him? He'd been so tiny and not even crawling when Chase left. Thea didn't play shy with him. Maybe Zane wouldn't either.

Big green eyes, the same color as Brock's, glanced up at Chase, and Zane lifted a chubby finger in the air to point. "Tummy."

"Yeah, Uncle Chase's tummy is making noise," Krista said. She bent down and put her face in front of her son's butt, taking in a big whiff. "Did you crap your pants, buddy?"

"Go poop," Zane said with a nod.

Krista glanced at Brock. "You couldn't change him?"

Brock's face of innocence had Chase pushing down a laugh. "I swear he hadn't shit himself a second ago. He did it on the walk over there."

Krista's eyes rolled, and she hoisted Zane into her arms. "Right. Same line every time."

"Is not. I change plenty of diapers."

"Sure you do," Krista teased, already halfway down the hall.

Brock peeled himself off the floor and, with a grunt and help from the arm of the couch, stood up. "Beer?" he asked.

Chase nodded and followed his brother into the kitchen. "So what's next?"

"What do you mean?" Brock opened the fridge and pulled out two bottles of Phillips Blue Buck pale ale, passing one to Chase.

"Next job." He popped the cap and tossed it into the trash when Brock opened the cabinet beneath the sink to put his cap in, as well.

"Take a breather, brother," Brock said, his tone turning boss-like and less brotherly. "You just got back."

"Yeah, from the cushiest, most boring job ever. I was a glorified babysitter. Had to attend her classes with her. Chick is majoring in English lit. Do you know how boring that was?"

Brock snorted and took a long pull from his beer. "Paid well, though."

"Still feels dirty taking that jackass's money."

"His daughter isn't a jackass, though, and you—we—took it to protect her. Our services aren't free. We all got bills to pay." Brock ran his hand over Zoe's hair when she skipped into the kitchen and wrapped her arms around his leg lovingly.

"Need another job. Don't want to sit idle." Chase sipped his beer. Fuck, how he'd missed beer. He never drank on the job, and seeing as he was technically "on the job" twenty-four seven while down in Georgia, he hadn't had a sip of anything in half a year. Not that he was keen on American beer anyway. Maybe some micro-brews but none of that domestic crap. So to have a cool, crisp Blue Buck pale ale as his first beer in forever was almost worth crying over.

"You seen Stacey?" Brock asked, ignoring Chase's eagerness to get back to work.

His jaw tightened, and he nodded. "She was at Mum's picking up Connor."

"Yeah, Mum loves those kids, asks for them all the time. When she doesn't have my kids, she's got Stacey's. If it didn't give me the willies, I'd say she needed a man in her life."

"Who says she doesn't have one?" Krista said, joining them in the kitchen and plunking Zane down next to his sister.

"Does she?" Chase asked, pivoting quickly to face Krista, who was now pushing the mushrooms and onions around in the frying pan with a spatula. He turned back to Brock. "Does Mum have a boyfriend?"

Brock's shoulder lifted. "Not that I know of." He glanced at his wife. "Is my mother seeing someone?"

Krista had her back to them, so all she did was shrug. "I can't say for certain, but you're doing an awful lot of assuming that she doesn't have a romantic life. Just because you haven't *met* a man in her life doesn't mean there isn't one."

"You better be teasing, woman," Brock said quickly.

"And that's exactly the type of he-man, barbarian attitude that will keep you from ever meeting a man in your mother's life. She raised four alpha-male Neanderthals. What man would she ever want to inflict you four on?"

Chase and Brock exchanged uneasy glances.

Did their mother have a boyfriend? And if so, how serious was it? What was his name? What did he do for work? What was his criminal background? All Chase needed was a name and then he could go digging. Find out how often the man visited the dentist, what his shoe size was, how often he visited porn sites and what his preferences were.

All he needed was a name.

"This guy got a name?" he asked, hoping his tone came off casual. He leaned back against the wall and crossed his ankles for good measure.

Krista cast him a glance over her shoulder, her smile coy. Brock's wife was no dummy. "Nope. Like I said, I don't know. But the fact that you guys just *assume* she doesn't have any romance in her life is sad. She deserves it, and I hope she has it, and that's all I'm going to say about that." She let the spatula rest on the spoon rest and turned back to face Chase. "Your love life, on the other hand, is pathetic. *You're* pathetic. And that's *not* all I'm going to say about that."

Brock choked on his beer, but that didn't seem to stop him from laughing. "God, I love you woman. No punches pulled, just how Chase needs it."

CHAPTER FOUR

EVERY WEDNESDAY NIGHT, Stacey and one of her best friends, Emma, went for a run. Rain or shine, wind or hail (okay, maybe not hail), they geared up, put on their headlamps and reflective gear and went for a much-needed, energizing run.

Emma's husband, the gorgeous, brilliant, wealthy James, stayed with all their children (he and Emma had twin girls, Claire and Grace, who were about eight months older than Thea) while the mothers got their exercise. He fed the kids, bathed them and had Stacey's children in their pajamas by the time she and Emma returned home sweaty, red-faced and feeling like they could take on the world.

Where Emma found James, Stacey would like to know.

She wasn't sure they made men like James Shaw anymore.

At least, she hadn't been able to find one.

Her late husband had never offered to watch Connor while she went for a run. Ted rarely felt comfortable to be left alone with his kid at all. It'd always struck her as weird, but eventually she accepted his preferences, and when Ted was home, the three of them were always together. Then Ted would leave for two weeks—to go be with his other wife, Freya, it turned out—and Stacey would be back to doing things all on her own. It was actually easier when Ted wasn't home because she had one less person to pick up after. He was also a really picky eater—pickier than Connor—so when Ted was away, they could eat what they liked.

Thankfully, today was Wednesday, and after running into Chase at Joy's house earlier in the day, Stacey was in desperate need of some girlfriend time. Not that she hadn't been rehashing the Chase stuff for months with Emma, but a lot of it had been put to rest over the last while, simply because he was out of sight so, for the most part, out of mind, as well.

At least she liked to pretend he was out of mind.

Until she struggled to sleep and their one incredible night together came back into her mind and she was forced to grab one of her battery-operated stress relievers and take a withdrawal from her spank bank.

"Was it awkward?" Emma asked, not nearly as out of breath as Stacey was as they climbed the hill just down the street from Emma and James's lavish home.

"Incredibly. I also hugged him when I saw him, which I know just amplified the awkwardness."

Emma's curly blonde hair was tucked into a ponytail and a white cap, but beneath her headlight, Stacey could see her friend's hazel eyes go wide. "You hugged him?"

"It was instinct. I'm in love with him. I haven't seen him in five months, and the last time I saw him, we'd had sex. Well, I mean, besides when he came by the house, saw Rex there and then left." She let out a long sigh. "The man treated me like a one-night stand. A piece of meat. And yet I'm still in love with him? What does that say about me?"

Stacey was wearing her black running hat and headlamp, along with her gray leggings, a black, long-sleeved Sugoi shirt and a white vest. It'd been chilly when they first started, but as they continued to climb the seemingly never-ending hill, her body began to get warmer and sweat started to sting her eyes.

"I mean, when it comes to men, I really know how to pick 'em. First Ted, the polygamist, and then Chase, the dick dip and dasher."

"Dick dip and dash?" Emma asked, throwing Stacey some amused side-eye.

"Yeah. Dip your dick, and then dash before they cling. If it's not a saying, it should be."

Emma made a noise of impatience. "This is all so messed up. I wish men would just *talk*. You know? If men talked even a fraction more than they do, the world—relationships, marriages, governments—would be so much better off. I doubt the world would be involved in half the wars it's in right now if men talked more and compared dick sizes less."

Stacey nodded. "Imagine how peaceful the world would be if women were in charge?"

"Sing it, sister. Look at all the countries in the world run by women. They're not at war. Coincidence?"

"I think not," Stacey panted. She was struggling to do much more than hum her responses.

"Instead, they just grunt, buy a bigger missile than the other guy—because dick size compensation and all that—then they get mad or butthurt or whatever and leave for five months."

"True dat." They reached the top of the hill and, like always, stopped to stretch and take some much-needed deep breaths.

"Honestly," Emma started, adjusting her blinking green safety light on her vest, "I think you should just go to his house, knock on the door and demand he tell you what the hell happened back in September. Don't leave until he does. Otherwise, you'll always be left wondering ..."

"Like was it the sex?" Stacey asked, lifting her arms above her head and lacing her fingers over her ponytail to bring more oxygen into her lungs. "Was it bad? I mean it'd been a while for me, and I'd just had a baby, so things definitely weren't as tight as they'd once been, but I didn't think it was *bad*."

"It wasn't bad." Emma's head shook. "I've never even had sex with you, but I know that it wasn't bad. You said you had sex three times."

"Yeah, but maybe the first time sucked so he was like, *Let's try this again. Maybe the first time was a horrible fluke.* And then he thought the same thing after the second time, and the third time sucked so much he just couldn't bear the thought of doing it again and he left. Went to find some young, tight college vagina that hasn't pushed out two children and has been growing cobwebs ever since."

Emma snorted and swatted her. "Shut your hideously beautiful face right now. The sex was *not* bad, and don't you dare say it was again." She jerked her chin, and the two started running again. "Chase has been through some shit."

"Yeah, I know. Joy mentioned one of his missions from a few years back really messed with him. She said it's not her story to tell though." She reached out and grabbed Emma's shoulder, stopping them both from running. "Do *you* know?"

Emma's head shook, and they started running again. "No. I've heard whisperings that he may have been kidnapped or something during his time in Peru, but I don't know the details. The Hart brothers are tough nuts to crack. Heath is the easiest, but even he's changed since he was taken hostage for ransom."

Yeah, that had been a terrifying and dark time for all of them.

"Joy has invited everyone over for Saturday night dinner next week—including me and the kids."

Emma sucked air in between thinly parted lips. "Oh, awkward. You haven't seen much of Rex lately, have you?"

"No. He's been away on a lot of jobs. Was down in Seattle with Heath for a while working that Russian mobster job, then back up here for a while running surveillance. Now I think he's up in the Yukon, no idea why. Joy just tells me what she knows, but as you know, it's not much, based on how tight-lipped her sons are. She says he's back next Friday, which is why she wants to do the dinner Saturday night."

"You gonna go?"

"Can anybody say no to Joy?"

Emma's chuckle was wheezy. "Good point. Things between you and Rex okay?"

"They were never *not* okay. As you know, Rex is a great guy and a really good friend ..."

"But you love Chase."

"But I love Chase. Even if I *did* like Rex beyond friendship, I couldn't be with him after I've been with Chase. It just wouldn't feel right. I could never come between the brothers like that. But I don't love Rex—at least not the way I love Chase."

She wasn't sure she'd ever loved or would ever love anyone the way she loved Chase.

Which was so fucked up, given the way everything had transpired. They hadn't been on one date. Had kissed that one time, had sex that other one time, and then he vanished without even a wave goodbye. And yet, in their few months together, she fell in love with him anyway.

She didn't mind that he was quiet or stoic.

Still waters run deep, and she knew that for a man like Chase, his waters probably ran deeper than most.

They came to their halfway point, which was where they always stopped to do another stretch and take another deep breath. Emma turned to Stacey, put her hand on her shoulder and leveled her hazel gaze directly at Stacey's brown one. "Then I suggest you tell him. Before it's too late and he heads off on another job—or worse, falls for someone else."

––––––

AFTER A DELICIOUS DINNER made by his sister-in-law, some much-needed and sorely missed playing with his niece and nephew, Chase climbed back into his truck and returned to his cold, nearly barren apartment.

Seeing Stacey—not to mention her kids—had fucked up his mind for the rest of the day. He'd done his best to push all his feelings aside and focus on his family, focus on hearing about Zoe's preschool and how Zane loved his daycare, but no matter what, his thoughts always drifted back to Stacey.

That's how it'd been for the last five months. Particularly when he was alone in his bed or in the shower and he knew Charlene and Bobby-June were in their room.

The last thing he needed was for the charge he was hired to protect hearing him jerking off in the shower. Not that he was loud or anything, but either way, that wasn't something he needed.

Stacey had fueled his fantasies, his daydreams and his night dreams. Her soft body, the little noises she made as he made her come, the way she tucked her hair behind her ear—always on the left side, and always with her pinky finger—and wrinkled her nose when she was thinking extra hard. Everything about her turned him on. Everything about her made him want her more, made him conjure up the memories of their brief but incredible night together.

He turned on a few lights in his place, retracted all the blinds to open up the place and stripped down to nothing, tossing his laundry into the hamper. He didn't fucking care if anyone saw him through his windows. He wasn't ashamed of his body, but he couldn't have the blinds drawn. That was just one more layer between him and the outside world. He also didn't have a proper bedroom, since his place was a studio-style loft. Less walls, the better.

He turned the water on in the shower and let it get warm. He even had a see-through shower curtain. Since it was just him, what the fuck did it matter? And it kept the space just a little more open. He was a big guy, and these micro-loft condo bathrooms didn't lend much in the way of open and spacious.

He glanced at himself briefly in the mirror as it started to fog up. He'd peeled his wool cap off and could see a faint shadow forming on his scalp. He needed to shave. He also needed to shave his face. He was fine with the scruff, particularly since the thicker it got, the darker it got—unlike Heath's beard, which was just a blond fluffy mess on his face if he didn't keep it cropped to his jaw.

He hopped into the shower and pulled the curtain closed, letting the much-too-hot water soothe his aching muscles. Economy-plus seats were not designed for men his size. And as hard as he'd tried, he'd been jammed into a window seat to boot, forced to contort himself like a circus performer to accommodate the girth of the man in the middle seat.

They'd only had one night together, but that night had stuck with him for five long, lonely months. He'd been determined to keep things professional with Stacey. She was a new widow, a single mom and her family was in danger. But a woman like Stacey proved impossible to stay away from.

They'd taken the kids to the park in the afternoon. Not something he'd been keen on doing since there was a threat out there, and they *had* been approached by Spiros Petralia once already, but Connor was driving Stacey nuts, so they walked up the street to the nearby playground.

Connor had fallen from the top of the slide, taking a tumble and cutting his chin pretty badly. Chase, of course, had scooped him up and they raced to the hospital, where the little guy needed four stitches.

He'd been a trooper through the whole thing—letting the doctors do what needed to be done, all with a brave face and stiff upper lip. His mother, on the other hand, like most mothers when their child was in any kind of peril, was a basket case, and Chase had to do more in the way of calming down Stacey than he did Connor.

Once they got home—after McDonald's for dinner as a treat—she put Connor to bed, nursed Thea until the baby passed out, and then they were alone. He wasn't sure how it started, but before he knew it, she was straddling him on the couch, asking him to take away the pain, to take away her fear and just help her feel... normal.

Chase couldn't remember the last time he felt any kind of normal, so he wasn't sure how he could help her feel it herself. But when she pulled her nursing tank top off—the one with the built-in bra—and arched her back, what red-blooded man would be able to resist sucking those nipples into his mouth like they were damn lollipops?

"Just for the night," she kept saying. Even though how anybody could get their fill of Stacey Saunders in one night was beyond him. He took her three times, made her come a hell of a lot more.

They'd only gotten one night.

Just one.

But that one night had changed everything.

After making her come enough times she passed out in his arms with a smile on her face, Chase fell asleep, too. But he wasn't out for long, and woke up in a cold sweat and with heart palpitations so severe he was sure she could hear them while she slept.

He'd had another dream.

This time he was back in solitary confinement. In the dark with nothing but the rats and cockroaches as his companions. Noises from beyond the door were eerie. Wails of sorrow and pain. Cries for help. Screams of the criminally insane.

As his brain began to play tricks on him, those cries turned into howls, and the scratching of the rats' nails on the wall sounded more like the scraping of long, sharp monster talons.

Rats didn't snarl, but he could have sworn he heard a snarl and felt the hot breath of a beast on his neck right before he woke up, his chest and forehead damp, pulse thundering.

Stacey had drawn the blackout blinds, and the room was dark. She'd turned off the bedside lamp.

He'd panicked when he opened his eyes. The walls instantly began to close in around him. The dark fucked with his eyes, causing things and creatures to appear where he knew there weren't any.

A funny thing, the brain. He knew in the logical part of his mind that the things he was seeing didn't exist, but the fucked-up part of his brain made them appear anyway. And that just fucked him up even more. He could tell himself all day long that the things weren't real, that monsters didn't exist, but when he saw them, when they blinked at him and made noises, it became tougher and tougher to discern what was real and what was just him losing his mind.

A big part of him thought he really was going crazy.

And when he woke up in Stacey's bed, in the dark with the blackout blinds pulled down and the door closed, the monsters began to reveal themselves.

Nobody deserved to know those monsters besides Chase, least of all Stacey. She'd had a rough enough year as it was without having to endure Chase and all his fucked-up baggage.

What grown man was afraid of the dark? What grown man believed in monsters and couldn't sleep in a bedroom with the door closed?

He wasn't right. He wasn't whole. And he definitely wasn't right for Stacey.

He couldn't give her the family she wanted, the whole man she deserved.

So, since the Petralia threat had been pretty much neutralized and he was only really hanging around Stacey and the kids because he wanted to be with them, he did what he figured was best for Stacey and her family.

He let Brock know he needed a break for the day to collect his thoughts, to figure out a way to let her down, even though he'd already fallen in love with her. But when he returned, Rex was there with Stacey and the two were ... cozy.

He remembered carrying Stacey down the hallway to her bedroom, laying her down gently and covering her body with his. She'd reached for him, tugged furiously at his shirt and pants, demanded he get naked so she could feel all of him.

She'd paused for a moment when she realized she didn't have any condoms. Neither did he.

He didn't need them.

But he wasn't ready to tell anyone—even Stacey.

He was still coming to terms with his fate. With the ramifications of his choices and all that he'd gone through for those soul-crushing six months. Saying it out loud would only make it feel more real.

More permanent.

So they pulled out.

The first time, she'd let him finish in her mouth, the second time on her chest, and the third time her back. He always cleaned her up afterward, and she'd smile at him as he brought the warm washcloth from the bathroom and gently mopped up his spill.

She'd joked just before falling asleep with her head on his chest that they'd have to buy condoms at the drugstore the next day, and he'd nodded, agreed and stroked her back. That was the first nail in the coffin of their budding *whatever*.

Thoughts of Stacey's luscious tits bouncing back and forth beneath him as he hammered into her brought him to the edge of reason, to the edge of sanity. He remembered the look in her eyes as she wrapped her mouth around his cock and let him finish in her mouth, the sexy curl of her lips as she swallowed and licked the remaining drops away with her tongue.

Back in reality, he opened his eyes through the thick spray of the shower and looked down. Like always, thoughts of Stacey and their night together had his cock hanging hard and heavy between his legs, the precum dripping from the tip getting washed away with the pummeling water. He took his length in his fist and slowly stroked it from root to crown, squeezing the head until it turned a deep, dark purple.

He felt his balls tighten. Heat pooled in his lower belly, and sparks flew behind his now-closed eyes as he took a deep breath and finally released his load. His hand paused on his shaft as the orgasm hit him full force, his cock pulsing with each spurt. After he reached his crescendo, he opened his eyes and began to stroke himself again, working out the last bit of cum, prolonging his pleasure for as long as he could.

Eventually, he was empty, his balls relaxed and his muscles loosened.

They'd only been together one night, and he hadn't been with anybody since.

He didn't want anybody else. He was sure Stacey had been with other men by now, including his brother Rex.

He needed to stop thinking about her, stop thinking about that night and move on.

He knew now that he wasn't a man meant to have a family.

He wasn't meant to be a father—Mother Nature had made sure of that—so now he needed to focus on other things, which was getting the fuck out of this concrete prison of an apartment and onto some land.

Stacey and those kids were not his.

They never would be, and he needed to stop living in the past.

His future involved him and him alone, on his farm with wide open spaces, no walls, no boxes and plenty of light.

He wouldn't live in the darkness ever again, even if that meant he lived alone.

CHAPTER FIVE

Thursday, Stacey found herself in the grocery store with a snoozing Thea on her chest in the Ergo and an overly chatty Connor in the front of the grocery cart. He was babbling away about his favorite Paw Patrol characters and which pup he would like to be for Halloween—a full eight months away—while Stacey tried to remember whether the recipe she planned to make needed parsley or cilantro.

She'd lost her shopping list somewhere between her vehicle and the front door of the store. Not the first time. Wouldn't be the last time.

With her head down as she shoved a bunch of apples into a bag, murmuring something about needing to also get more chickpeas, she nearly fell on her ass when she turned back to her cart and hit a solid wall of muscle. Thea in the carrier made a grunt but didn't wake up.

"Easy now," rumbled a deep, sexy voice. A hand fell to her elbows and righted her where she stood.

"Chase!" Connor cheered. "You buying groceries, too?"

"Sure am, little man," Chase said.

Stacey took a step back, lifted her head and blinked, taking in his full stature.

Damn, he looked good.

With a black sweater with a quarter zipper at the neck, dark wash jeans and a black knit cap, the man oozed danger and sexiness like a doughnut oozed raspberry jam. His muscles strained against his sweater, and the way his jeans hugged his thick thighs had her panties instantly getting damp.

"Hello," she said, swallowing all the saliva that had flooded her mouth.

He nodded. "Hello."

Why did you leave? Why didn't you call me? Did that night mean nothing to you? Did I mean nothing to you?

All the questions that had been burning inside her for the last five months hung heavy on her tongue, but when she opened her mouth, nothing more than silent air came out.

"Whatcha buying, Chase?" Connor asked, peering into Chase's modestly full black plastic shopping basket. Where Stacey lacked the words, her son had them by the bucketload.

"Just a few groceries, little man. Fruits, veggies, a couple of steaks." He was speaking to Connor, but his eyes remained on Stacey.

It didn't used to be this awkward between them.

Sure, at first, they'd tiptoed around each other, as she wasn't sure how to act around a bodyguard and he'd been on high alert.

But after a couple of weeks, they fell into a pattern and their friendship blossomed. They talked. They laughed. He played with the kids. They even cooked meals together.

He was, surprisingly, a very good cook.

Those few months that they spent together living like a family, even though he was on the job the entire time and she was hiding from a Greek mob boss, were some of the best days of her life.

Connor and Thea adjusted to the move quicker with Chase there, and he even helped bathe and put the kids to bed.

For all intents and purposes, he acted like her partner more than he did her bodyguard.

And it had been really nice.

Though she wasn't afraid to admit that from the first moment she laid eyes on him, she'd been attracted to him. Hell, attracted seemed like an insufficient word for how she'd first thought of Chase—muscles dripping with sexiness, power and danger. Was there a single word for that? Entranced? Fascinated? Completely consumed?

Yeah, she'd been all those things with Chase and more.

So even though a real friendship had formed, in the back of her mind and deep down in her heart, she'd hoped and wished for more.

Then more happened.

Just once. Well, twice, in the fact that they'd kissed once, and then a few weeks later he'd taken her on a whirlwind trip to Bone Town.

Then he disappeared.

"Hey look, Chase, I have a sword," Connor said. He'd found a long stick of lemongrass and was waving it around like a weapon.

Stacey's body instantly grew hot, and a wickedly sexy grin tugged at one corner of Chase's mouth.

He was remembering that afternoon all those months ago just as vividly as she was. Back down into the rabbit hole of her memories she went. To that not so fateful, uber-embarrassing day, where her child revealed to the sexy bodyguard just how rampant Stacey's sexual appetite and proclivities were.

"Hey, Chase?" Connor called from down the hall, late one June afternoon. Stacey couldn't tell if Connor was in her room, his room or Thea's room.

"Yeah, little man?" Chase responded, bouncing Thea on his knee on the couch while holding the bottle for her.

Stacey's brain was in a serious state of confusion. She was pissed off that Chase seemed to be the only person Thea would currently take a bottle from, but she was also so unbelievably grateful that at least her baby would take a bottle from someone.

And if she was being completely honest with herself, she was also a little turned on at how Chase turned out to be the colicky baby whisperer.

He'd worn her in the Ergo to get her to sleep the other day, and Stacey had nearly had an orgasm on the spot.

"Wanna play sword fight with me?" Connor asked, stomping down the hallway like a rhino calf.

"Sure," Chase said from his spot on the couch.

She shot Chase a look. "No, no sword fighting. We do not encourage violence in this house."

He rolled his eyes. "You need to chill out. He's a boy. Boys like swords ... hell, girls like swords. My little niece loves to play Darth Vader and Luke Skywalker with me. We use wrapping paper tubes and paint them to look like light sabers. If you're that worried about it, change the name. Call it jousting or light sabers. But as long as they're not real knives or swords and no one gets hurt, let him be a kid."

Her jaw dropped, and she went to say something but stopped herself when he gave her a look that said, "Trust me."

Yeah, well, easier said than done.

She had trust issues.

Loads of them.

With men.

Thanks to her lying, cheating, two-timing, wife-hiding dead husband.

However, Chase had yet to give her a reason not to trust him, and since everything with Ted and the Petralia family had come to light, she hated to admit that she'd become a bit of a helicopter parent.

She needed to chill the fuck out.

So after some careful thought, she gave him a curt nod. "Fine. But if he gets hurt or sacks you in the nuts, it's on you. Blame him if you're unable to have children."

A look she couldn't place even if she tried passed across Chase's face for the briefest of moments. Sadness? Frustration? Anger?

She wanted to ask what she'd said, but his expression stilled quickly and he gave her a small smile, saving his bigger, more genuine one for Thea. "Sure, buddy, let's sword-fight," he said again, making googly faces at Stacey's daughter.

Stacey paused what she was doing in the kitchen. "I'm not even sure what swords he's talking about. I don't think he owns any." Had he gotten into the gift wrap cupboard? Would she go into the laundry room to find tissue paper and bows everywhere?

But her innocent little boy answered that for her when he came careening around the corner waving his "swords" in the air.

"See, swords. Mummy has them in her nightstand. Mummy, why you have swords in your nightstand?" He ran over to Chase and handed him Stacey's hot pink vibrator while pretending to stab the big burly bodyguard in the stomach with her dark blue dildo.

Chase's eyes went wide, and he nearly dropped Thea on her head as he fumbled awkwardly and uncomfortably with the "sword" Connor had just handed him. He was also simultaneously trying to evade another impalement with the dildo Stacey had secretly nicknamed her "Navy SEAL." Meanwhile, she was glued to the floor, her jaw threatening to knock her knees, and her eyes were as wide as dinner plates.

She could not move.

"Connor!" Stacey finally exclaimed, making the poor boy nearly leap out of his skin. "We DO NOT go into Mummy's night-stand. Those are *not* toys." She lunged forward to take the big blue one from him, his lip quivering as he realized he was probably in deep trouble.

He handed it to her without fuss. "Sorry, Mummy," he said sheepishly. He was such a good kid. Her heart broke from his tone and the remorse that came out with his words. He'd been through so much in the last while, and through it all he was such a trooper. He was still always happy, smiling and easygoing.

She'd completely expected him to lash out with bad behavior after losing his father, having a new sibling and being forced to move, but he hadn't. He'd taken everything in stride.

Chase was avoiding eye contact with Stacey now, but he thrust the pink one in the air and she snatched it from him.

"They *are* toys," she heard him mumble under his breath, while *booping* Thea on the nose and giving Connor a big grin. "It's okay, little man. We'll go find you a different sword, a better one. Maybe your mum has some wrapping paper tubes we can use." His gaze finally drifted up to Stacey's. He had unshed tears in his eyes while his mouth struggled for all it was worth to hold back a smile. He was crying from laughing.

Oh my God, kill me now.

She shot him an irritated glare, but she couldn't hold it for long, and finally her mouth drew up into her own smile. "I'll go see what I can find in the laundry room. Connor, sweetie, these are *not* toys. Okay?"

Connor nodded, climbing up into Chase's lap, forcing him to juggle Thea in his arms. Connor started rubbing his hands over Chase's bald head while saying, "It's so shiny."

Later that night, once the kids were in bed, the dishes were done and the laundry was folded, Stacey finally found a moment to herself and sprawled out on the couch, the remote in her hand and the channel menu scrolling past her glazed-over eyes.

Chase wandered into the room with his laptop and set up station in the chair adjacent to her. He'd changed into flannel pajama pants and was wearing a tight black tank top, his muscles so well defined through the thin fabric, she could practically count each ab. And those arms, Jesus Christ, those arms. If the knowledge of him knowing she had those toys wasn't enough to make her want to toss them out with the next garbage pickup, she'd be using her *Navy SEAL* later that night and thinking of those arms.

"So ..." he started, opening up his computer and waiting for it to turn on, his face suddenly being cast in a big blue glow from the screen. "I don't care about earlier. Not judging you. It was funny, but no judgment."

Her cheeks started to get warm. Hell, her entire body was getting hot. Her heart rate picked up speed, and her ears filled with the thunderous beating of her pulse. She swallowed and licked her lips nervously. "I, uh ..."

His smirk stole her breath. "It's hot ... knowing that you touch yourself. That *women* touch themselves. I'm not intimidated or disgusted by it. It's a turn-on. To know a woman likes pleasure and knows how to pleasure herself ..." He lifted one shoulder casually. "Nothing wrong with that."

He pulled his glasses out of his pajama pants pocket, gave them a quick clean on the hem of his tank top, offering her a peek at the abs beneath.

Oh mama.

He put his head down and started typing on his laptop like a mad fool, ignoring her existence for the rest of the evening. Meanwhile, Stacey was left sitting there stunned, turned on, and until she went to bed, there wasn't a damn thing she could ... or would do about it.

"You going to move back into our house, Chase?" Connor asked, drawing Stacey out of the past and back to the present, back into the grocery store, where Chase wasn't in his pajama pants or tank top and he hadn't just told her he was A-OK with the idea of her using her vibrator in the room that shared a wall with his.

Chase's head shook, and regret filled his eyes. "Afraid not, little man."

"But you can have your old room back," Connor said, his confusion and desperation something Stacey felt in every cell of her body. Mostly because she felt all those things, too—and more.

"You guys are doing okay? You have Rex, and I don't know how much longer I'll be in town anyway." He picked up a broccoli crown, pulled a thin plastic bag off the roll and stuck the crown into the bag before tossing it into his basket.

"What do you mean we have Rex?" she asked, her body temperature rising but not for a good reason. Did he think she was with Rex?

He shrugged and turned his head. "Doesn't matter. I gotta get going."

Connor's face fell. So did Stacey's heart.

"See you at Nana Joy's for dinner, right?" Connor asked hopefully. "We can play together then, right, Chase?" God, the eagerness and love in her son's tone was gutting. He loved Chase so much, forgave him instantly for his absence, and now Chase was just giving him the brushoff.

Chase reached out and ruffled Connor's hair. "Sure thing, little man. Plenty of time to play." He lifted his chin toward Stacey, muttered a half-assed "See ya" and took off toward the onions and potatoes.

"Is Chase mad at me, Mummy?" Connor asked, relinquishing the lemongrass stick to Stacey so she could put it back.

She glanced up at her son. "Not at all, sweetheart. Chase is just having a hard time getting back into his life here in Victoria. He was away for so long that it can be a bit of an adjustment when you finally return home."

The fact that Connor now thought Chase was upset with him only made Stacey angrier. How dare he leave them the way he did five months ago.

Forget his dick dip and dash on her.

He'd left her kids without a fucking word. Not a goodbye. Not a see you later. Not even a motherfucking text message. Particularly Connor, who had just lost his father. Then Chase up and let without a word, just like Ted had.

Who did that?

Assholes, that's who. And next time she saw Chase Hart, next time she got him alone, she would be sure to tell him just how big of an asshole she thought he was.

CHAPTER SIX

THE KIDS WERE IN BED, and Stacey paced her living room. After running into Chase at the grocery store and once again getting the brushoff, she'd been seething for the rest of the day.

Did he think she was with Rex?

Was that what all of this was about? His dick dip and dash? His lack of any communication whatsoever for the last five months?

Why the hell didn't he just come out and freaking ask her?

Men and their goddamn lack of communication. That was going to be the end of her, she just knew it. It was going to be the end of the world.

Women needed to take over. Run the governments, the military, the space programs, all of it. Wars would end, countries would stop fighting over the moon, and instead of destroying the Earth, people would start to take care of it and rebuild it. Preserve it for their children and grandchildren. Women were nurturers, and the world needed nurturing.

But men? They just liked to fight and destroy. Compare dick sizes and battle until there was blood. Or heartbreak. Or both.

First, Ted and all his fucking secrets, and now Chase with his grunts, silent treatment and ghosting. Two men in her life who had taken her heart and stomped on it.

Even if she was terrible in bed and a terrible roommate, she didn't deserve to be treated the way Chase had treated her. Especially not after everything they'd been through.

The clock on her phone said it was eight o'clock. She usually didn't go to bed until around eleven, since the evening was the only time she had to herself, even if her children thought sleeping in was for idiots and squawked at her for sustenance at six fifteen on the dot every morning.

With her molars clenched painfully tight, she brought up the contact list in her phone and found the number for the babysitter she and Emma occasionally used.

Elena was a very responsible seventeen-year-old with her own car, awesome references and an up-to-date criminal record check. She also loved kids and planned to become a kindergarten teacher. Connor and Thea adored her.

Stacey shot Elena a quick text, asking her if she was available for an impromptu gig, and Elena messaged her back right away with a thumbs-up because teenagers lived on their phones.

By eight forty, Stacey was circling the block downtown looking for parking.

God, she hated downtown.

Not that it wasn't beautiful in its own way, but she just hated how cramped it felt. She was appreciative of James and Emma for renting her the townhouse that they owned, but she hoped to one day own some land.

She finally found a spot two streets over from where she needed to be. It was dark and cold, as Februarys in western Canada were prone to be, but at least it wasn't raining or snowing.

Since all the shit with the Petralias had gone down, she'd gotten good at watching her back and becoming more aware of her surroundings. She carried bear spray in her purse as well as a rape whistle on her keychain, and just for extra protection, she had a very sharp two-spiked "safety kitty" made out of resin that she kept on her keychain as well. She'd found it on Etsy and bought enough for all the women in her life. The ears were sharp as hell, and she'd drawn blood on herself more than once reaching into her purse for her keys. It did not bode well for anybody trying to snatch her.

As she walked to the front door of Chase's building, nothing sinister percolated in the air and no weird tingle danced along her spine.

She wondered if he'd let her up if she buzzed him but realized she didn't have to buzz him when a couple exited the elevator and opened the main door. She slipped in after them and stepped into the elevator before the door closed.

Chase was going listen to her whether he liked it or not.

If he left for all this time simply because he *assumed* she was with his brother—the day after they had sex, no less—then she was going to tear a much-needed strip off this Hart brother.

————

CHASE WAS in the shower when he heard the pounding on his door.

Angry pounding no less.

Who the fuck?

What the fuck?

He hadn't had any dreams recently or made any unnecessary or disturbing noises, so it couldn't be his neighbors.

He shut off the water, grabbed a towel from the bar and did a quick dry over his torso and head before wrapping it around his waist and heading to the front door.

The angry strawberry-blonde on the other side of the door was not at all who he expected to see when he peered through the peephole.

Her hands were on her hips, and she was glaring at him. She knew he was there.

"I know you're there, Chase. Open up."

Exhaling deeply through his nose, he unlocked the deadbolt and opened the door with the latch.

She pushed her way inside, a streak of anger across her fine features. But that anger quickly dissolved when she took in what he was wearing—or in this case *wasn't* wearing.

"Put some damn clothes on," she demanded, spinning on her heel and crossing her arms over her body with a huff. "It will be impossible for me to yell at you when all I want to do is rip off that towel."

His lip twitched, but he did as he was asked and wandered over to his bedroom area. He tugged on a pair of gray sweatpants. "Better?"

She spun around. Did a dramatic eye roll. "No. Put a fucking shirt on. And you know damn well gray sweatpants are fucking lingerie to women."

He didn't know that, but that was good to know.

He grabbed a black tank out of his drawer and pulled it on over his head. "Better?"

She let out a loud huff. "A little, yes. Though a winter parka and some very baggy painter's pants would be preferred."

"Don't have either of those." He ran the towel over his still-damp arms again before tossing it into the hamper beside his dresser.

Fuck, she was gorgeous. Stunning, really. Even pissed off like he'd never seen her before, with her foot tapping and hands on her hips, she was drop-dead stunning.

And it wasn't just the big, expressive eyes the color of milk chocolate with the thick, long, fair lashes that held intelligence. It was the way her nose wrinkled when she thought hard or the lift of her brow when someone surprised her. The perfect shape of her lips. Plump and full. The color of her hair. Strawberry-blonde and poker straight. He was surprised to see it down at all, hanging loosely around her shoulders. She said a "messy mom-bun" was just easier. Kept the kids' hands off it and out of her face and Connor's yogurt. It appeared a little disheveled, though. Like she'd been pacing her living room—or perhaps his hallway before knocking on his door—and had run her fingers through it half a dozen times.

"So you wanted to yell at me?" he asked, lifting one brow.

"Yes."

"What for?"

Her nostrils flared, and color filled her cheeks. "Do you think I'm with Rex?"

He lifted his shoulder, trying to remain cavalier, even though he was anything but. "Aren't you?"

"No!"

Well, that got his attention.

But wait. He needed to find out if she *was* at any point with Rex. Whether they were together now or not didn't mean they hadn't been. "Were you?" he asked slowly.

"NO!" She stepped toward him, her finger pointed at him. "Is that why you left? Because you just *assumed* that I was bed-hopping the Hart brothers?"

Well, when she put it like that ... no. He scratched the back of his neck and glanced away from her.

"I thought we had something," she said, her ire appearing to subside. "And then you did a dick dip and dash." Oops, nope. Ire was back. The flash of fire and hurt in her eyes was unmistakable and also gut-wrenching. "Was it bad?"

"Was what bad?"

"The dick dip? The sex? Is that why you left?"

Jesus Christ. Is that what she thought?

Fuck.

He opened his mouth, but she cut him off.

"It's one thing to fuck me and leave. I'm a big girl. I can take it. But to not even say a proper goodbye to Connor ... The kid was torn up when you left without a word. He thought you were mad at him. Asked me the same shit again today. If the reason you weren't coming back to live with us was because you were mad at him."

Like a knife to the fucking heart.

"So what was it, hmm? Bad sex? Assuming I was just making my rounds through the Hart brothers? Do you think I've taken a trip to Bone Town with Heath, too?"

Bone Town?

In his entire thirty-eight years, he'd never heard a woman refer to it as *Bone Town.*

"Do I have too much baggage? Dead husband, two kids, was a former polygamist sister-wife? What was it, Chase? What could I have possibly done to make you leave right after sleeping with me and not send me one goddamn message over the last five months? What?" Her words were coming out like a forced croak, and tears brimmed her soft brown eyes. Her chin and bottom lip wobbled, and she wiped the back of her hand beneath her nose.

How could he tell her it wasn't anything she did but it was what his past was doing to him?

Using her being with Rex was the easiest excuse, when deep down he knew he just wasn't good enough for her. He was too much of a mess. He couldn't drag her, let alone her two innocent children, into his world, into his brain, where monsters lurked in the dark and shadows.

She stood there, six feet away from him, trembling with hurt and rage, her tiny fists bunching at her sides as she did everything in her power to not break down.

He wanted to go to her. To take her in his arms, absorb all that hurt—hurt he'd caused. But wouldn't that be leading her on? He'd done enough of that already.

"So what is it?" she asked shakily. "Am I just a terrible lay?"

Fuck.

He was in her space, holding her, wrapping her tiny frame in his arms before he knew any better.

And fuck if that didn't soothe the ache he'd been feeling in his own heart for the last five months. He felt her shudder and she tried to push him away, but he wouldn't let her. Eventually, she gave up the resistance and melted into him, her breathing still hitched, but her body was beginning to relax.

He didn't want to let her go.

All he wanted to do was touch her. To keep touching her.

Take away all her pain and doubt and apologize for not only his countless fuck-ups but the fuck-ups of all men. She'd been hurt by too many, and he hated that he was on that list.

He wanted to be with Stacey, hold her.

And never stop.

Although their one night together had been thorough and memorable, he'd need more time to commit every inch of her to memory.

He needed more time exploring her body so when she finally saw him for the damaged soul that he was, he could remember the taste of her across his tongue on his lonely nights alone.

Until he could conjure her scent and recognize it on a breeze.

Until he heard her voice, her cries of pleasure in his dreams.

Dreams to drown out the nightmares.

When her breathing relaxed, she lifted her cheek from his chest and glanced up at him. "You still haven't answered my question."

"You weren't bad in bed," he said softly. "Far from it."

"Then why did you leave?" A plump tear slid down the crease of her nose. "I thought ..." The delicate line of her throat moved on a hard swallow. "I thought we had something." She shook her head and glanced away. "Or was it all in my head? The hopeful manifestations of a lonely single mother? I saw feelings when all it was was sexual attraction?"

Chase squeezed his eyes shut and shook his head. "No. I had—*have*—feelings for you."

"Then why did you leave?"

"I had another job."

He should have expected the anger.

Flames of fury ignited in her eyes, and she pushed out of his arms. "Another *job?*"

Damn it, he really hated not being honest here, but he also didn't want to burden her with his problems. They weren't solvable. They wouldn't go away. Like a fucking inoperable tumor in his brain, they would forever be there, fucking with his head, with his life.

"So that's all I was to you then, just *a job.*"

He ran his hand over his bald head and glanced out the window into the dark sky, the city's light causing the air to hold a soft orange glow. "I got confused after our night together. So I went to think. Then I came back to find you and Rex hugging—and he wasn't wearing a shirt—and I had a knee-jerk reaction. I told Brock to give me a job anywhere that wasn't here, and he handed me the Georgia mission."

All of that was true. He'd just omitted a few key elements.

Like he woke up in her bed in a cold sweat, saw figures looming in the dark corners of her room and felt the walls closing in around him.

Or the fact that even though it gutted him to think of it, Rex was the smarter, safer choice of partner for Stacey and the kids. He hadn't been locked away in prison and solitary for six months, left to make friends with the voices in his head, the cockroaches and rats in his cell.

"You broke my heart," she whispered. "You broke Connor's heart."

Damn it all to hell.

He hated that he'd broken her heart. Broken her son's heart. Made her question whether she was decent in bed or not.

He was so fucked up in the head that when he thought he was doing what was best, thought he was protecting Stacey and her family, he was hurting them.

"I ..."

What could he say?

I'm sorry for breaking your heart, but if you knew who I really was, you'd be afraid of me?

Fuck no.

But he knew that he wasn't right for her. As much as he wanted that to not be the truth, he knew it was. He was too fucked up to be a good man for any woman or family.

The rage in her eyes seemed to wither, and she took a step toward him. "What happened to you?" She took another step and reached out with a shaky hand, taking a clump of his tank top into her fist. "Nobody will tell me. It had to be a job ... a mission. What happened? Help me understand."

"Nothing you should know," he said through a tight throat. "Once you know, you can't unknow, and I don't want to put that on you."

Her bottom lip wobbled, and she looked up at him with glassy eyes that felt like a machete to his solar plexus.

"Do you love me?" she asked. He could tell she was trying her damnedest to be strong, but the worry that he didn't love her in return flashed behind her shiny eyes.

Slowly, he nodded.

He hated lying to her about his past, not confiding in her, but that also wouldn't be fair. She had enough on her plate as a single mom. She didn't need his issues to become her issues, too.

But he wasn't lying about loving her.

He'd fallen in love with her almost instantly. The sass, the strength, the smile that made the whole world smile, too.

What sealed the deal for him, though, was when Connor brought out those damn sex toys and wielded them around like swords. He'd never seen a person go *that* shade of red in the face. But it'd suited her all the same.

"I love you, Stacey," he whispered, gently prying her fingers from his tank top and bringing them to his lips. "I can't promise you a future though. My head—"

She lifted up onto her tiptoes and pressed her lips against his. "Let's worry about the future later. You have five months of making me wonder, of worry and anger to apologize for. I suggest you start now." She surged up on her toes and took his mouth more fully as she wrapped her arms around his neck and pulled him down to her.

Initially, he'd been reluctant to take her kiss. He didn't want to lead her on. But that reluctance shattered when her tongue wedged its way past his lips. Hesitance became starvation, and he quickly took control and pulled her tighter against him.

His cock woke up in his sweatpants, and his heart was telling him to take the risk. That she was worth the risk.

He also knew that if he pushed her away now, she'd never forgive him.

He also knew that if he pushed her away now, he'd never forgive himself.

Wrapping his arms around her back, he spun her around and walked her backward to his bed.

They fell into his king-size bed, their lips becoming unglued. She gazed up at him with those soft brown eyes of hers, the flecks of gold around her pupils muted by the dim lamplight.

Fuck, he loved this woman.

She reached for the hem of his tank top, her smile now radiant. He helped her, and the way her eyes widened and her tongue slid across her lips like she was staring at a juicy steak had him grinning.

"Goddamn it, you're hot," she said on an exhale.

"You're hotter," he said, tucking his fingers into the elastic of her yoga pants and pulling them down to expose her white cotton briefs. He tossed them to the floor.

She let out a bark of a laugh. "HA! Sure. Frumpy single mom of two. A widow. I barely have time to run once a week with Emma, and I eat more PB and J crusts than any person should."

With a long pull of air from his nose, he surged forward and took her mouth. "Hot as fuck and don't want to hear another word contradicting me, got it?" he said, breaking the kiss, which left her starry-eyed and smiling.

She touched her bottom lip with her finger. "Ditch the sweats," she said, her voice now erotic and hoarse.

"Thought they were lingerie for women," he said.

"Lingerie is meant to seduce and then be removed. They've done their job." She tugged her shirt over her head, exposing her black sports bra.

"Take that thing off. Does nothing but hide your tits."

Grinning at each other, they did as they were both told. She tugged the bra over her head, and he dropped his sweats to the floor.

His cock was at full attention now, a thick string of precum hanging from the tip. She eyed his crown like it was the hottest day in summer and he had a Popsicle between his legs.

"I've got nothing to apologize for," she said with a gentle head-shake. "Not planning on putting that in my mouth for a while."

His grin hurt his cheeks now. Fuck, he loved her sass.

When she wanted something, she went for it.

"Not gonna ask you to." Though if she wanted to, he'd never turn her down.

He removed her panties and allowed himself a moment to just take in the beauty, the rawness of Stacey naked on his bed. This image had kept the monsters at bay during his stint down in Georgia. When he felt the walls closing in, the darkness beginning to get thick, he thought of Stacey spread out before him, a flush to her skin, her nipples beaded, pupils dilated, arms out reaching for him.

The downy patch of blonde hair between her legs was damp, and he dropped to his knees and pressed his nose to it, inhaling her scent. Imprinting it on his memory for later. Like when the monsters returned.

Her fingers tracing a gentle path on his bald head had him tilting his gaze to her. "Inside me, Chase. It's been too long."

She didn't have to tell him twice.

Pressing a knee into the bed, he pushed her legs apart and made to settle between her thighs when she stopped him. "Condom?"

Right.

He had a few still kicking around, but since he didn't need them and hadn't gotten laid since Stacey, he hadn't really had the need to keep a healthy supply.

But he knew he'd spied at least three in his nightstand drawer.

With a nod but no words, he stood up again, went to his nightstand, found what he needed and sheathed himself.

He could tell her that they didn't need to use them. That he was clean and he assumed she was. Fuck, no condom would feel a hell of a lot better.

But even so, that just wasn't something he was ready to share.

He'd known his fate, his lack of virility for almost a year now, and it was still tough to accept.

He'd never have children of his own. Never be a father.

Maybe that was for the better anyway. How could he chase away the monsters from under the bed when he was afraid of them himself? How could he help his children overcome their fear of the dark when he was nearly forty and hated the dark himself?

"Chase?" Her gentle tone drew him from his darkening thoughts. "You okay?"

Nodding, he left the condom wrapper on his nightstand and went to her.

She reached for him, her expression serene and welcoming. The connection between them crackled, and her brown eyes—still shining a little—invited him for a swim in her thoughts. He dove in willingly. Anything to escape his own mind, even for a little while.

He settled between her soft thighs, brushed the hair off her face with his palms while his elbows rested next to her shoulders. He dipped his head, soaking in her gaze, and fought the shiver that wracked him as she shimmied beneath him and the wet heat of her center brushed against his cockhead.

She reached between them and guided him home, the sizzle that shot across his skin from her touching him there like fireworks through his whole body.

He slid inside, and they both sighed.

"I love you, Chase," she said, gazing up at him. "Welcome home."

CHAPTER SEVEN

It was like coming home after being away for way, way too long. Chase's weight on her, his manly, fresh scent enveloping her, helped mend the broken heart he'd left behind all those months ago. His kisses were powerful enough to make her forget her anger toward him and only bask in the now, in the fact that he was back and apologizing to her with his body in the best way he knew how.

He wasn't a talker.

Had never been.

So if he needed action to apologize, then she'd take it.

"I've missed you, Chase," she said, relishing him finally being inside her again. She hoped to God she was tighter now. It felt like she was. She did her Kegel exercises whenever she remembered—which wasn't that often, but hopefully it was enough.

When he hit the end of her, they both groaned, smiled at each other like idiots in love, and then he began to move.

Like a dark sky at night struck by a bolt of lightning, her whole body lit up when Chase slid across her channel, when his mouth fell to hers and he pried her lips apart and wedged his tongue inside.

He leveraged up on one hand, pushing it into the mattress until his forearms bulged with ropey veins and his muscles popped. With his other hand he tugged on an already tight, achy nipple.

God, how she'd missed him.

They'd only had one night together, but it'd been a memorable one.

An incredible one.

It had kept her warm these past months as she remembered the way he moved, the flex and dip of his hips, the gentle yet firm caress of her breasts. His strong grip on her thighs as he palmed them open to put his face between her legs. The rough pads of his thumbs as he strummed her clit or nipples—she'd woken up several times over the last several months panting from a sex dream. A sex dream about Chase and just how *good* he was at making her come.

Each pull back had her squeezing her body around him, unwilling to let go of even an inch, only to be satisfied once again, moan and smile into his kisses as he thrust back inside, ending each drive home with a manly grunt she felt down to her toes.

She wasn't going to last much longer.

The intensity of his passion, of his need for her, of their time apart was too much. Her emotions were hanging precariously near the edge. She was close to tears. To feel him inside her, above her, around her, on her. The man consumed her in every imaginable way.

She raked her nails down his hard, muscular back.

The man's muscles had muscles.

He was a killer.

A warrior.

A hunter.

And yet, when he needed to be, when he wanted to be, like when he was with her or her children, he was as gentle as if holding a new lamb. His patience abounded for Connor's millions of questions, and Thea preferred him to give her a bottle and calm her down almost more than she preferred Stacey—at least she did. And the baby had been drawn to him again when he arrived at his mother's house earlier in the week. As if she remembered Chase having the warm arms she loved to fall asleep in.

There was no doubt about it; He had a protective presence that she knew even her children felt.

When Chase was on duty or around those he cared for, nothing —and no one—would ever hurt them.

Chase broke the kiss and dipped his head to draw a beaded nipple into his mouth. She loved it when he scissored his teeth over her puckered bud, tugged until an ache sprinted down her body, landing firmly on her clit.

He picked up fervor, and she felt the orgasm begin to build in her lower belly. Like a pot threatening to bubble over, she was incapable of staying at a gentle simmer. He filled her up until she was overflowing.

With another hard thrust in, his lower belly raked across her clit, and she detonated. Squeezing her eyes shut until they were sore, she bowed her back and let the climax crash through her. It broke the dam and flooded every corner, nook and cranny of her body. Her fingertips tingled, her scalp prickled and her toes curled until a charley horse threatened to ruin everything.

Chase kept moving. He slowed down, exaggerated his hip dips and finished each decadent plunge with a delicious swirl that had her seeing even more stars.

She released the breath she hadn't been aware she was holding and collapsed into the pillows, satiated and so damn in love it nearly killed her.

"Did you ...?" she asked, opening one eye and glancing up at him.

He released her nipple and smiled. "Not yet."

Chase dropped his head again and slid his tongue down between her breasts to her belly until his cock slipped out of her.

He shimmied down the bed farther, planting warm, wet kisses over her tingling torso, setting her entire body into a frenzy. His feet broke free of the sheets, and he was face-to-face with her pussy.

Those big, warm, calloused fingers pushed her thighs apart, and he nuzzled her mound. "Fucking dreamt of this, Stace. Your scent, your taste. Fucking craved them." His tongue flicked out and hit her clit dead center. She was already sensitive from her first orgasm, so when her whole body jerked, it was no surprise.

The flat of his tongue swept up from her perineum to her clit and back, sending every neuron into a spasm. She quivered when he fingered her slick entrance, pushing one digit in and then another, pumping like his cock just had. He pressed up hard on her sweet spot, and another surge of pleasure speared her.

"Chase ..." she whimpered, her hands running over his smooth, bald head.

She'd never been a big fan of bald men, but Chase—and Rex for that matter—both pulled it off like they'd been born to be bald. Vin Diesel had nothing on Chase.

He tilted his head to the side and pulled his fingers free from her, moving them down to her crease. One finger pressed against her tight hole, and she puckered against it.

"Let me in," he said with a gruff grumble.

She did as she was told, relaxing her body so he could slide a finger into her anus.

Despite the invasion, she relaxed.

His other hand came up, and he rested his forearm on her belly, his thumb finding her clit again while his tongue slid into her pussy and began to fuck her.

The sensations were new, unlike anything she'd felt before. Even though she'd had a thumb on her clit and a finger in her ass, his tongue inside her pussy, slippery and strong, fucking her hard was new and exhilarating.

"Oh my God ..."

"Good?" he murmured, pushing his tongue deeper into her pussy.

"Unlike ... anything ... God, this is like ... my new ... my new favorite thing."

Her hips churned and her core clenched. She was on the verge of another climax, this one setting itself up to be even wilder, even more intense than the last.

She tapped his head. "Close. So ... close."

He pushed his tongue into her deeper, added another finger in her rosette and went double time on her clit. She was coming before she knew what was happening. Her body arched against the bed. Her head dug into the pillow beneath her as he fucked her thoroughly with his mouth and fingers.

Every muscle tightened inside her; the euphoria blossomed from her center outward, unfurling like a flower blooming in summer sun, the petals extending out to her fingertips and toes.

The orgasm began to ebb, and her body went limp with a heavy sigh—she was exhausted. All the crying, the stress and now being with Chase again at long last had finally brought her to a point where she figured if she closed her eyes long enough, she might finally get some sleep.

Chase removed his fingers and thumb and raised himself up to his knees, covering her once more. He slid inside her and began to move again.

She wasn't sure she could come again, but the feeling of being full of Chase brought her a different kind of pleasure. This was a pleasure she didn't necessarily feel in her erogenous zones but deep in her chest. He was picking up the pieces of her fragile, shattered heart and closing up the cavity where it'd been ripped from her body.

Her heart had been broken when they met, and he'd mended it back then. Then, he'd broken it again by leaving. Now, he was healing her again—and hopefully for good.

As much as it sucked that she'd been threatened by a Greek crime family, she owed Ted that small bit of gratitude, because if the Petralias hadn't come after her and Freya, she never would have met Chase. She never would have been inducted into the Hart family or found friendships in Emma and Krista that she would hold close to her heart probably for the rest of her life.

"I missed you," she said, feeling fresh tears sting the corners of her eyes and her throat begin to get tight again. "So much."

"Missed you, too, baby."

"Don't ever leave like that again ... promise?" Her words felt almost like a warning, but she didn't intend them to be. She just wanted him to know how much he was loved, how much he'd been missed, and how much the last time he'd left had broken three hearts.

He picked up speed and started hammering into her with more intent, his face taking on a sexy, almost mean expression as he bared his teeth, furrowed his brow and flared his nostrils.

"Chase?"

Her nails traced a delicate path down his back, and she felt the muscles of his ass clench and squeeze with each thrust. She'd noticed and appreciated his delectable ass nearly the moment she met him. And then when she finally got to see it in the flesh that first time, she'd been unable to stop herself from biting it.

Fortunately, Chase didn't seem to mind.

"Promise," he grunted, lunging forward and capturing her mouth at the same time she felt him still inside her and his breathing became shallow and erratic.

A low, gravelly groan burbled up from the depths of his throat and into her mouth at the same time his quick pants came out in forced breaths through his nose, hitting her upper lip.

He pulsed inside her as he came.

She locked her legs around his back and squeezed her Kegels, hoping she was enhancing his orgasm even just a little bit.

With a deep exhale, he collapsed on top of her and broke the kiss, his chest still heaving against hers, his weight heavy but not unwelcome.

He slid out and off her a few moments later, and she quickly and quietly swung her legs over the side of the bed and went to the bathroom.

"Come back when you're done," he said behind her, which only prompted her to grin at him over her shoulder and wiggle her butt.

She finished in the washroom, let Chase go in after her, then the two of them climbed back into the bed. He promptly tugged her back against his front and buried his nose in her hair.

She had to get home, get back to her kids and relieve the babysitter. But being there in Chase's arms, finally, was an indulgence she would allow herself, even if just for a few more minutes.

He squeezed her tighter. "When do you have to go?"

"Soon," she said, her throat feeling tight. "Got a babysitter, but she has school in the morning."

He made a guttural noise.

"Come over tomorrow night. When you can. If you want to see the kids, come over for dinner. If you're not ready for all of that again, come over when they're in bed. But—"

"I'll come for dinner," he said, pressing a kiss to her neck. "Connor and I can have another sword fight." The thick, deep gravelly laugh had her nipples pebbling.

"Been using those swords a lot these last few months," she chided. "Particularly the big blue one."

Cupping her breast, he pulled on a nipple until she gasped. "Put 'em away. I'm back now."

He was already hard as an iron bar behind her again. She shimmied her butt against him. "Yes, you certainly are."

CHAPTER EIGHT

"AND THEN WE jumped off this rock as big as a dinosaur and Ms. Allegra screamed because she was so surprised and scared to see us," Connor said with so much enthusiasm and gusto, Stacey tossed her head back and laughed. It didn't matter that she'd heard this story at least five times since it happened earlier that day while Connor was at preschool. The way her son told his tales was Oscar-worthy for sure and deserved to be appreciated with a laugh and a clap.

She might not be *so* enthralled when he told her for the fiftieth time come Sunday evening, but for now, it was still fresh enough to be funny.

But now, he had a new audience.

Chase sat patiently at their dinner table, listening to Connor's full story, giving the little guy all his attention as Connor pantomimed and made noises describing his fun-filled day at Seedlings Preschool.

Chase's green eyes went wide when Connor roared like a dinosaur. "Great dinosaur impression, little man. What is that? A T. Rex?"

Connor nodded. "Yeah, how'd you know?"

"Know my dinosaurs." Chase shoveled another forkful of the sundried tomato alfredo and fettuccini Stacey had made into his mouth.

Thea, who had a bowl of noodles cut the length roughly as long as her little finger, was wearing the majority of her sauce on her face and would most definitely need a bath afterward. But she seemed to actually be getting some of the pasta into her mouth as well and watched her brother with such love and amusement, it was hard not to smile despite the mess Stacey knew she'd have to clean up later.

"Are you staying the night, Chase?" Connor asked, reaching for a cucumber from the tray of sliced veggies Stacey always had on the table. He dipped it into his small ceramic bowl of ranch dressing. It was the only way she could get her kid to eat his veggies.

Chase shook his head. "Afraid not, little man. Just came by for dinner and a visit. Missed you guys."

"We missed you, too," Connor said. "I thought you were mad at me."

Chase and Stacey exchanged glances across the table.

After their encore of sex last night, they discussed, albeit briefly as she got dressed, how they would approach things with Connor. He was such a happy child, even after all the crap he'd gone through over the last year: dad dying, new sister, moving, threat to the family, Chase leaving without saying goodbye.

Connor didn't deserve everything he'd had to endure, not at four years old. Hell, she didn't think she deserved it at thirty-three, but her well-being wasn't her priority; her children's was.

"Not mad at you, little man. You didn't do a thing wrong," Chase said gently.

They needed to make it clear to Connor that whatever was happening between Chase and Stacey wasn't going to affect the way Chase felt about Connor and that Chase would always be in his life.

Chase had made that abundantly clear last night.

He hadn't made Stacey any promises about the future, besides the fact that he wouldn't leave like he had without saying goodbye, and she knew after speaking to Joy and Emma and seeing the agony in Chase's face when he toyed with the idea of telling her more that that was all he *could* promise her.

For now, she'd take it.

They had time to work on whatever they were.

He loved her.

She loved him.

That was enough to build on for now. No matter how slowly they needed to build it.

He said no matter what, though, he would be there for Stacey and her kids. That all the Harts would be, regardless of whether Stacey and Chase were together or not. He said he saw how much his family had embraced her and how much they meant to her and the kids and that after everything they'd been through, he would never dream of ripping that away from them.

She'd nearly peeled off all her clothes again and tackled him to the floor, but it was late, and Elena the babysitter had texted her asking what time Stacey expected to be home.

"I'm glad you're not mad at me," Connor said. "I was mad at you for leaving and not saying *goodbye*, but then Mama told me you had to leave for work, so I forgave you." He made a pouty face and glanced up at Chase. "Can you say *goodbye* next time, please?"

Chase looked like someone had just knifed him in the back. He nodded slowly before reaching over and ruffling Connor's shaggy head. "I will, little man. And I'm sorry."

Just like kids did, Connor bounced right back like a rubber ball, and his radiant smile curled the corners of his lips once again. "Thanks, Chase."

Chase wasn't as quick to bounce back as Connor, but he smiled nonetheless and pointed to Connor's half-eaten plate of dinner. "Eat up, little man. Your mama's pasta is delicious, but I brought dessert."

Connor's blue eyes lit up. "Is it ice cream?"

Chase shrugged but grinned. "Dunno. You'll need to eat more dinner to find out."

Connor bounced in his seat and looked excitedly to Stacey. "Did Chase bring ice cream?"

Stacey played along and shrugged as well, exchanging coy glances with Chase. "You'll have to eat more to find out."

Connor's smile grew even more. Like the Grinch's heart. He dove back into his pasta and started hoovering big heaping forkfuls.

"Easy, little man. You don't want to choke." Chase rested his arm on Connor's. "Slow down."

"Or get a tummy ache," Stacey said.

Connor did as he was told and seemed to finish his dinner in record time.

Chase helped Stacey clear the dishes, loading them into the dishwasher and sink, then he opened her freezer like he would at his own house and pulled out a tub of Chapman's Tropical Wave Sorbet.

Connor's eyes were as big and round as the dinner table. "That's my *favorite*," he said.

"Is it? I had no idea." Chase tapped his chin playfully, brought down bowls from the cupboard and grabbed spoons and an ice cream scoop from the drawer. Again, like he would at his own house. All that time away did not seem to change his comfort or familiarity in Stacey's home. He fell right back into the groove he'd carved out for himself as if he hadn't been gone a day, let alone half a year.

Connor nodded in earnest. "Yeah. My very favorite."

Stacey finished wiping Thea's face, though the baby still had alfredo sauce in her hair, and she sat down at the table.

"Well," Chase started, popping the lid on the sorbet, "a little birdie *might* have told me what your favorite flavor was. And I *might* have bought it as an extra way to say that I'm sorry for leaving without saying *goodbye.*"

Connor was standing on his chair, his hands on the table, watching Chase scoop the sorbet. "I forgive you, Chase. Even without the ice cream. But I really, *really* forgive you now."

Chase put a single scoop into an orange plastic IKEA bowl, added a spoon and passed it to Connor. "Good to hear, little man."

Connor sat back down in his seat and dove into the ice cream.

Chase's gaze swung to Stacey. His eyes held an avid heat and intrigue that made her belly turn molten hot.

He finished scooping up bowls for the rest of them, including Thea, who actually shivered and made a hilarious face when she tried hers—not sold or sure of the sweet, icy blob in front of her— then he sat back down at the table.

"This is so yummy," Connor said. "What's your favorite flavor, Chase?" He pointed to the tub. "There is pineapple, coconut and lime. My favorite is the pineapple. But I also like the coconut ... and the lime."

Chase took a spoonful of his ice cream but then erotically, slowly pulled it out of his mouth, all while keeping his gaze laser-focused on Stacey. "Strawberry-blonde," he said. "That's my favorite flavor."

Stacey's face caught fire, and she was forced to glance down at her bowl out of fear the look Chase was currently giving her might cause her to have a spontaneous orgasm.

"That's not in here," Connor said, completely oblivious (thank God). "See. Pineapple, lime and coconut. You're probably thinking about the berry flavor. But we can't have that one because Mama is allergic to strawberries. Right, Mama?"

Stacey had lifted her head again and was having one of those dirty, delicious, wordless conversations with Chase. He slid his tongue across his bottom lip, and her pussy actually quivered.

She thought that was something that only happened to women in those romance novels she devoured during her first pregnancy—you know, when she had all the time in the world for such things—but no, her pussy actually quivered.

"Mama?" Connor probed. "You're allergic to strawberries, right?"

She shook the dirty thoughts from her head and glanced at her son. "That's right, baby. Mama can't have strawberries."

"I can though, right?" Connor asked, still blissfully oblivious, like a four-year-old should be.

"So far you haven't had any allergic reaction to anything. Neither has your sister, which is really good." She put another spoonful of sorbet in her mouth, hoping it would cool her off. The man sitting across from her had her temperature spiking. She could probably power a small village with how much heat she was generating.

"What time's bedtime?" Chase asked, drawing her attention to his lips, his very talented, very soft and kissable lips.

She was going to burst into flames if he didn't calm the hell down soon.

Glancing at the clock on the stove, she swallowed the sorbet in her mouth and let it slide down her throat before answering. "In about forty minutes."

"Thea go to bed at the same time as her big brother now?"

"Yeah, we do," Connor answered. "Though she still sometimes wakes up to eat because she has a tiny tummy and wants Mama milk at night." He held his arms out and flexed them. "But I'm a big kid now and can sleep without getting up to eat. My muscles are huge. Feel them, Chase."

Chase reached over and squeezed Connor's biceps, making a

face like the kid had navel oranges under his long-sleeved shirt. "Holy cow. Do you work out? Those are some serious guns you got there, little man."

Connor was all grins. "I help Mama bring in the groceries. I have seven muscles now. I had nine, but because I can't ride my bike in the rain, I only have seven now. I hope to have twelve in the summertime when I can ride my bike more."

Chase's lips twitched as he tried to hide his laugh. "Seven muscles are still a lot of muscles, and I like to hear that you're helping your mum."

Connor nodded. He pinned each one of them, including Thea, with a look. "I like that we're all together as a family again. I'm glad you're home, Chase." Then, like he hadn't just launched a love grenade into the center of the table, he happily dove back into his ice cream.

Chase and Stacey exchanged looks over the table. Hers was wary but hopeful. She knew it because that's how she felt in her heart. His was really confusing.

She could see the love there. See how much he enjoyed spending time with them, being a part of their little nest. But she also saw the fear. The fear of whatever it was he couldn't bring himself to tell her.

Eventually, he shook himself free from her gaze and turned to Connor with a lopsided smile. "I'm glad to be home, too, little man."

———

"Sorry, little man. Six books is my limit," Chase said, his hand on the door to Connor's room, body halfway out into the hall.

"You can read me more tomorrow, Chase. That's okay," Connor said, turning over onto his side and tucking a stuffed bear tightly under his arm. "Your eyes are tired. Go rest them."

This kid was something else.

He'd won Chase's heart pretty much the second Chase met him, and even now, he was funny, kind, understanding and so damn lovable.

"Thanks, little man," Chase said, trying to close the door. "I might just do that."

"Chase?"

He opened the door a bit wider again. "Yeah?"

"I love you."

Jesus Christ. The kid had a whole quiver of love arrows, and he was firing them all directly at Chase's chest tonight.

Chase nodded. "Love you, too, little man. Now get some sleep."

Connor smiled and snuggled deeper into his pillow. He yawned and closed his eyes. "Night-night, Chase."

"Night-night, little man." He closed Connor's door almost all the way, leaving it open just a crack, as he knew the kid preferred.

Hell, if it were Chase, he wouldn't want the door shut even a smidgen and would insist upon having his blinds up and the window open. Connor's room was on the smaller side, and even just sitting on the floor reading the kid books had made Chase's heart beat like a hamster's in his chest.

The door next to Connor's closed, and Stacey emerged. "That is one tired baby," she said with a yawn. Not bothering to ask him to move, she leaned in and peered through the crack in Connor's door. "And this one is out like a light, too."

"Carbs and ice cream will do that," he joked.

She glanced once more into Connor's room before turning to him. "Are you tired?"

He shook his head. "You?"

"Only of seeing you in clothes." Her brows bobbed. "But I want to shower first ..."

"That an invitation?"

Her interest was piqued. "It can be."

"Give me a minute to finish the dishes in the kitchen and I'll meet you in there. Don't *start* without me though, got it?" He rested his hand on her hip, pushing the fabric of her pale blue T-shirt and leggings out of the way so he could have his hand on her skin. Caressing the gentle curve with his thumb, he felt her skin heat beneath his touch. She blushed, and he caught the scent of her shampoo or soap—or maybe it was the kids' soap, since she'd just bathed them. Either way, he wanted to inspect it closer by sliding his nose along her skin, pressing it into her hair, and he would.

The gentle smolder in her eyes licked up into flames, and she grinned, lifting up onto her tiptoes. He thought she was going in for a kiss, but her mouth fell next to his ear instead. "Don't take too long. I've gotten good at *taking care of myself* all these lonely months."

A growl of possession rumbled in his chest. "Not anymore." He dropped his hand from her hip to her ass and squeezed. "Your orgasms are mine."

"Then come and get them." She trailed her tongue over the shell of his ear before cupping his erection with her hand for just a fleeting moment and then disappearing into the bathroom.

Chase adjusted himself in his jeans, grunted and headed to the kitchen.

He was going to break the damn world record for fastest dishes ever washed, even if it killed him.

CHAPTER NINE

Turning on the water in the shower but not stepping in just yet, Stacey glanced at herself in the mirror and poked at her belly. Would she ever be rid of the slight pouch that hung just below her belly button?

The more mothers she spoke to, the more confirmed that no, she probably wouldn't ever be completely rid of it. It was a badge of honor—just like stretch marks—from bringing life into the world.

She tested the water with her hand and stepped inside over the tub, letting the water spray her in the face for just a moment before turning around so it could soak her hair and back.

The slight *click* from the bathroom door said he was in the room.

She glanced through the steam-covered glass doors to find a man she could stare at naked every hour of every day, peeling his long-sleeved gray waffle shirt over his head. His jeans and boxers were next, followed last by his socks.

She allowed the water to cover her head and soak her hair, to take her worries about this new *whatever it was* with Chase down the drain and out to sea.

The glass door slid open and a big, bald force of nature, more naked than Adam with his modest fig leaf, stepped over the tub.

"Hope you didn't start without me." His voice was slightly hoarse, his cock heavy and hard between his thick thighs.

She smiled and stepped into his space, feeling small and protected by his size and strength. "I did not. I was waiting for you."

"Good woman." He wrapped his arms around her and dipped his head to take her mouth.

She pushed up on tiptoes and let her arms float up and over his shoulders, opening her mouth for him and letting him lead the kiss.

He'd stepped into the shower with an erection fit to make a nun blush, but even so, she could swear she felt him grow even more against her hip. It certainly twitched.

Their kisses quickly turned carnal, and he had her backed up against the shower wall, her hips hiked up around his waist, and he was teasing her core with the head of his shaft until she was almost ready to scream.

His fingers drove into her hair, and he crushed his lips to hers, prying her mouth open and sliding his tongue inside, tasting her.

A claim. At least that was what it felt like.

She kissed him back, mirroring his fervor. Their lips moved, their tongues tangled, and when they finally paused and he pulled his lips away, they both had to suck in air.

Everything about Chase was electric. His touch, his kiss, the way his voice raked through her. Gravel coated in syrup in a rock tumbler. It was a weird comparison, but it was all she could come up with.

Damn if she didn't want more.

So much more.

Her heart thumped heavily, and his cock twitched against her entrance. But he didn't move his hips. Rather, he slowly, agonizingly so, traced her face with his fingertips, as if he were trying to commit every freckle—and she had a lot of them—to memory. Over her forehead, down her nose, over her lips. His thumb swept demandingly across her bottom lip, tugging it until his fingers moved down farther and curled gently around her throat, pausing for another moment over her wildly hammering pulse.

She watched him. In awe of how not only gentle, but powerful and demanding he could be.

He released her, which wasn't at all what she was prepared for, and stepped back.

She blinked through the spray, confused. Was he having second thoughts about them?

His eager cock and the shiny head covered in precum would say otherwise.

But still.

He always had her second-guessing his feelings, and it drove her nuts.

"Chase—"

He shook his head and pressed a finger to her lips.

She waited, her hands by her sides, chest heaving, water soaking her body.

He stepped toward her again, but he didn't touch her. His fingers hovered over her body, like he was doing some kind of weird Reiki. *He* wasn't touching her, but his energy, his want for her was.

She shook as the back of his finger made contact with her arm, the touch so delicate, had she not been on pins and needles and acutely aware of everything he was doing right now, she might have missed it.

"Fucking beautiful," he whispered, tracing that same finger beneath the curve of each breast and finally lifting his head to pin her with his gaze.

Her nipples were painfully peaked now, and as much as she was enjoying whatever bizarre and torturous foreplay this was, she was going to combust or take matters into her own hands soon if he didn't do more than just skim his finger across her skin.

"Chase, you need to—"

He stepped forward and dropped his head, drawing his tongue over one nipple and playing with the other one between his thumb and forefinger.

She nearly came on the spot.

He switched nipples. Twisting one and sucking the other. Gentle nibbles and erotic tugs.

All of it was driving her closer and closer to the edge.

Goddamn it, how she'd missed intimacy, how she'd missed Chase.

He lifted her up again, and she wrapped her legs around his waist.

Her thought of whether he could hold up okay was only fleeting when he tugged hard enough on her nipple, her clit spasmed.

With one hand wrapped around his neck, she used the other to hold onto his shoulder as he entered her.

She tilted her head back and hit the shower wall behind her, allowing the moment, the feeling of being so consumed and full wash over her like a cleansing summer rain.

He lifted his head from her breast. His lips skimmed down her arched throat, and he sucked at the hollow of her neck.

"Chase ..."

He scraped his teeth down her jaw and neck. "Hmm?"

"Stop teasing me."

Even without seeing him, she could tell he was smiling. A rarity for such a serious man, but when he did—look out!

"They say the first inch inside is the most sensitive. Isn't that what I'm hitting?"

"Who says that?"

"*They* do."

"Who's they?"

She felt his shoulder rise beneath her forearm. "No idea."

With a growl, she lifted up on his hips, positioned him perfectly at her entrance and then slowly slid down. Inch by measured inch.

She had the intense urge to ride him like a stallion. With wild abandonment until she reached her destination. But she remained still, just like last night, enjoying that delicious stretch as he filled her right up.

When he finally hit the end of her, he paused.

Their moans mingled and echoed around the small space.

"Much better," she said, bobbing up and down on him. "Don't you agree?"

"Mhmm." His fingers dug harder into her ass cheeks, to the point where she knew she'd have bruises later. But it was when he started to move in that sexy flexy hip way of his that she really started to see stars. Emma said she could speak another language—she had no idea which one—when she and James had epic sex.

Now Stacey understood what her friend was talking about.

She was murmuring things even she didn't understand, but they somehow felt like the right things to say.

He pressed her harder into the shower wall and released one hand from her butt, drawing it up the side of her body and cupping a breast.

She drew in a sharp breath when he plucked the nipple like the string of a guitar. Her breasts were regaining their sensitivity. She could feel her orgasm building, the intense heat in her belly growing, her limbs beginning to tingle.

The slightly-too-warm water pummeled their bodies, steam filled the air, and Chase's manly grunts and groans brought her perilously close to the edge.

She was about to take the leap. To hold her breath, spread her wings and cross her fingers for a soft landing when he pulled out, set her down on her feet and gruffly spun her around. His hand on her lower back encouraged her to hinge at the hips, and she did as he instructed, placing her hands on the wall for support.

He angled himself back inside her and thrust hard, hitting the end of her with one solid push, which ended in a grunt from both of them. Then he started to move again.

The new angle was divine.

He hit her deeper. He stroked new parts of her channel, and when she looked down and saw his wet, sexy feet planted firmly on the tub floor, her orgasm started to knock on the door once again.

Her hair hung in her face like a dark blonde veil, and water dripped down her nose and into her eyes. She relished the massage of the spray now hitting her between the shoulder blades. Thea's car seat was heavy while empty, but with her very health baby in it, Stacey's arms and shoulders got a real workout. Chase released his vice grip on her hip with one hand and hunched over her, reaching beneath her body and between her legs to where her clit pulsed and swelled.

Her legs wobbled and knees threatened to buckle when he found her nub and began to rub rough concentric circles.

"Oh God ..."

Even with the new, weird angle, his cadence barely waned. He kept up the speed, the vigor, the rhythm until Stacey couldn't hold on any longer and she let go. Her fingers curled and flexed against the shower wall and her feet rolled over to the sides as the climax ripped through her without remorse.

She squeezed her eyes shut and pushed back against Chase while grinding down hard against his fingers. Her body grew hot, the heat spreading out from her center into her chest, neck and limbs until even her nose tingled.

Her euphoria began to ebb, but she still felt incredible, and she squeezed her muscles around Chase, enjoying the very last surges of pleasure before they evaporated into the ether completely.

He released her clit, and she let out a sigh of relief. It was always super sensitive right after sex, and she would often spasm uncontrollably if it was touched post-orgasm.

He kissed her shoulder blades from one side to the other, sweeping her hair off her back as he did so, before finally pulling out. They'd had the conversation about past partners earlier in the week, and neither of them had been with another person since the last time they were together. She wasn't ready to go on the pill just yet, but she figured they could use condoms in the bedroom and pull out in the shower.

She pushed herself up to standing using the wall for support and turned to face him, once again looping her arms over his shoulders and lifting up on tiptoe. "I hope you're not planning on taking that ice cream home with you."

He grinned. "Wouldn't dream of it."

She nuzzled her nose against his. "Good. One less thing for me to worry about."

"Don't ever need to worry about me. *I* take care of you, remember? Ice cream, orgasms and all."

Regarding him with a sarcastic, wry expression, she pulled away from his face but let her arms remain where they were. "Right, because the big bad bald man can take care of himself."

His cock jerked against her hip, and her eyes flared.

"I *can* take care of myself, if you get my drift, but there are some things I'd much rather *you* take care of." His brows bobbed salaciously over those stunning green eyes.

Smiling, she released his shoulders and slowly sank to her knees, taking his hard length in her palm and angling it toward her mouth. "I can take care of you in other ways, too," she said before closing her eyes and pushing the crown past her lips.

His hand fell to the top of her head. "Yeah, but let's just start with this."

CHAPTER TEN

THURSDAY NIGHT, Stacey sat up in bed with a gasp, her heart palpitating wildly, body in a cold sweat.

It'd been months since she'd had a dream like that.

But it was no dream. Dreams were meant to be pleasant.

This was her worst nightmare.

Her family was being torn from her. Her children taken by faceless men wearing dark hoods, leaving her screaming and reaching out for them, but unable to move.

She wasn't bound, but her feet refused to cooperate.

It was like she had superglue on the soles of her shoes and was stuck to the ground forever.

The look in Connor's eyes still haunted her now that she was awake.

He was scared. Confused. And the way he called out to her and reached for her made her blood run icy through her veins.

With shaky hands, she turned on the bedside lamp and checked her phone.

It was only midnight.

Chase had left two hours ago, after a wonderful family dinner and a few energetic rounds in her bed.

She'd fallen asleep shortly after seeing him to the door, exhausted from her day with the children and running errands. No matter if she went to buy one item or thirty, a trip to Costco with two children was always mentally draining.

But even if a trip to Costco to stock up on baby wipes, diapers and multivitamins was the mental equivalent to writing the bar exam after a night of heavy drinking—or so she imagined—she wouldn't trade her life for the world.

She wouldn't trade that day for the world.

Her children were happy, healthy and safe.

Exhaustion was part and parcel with being a mother, and she knew these moments were fleeting. In the blink of an eye Thea and Connor would be grown and with families of their own. Hopefully, she'd have grandchildren to spoil and dote on, but she knew the day where her chicks left the nest would come faster than she could ever imagine. So even on the hard days, on the days that seemed impossible and never-ending, she kept her chin up and embraced the chaos, the endless laundry piles and toy-scattered living room. Because too soon it would all be gone.

"Mama?" Her slightly opened door opened wider and a sleepy-eyed Connor stood there with a concerned expression. "I heard you call my name."

Had she called his name?

She didn't remember that part of the nightmare.

She remembered screaming, but she hadn't woken herself up with a scream, let alone his name.

She called him over with a gentle flick of her fingers and he crawled up her bed from the foot. "I'm okay, sweetheart. Just had a bad dream."

He snuggled into the covers with her. "I had a bad one, too."

Holding him to her chest, she kissed the top of his head and swept her fingers over his sandy-blond hair. "Want to talk about it?"

"Bad men were taking me and Thea. You were yelling at them to give us back. I was scared." He cuddled in closer to her.

Crap.

This wasn't the first time they'd shared a dream.

It'd been happening for a couple of years now. And as Connor got older and could articulate and remember his dreams better, Stacey was realizing just how often it happened between them.

It was wonderful to discuss when their shared dreams were fun and magical, like the two of them holding hands and flying through the cotton candy clouds.

They usually talked about their dreams in the morning over breakfast—if they could remember them—and because she was in his so often, he would ask if she remembered this part or that part, thinking that she knew what he was talking about because she was there, too. They didn't so much *interact* in their dreams, but seemed to have similar ones. Shared experiences.

Either way, it was sweet and wonderful and something she looked forward to.

But when they were nightmares like this, she wanted to figure out a way she could sever this connection they had. Who was causing who to dream this way? Was she sending her dreams to him?

Because if so, it needed to stop.

He was only four.

He didn't deserve the nightmares that plagued her.

He didn't deserve to experience the horror and fear that she did.

Not at four.

Not ever.

The only person she'd mentioned this to was Joy, and of course, as a therapist, Joy was just fascinated. But she offered little in the way of a *fix*.

Stacey thought maybe hypnosis or as a last resort some kind of exorcism, but Joy merely laughed and said there wasn't much you could do. It was a mother-child bond, and one as tight as Stacey's and Connor's was nearly impossible to break, and not one Stacey should *try* to break. It would loosen on its own over time. But because it had been just Connor and Stacey for so long, their connection was strong, so strong they were even in sync in their dreams.

"It was just a dream, sweetie," she said, sliding them down so they were laying in her bed. "It wasn't real. Nobody is going to take you or Thea. You're safe here with me."

"And Chase, right? He'll protect us, too?"

For now. As blissful as their reunion was, the jury was still out on whether he was sticking around for good. She held onto hope that he was in this for the long haul, but every so often, a look he gave her or an off-handed comment he'd say had her questioning his permanency.

It was easier to just give Connor what he needed right now and she nodded and kissed his forehead. "Hmm. Chase will protect us, too."

"Why'd you call my name? Is it because you were there, too? Did we have the same dream again?"

She hugged him tighter. "I think maybe we did, honey. But it wasn't real. I promise."

Connor yawned and his eyes fluttered. "Can I sleep with you?"

"Of course, sweetheart." She reached over and turned off the light.

"Can you snuggle me until I fall asleep?" he asked, his voice soft like he was already half-way there.

"I'll snuggle you all night if you need me to, baby." She kissed his head again.

"I love you, Mama."

Oh God, this kid was going to rip her heart right out of her chest.

She kissed his head again and adjusted them into a more comfortable position. "I love you, too, baby."

"I'm glad Chase is here. I protect Thea, you protect me and Chase protects you."

"Something like that."

"But who will protect Chase? Thea is too little."

Such big thoughts for such a small person. He shouldn't be worrying about who was protecting who. He should be thinking and worrying about the next episode of Paw Patrol and what he wanted for breakfast.

"We protect each other," she finally said.

"Because that's what families do?"

Stacey squeezed her eyes shut and focused on her breathing. *In through the nose, out through the mouth.* "Yeah, kiddo," she finally said. "Because that's what families do."

But Connor was already asleep.

She spent the rest of the night holding her son, drifting in and out of consciousness, but never deep enough to dream. Never deep enough to bring back the bad men who were trying to snatch her children from her.

Because the only way that would ever happen, would be over Stacey's cold, dead body.

———

THEY'D BEEN DOING the family *thing* for over a week now.

Chase had dinner nearly every night with Stacey and the kids, then they'd bathe the kids, put them to bed, and then bang like they hadn't banged in months—because they hadn't.

Then he'd leave, kiss her goodbye and go battle his demons and nightmares on his own at home.

It wasn't perfect. Fuck, it wasn't even what he wanted, but it was the best he could offer them at the moment.

He wanted to be with Stacey, wanted to be with those kids and do the family *thing*. More than he ever thought he would want to. So for now, this scenario would have to do.

It was Friday night, and he knew from talking to Heath and Brock that Rex was set to arrive home from his job in the Yukon around six that night.

So with his balls thoroughly drained and his head feeling clearer than it had in fuck knows how long, Chase realized what he needed to do next.

Rex lived in another part of town, but since Victoria wasn't that big, another part of town was only a fifteen-minute drive from Chase's place, even less of a drive from Stacey's.

He left Stacey's after a thorough kiss goodbye and was at his brother's front lobby by eleven o'clock. Rex was a night owl, so unless he was in bed "entertaining" a guest, he was probably still awake.

Parking his truck on the curb, he locked it with the fob and headed toward the lobby, where a keypad was embedded in the wall under a small outdoor overhang.

He didn't even have to look up his brother on the tenant listing. Rex was in 411.

He punched in the number and waited for it to ring.

"Yeah?" Rex answered. Diesel woofed in the background.

"It's me."

The surprise in Rex's tone was unmistakable. "Come on up."

The front door clicked open, and Chase heaved on the handle.

He took the stairs, because given the choice between a small box and a few flights of stairs, he'd take the few flights of stairs any day. Hell, he'd climb fifty flights before he stepped foot into an elevator the size of a shoebox.

He reached his brother's door and knew it would already be unlocked.

He knocked out of courtesy and opened it.

Rex was standing in his living room with two open beer bottles on his coffee table. He tilted his head at one to indicate it was for Chase.

Chase nodded and murmured a thanks just as Diesel bounded forward and shoved in face into Chase's crotch. A couple of sniffs seemed to satisfy the pup and he loped back over to his bed beneath the wall-mounted television.

By the looks of things, Rex was sorting through his laundry. He had two piles on the couch and a hamper between them. He'd pick up a shirt, give it a sniff and then toss it into one pile or the other.

"So?" Chase's other bald brother asked.

"So why'd you go after Stacey?" Chase took a seat in the leather recliner positioned in front of Rex's enormous flat-screen television.

Rex's lip lifted at one side, and he bent down and picked up his beer from the coffee table, taking a long pull from it. "You weren't."

Chase closed his eyes and sipped his beer. "What makes you think that?"

Rex set his beer back down and went back to sorting his laundry. "Didn't see you making a move. Brock sent me to check on her, said you 'needed space.' Figured that meant you weren't interested." He tossed a pair of black jeans into a pile.

"We'd had sex the night before you went over to her place, took your shirt off and hugged her like you wished she was naked, too, and on her back." Chase fixed his brother with a steely gaze.

Rex lifted a shoulder. "Didn't know." He tossed a sock into the same pile as the black jeans. "Is that why you haven't returned one of my damn calls or messages? You've been pissed that I tried to move in on Stacey? Even though she turned me down immediately and said she only sees me as a friend? A low blow, I might add. Haven't been tossed into the friend-zone before. Not a fan."

Rex was roughly the same size as Chase. They were the closest in age, and although Rex and Heath shared similar coloring and the dark blue eyes, Chase and Rex were often mistaken for twins. Even growing up, people thought they were twins. Just shy of two years apart, they'd always been close growing up—all the brothers were.

So to not have Rex in Chase's life, even digitally, these last several months had been more painful than Chase was prepared to admit.

"You with Stacey now?" Rex asked, scooping up the pile with the black jeans and heaving it into his white laundry hamper.

Chase nodded slowly, staring straight ahead at the television. There was no sound, but a Canucks-Flames game was playing on the screen. "We're sorting through some shit. Taking it slow."

Well, they weren't *taking it slow* when it came to how much, how often and how hard he'd pounded her into the mattress over the last week.

They also weren't taking the *family thing* slow either. At least not in Connor's eyes. The poor kid had actually asked Chase that night if Chase was his new dad because his other dad was dead.

Knife. To. The. Gut.

But they were taking everything else slow. Whatever else there was left.

She'd pushed a little more for him to tell her his secrets, but he'd quickly changed the subject. He just couldn't see any way to tell her that wouldn't result in her going all buggy-eyed and questioning whether he was safe to leave alone with her children.

He was. At least awake.

Asleep was another story.

Not that he would hurt either of them, but the idea of Connor getting out of bed and seeing Chase in the middle of one of his nightmares was a nightmare in and of itself for Chase.

A knock at the door had them both turning around.

Diesel was back up from his bed with another *woof*.

"Hey, hey!"

The floppy-haired, blond puppy dog in the form of Heath came into the apartment carrying a six-pack of beer bottles, Brock in his wake.

Both Brock's and Heath's eyes widened when they saw Chase sitting in the recliner.

Diesel did his customary sniff of them both, got himself some head pats and ear scratches, then returned to his bed.

"Things good here," Brock asked warily, "or have you both just kicked the shit out of each other and are taking an intermission?"

"Neither have split lips or black eyes," Heath said, wandering over to Rex's fridge and stowing the beer. "I'd say they're mending fences."

Chase cleared his throat. "That's why I came."

Brock took a seat where the laundry pile had been, while Heath seemed content sitting on the floor beneath the television. He tipped a beer up to his lips.

Rex pinned his gaze on Chase. "Look, I'm sorry I tried to move in on Stacey. She's hot, sassy and sweet. Can you blame me?"

Chase grunted and narrowed his eyes. "Yeah."

Rex rolled his eyes. "Fine. But she turned me down, said she was in love with you. Shocked the shit out of me because I saw no more than high school puppy-dog eyes exchanged between the two of you."

"People move at different paces, bro," Heath said gently. "Some play the long game. Others"—he pointed at Rex and then himself—"go all in right away."

Rex's expression said he understood and agreed. He turned back to Chase. "I just didn't think you'd take it so fucking hard and ghost me for half a fucking year."

Chase's thumbnail picked at the label on his beer, and he stared at it for a moment, the paper lifting up and curling on one side. "Mumps and infection in Peru left me sterile."

The room went dead quiet.

Not that it was loud to begin with, but now you could probably hear a fucking pin drop.

He took his time lifting his gaze to his brothers.

All of them looked crestfallen. Like it was *they* who had been given the news they were shooting dust.

"How do you know?" Heath asked.

"Mom shanghaied me into getting tested about nine months ago. She had a suspicion, her being who she is and all."

"Nosy, meddling, obsessed with us," Heath said with a grin.

They all loved their mother more than anything in the world. Would kill and die for her. But she did have a penchant for meddling in her sons' lives and getting them to do things they wouldn't necessarily do without her prodding them like cattle.

"When did you find out?" Rex asked. He'd taken a seat on the other end of the couch from Brock, the laundry he'd deemed "clean" back in his duffle bag.

"Just before I took the gig watching Stacey. Fucked with my head big time. Still does." He took a long swig of his beer, hating the pity that stared back at him by three people he loved most in the world.

"Stacey know?" Brock asked.

Chase shook his head.

"She know anything about Peru?" Heath asked.

Chase shook his head again.

"You gonna tell her?" Rex asked.

That was the fifty-million-dollar question, wasn't it?

He wanted to tell her so she understood him better. Understood why he couldn't see them having a "normal" future together, why he couldn't give her more children if she wanted them. But he was also terrified of how she would react. That she might realize what he figured all along—Rex was the better, more mentally stable man for her.

"Haven't found a way to yet," he said, sucking in a breath through thinly parted lips. "She keeps asking. Can't figure out how to word it all."

"And not scare her the fuck away," Heath finished.

He pointed at his youngest brother. "Yep."

"Look, man," Rex started, "not being able to have kids doesn't make you any less of a man, if that's what you're worried about. And I doubt Stacey would fucking care. She has two kids already, and those kids fucking love you, and you love them, right?"

Like they were his own.

Even if they weren't.

"Don't see her caring that you're shooting blanks," Heath said. "Save money on condoms and shit." He cracked a half-smile, but it didn't stick around, his gaze suddenly turning serious again. "You don't think *we* think any less of you, do you?"

Chase tipped his gaze up to his brothers, leveling it on each of them individually.

Yeah, that was another one of his fears.

Brock didn't even have to try. He looked at Krista the right way and she got preggers. Both babies had been oopsies. Zoe was the result of a drunk one-night stand between Brock and Krista. They hadn't even gotten along at first.

"You should fucking know us better than that, dipshit," Brock said, real, genuine anger in his tone. "You want Stacey, you want those kids, they want you, then they're yours. Blood doesn't mean shit if you're the dad and man they need."

"That why you took off the way you did?" Rex asked. The unspoken words were also there. *Saw yourself as less of a man next to me?*

Chase nodded. "Yeah. Just a lot to process. Didn't think I was good enough for Stacey. Still don't."

"Fuck, and you think I'm good enough for Krista?" Brock asked, still angry. "That woman is leagues above me. But I try my damnedest every fucking day *to* be worthy of her."

"I'm sorry for trying to move in on Stacey," Rex said. "Didn't know you two had the connection that you did—that you *do*. Didn't know you'd *been together* or that you loved her. Never meant to come between you guys or for it to come between us." He reached forward and offered Chase his hand. "Know that I love you, brother, and am always here if you need to talk."

Chase took his hand and shook it, grateful to have his strained relationship with Rex be one less thing weighing him down.

"We're all here if you need to talk," Heath said. "Or if you'd rather not talk and just go a couple rounds on the punching bag. Either-or, bro."

Chase nodded and thanked his brothers.

They all tipped their beers up and drank in silence, pivoting their attention to the screen.

"Volume up?" Rex asked.

Brock grunted. Heath turned around fully, and Chase said, "Yes."

Then the four Hart brothers, together once again after over almost six months apart, watched a recorded hockey game and drank beer together. Just like old times.

CHAPTER ELEVEN

It was Saturday afternoon, and Joy had offered to watch Thea while Stacey took Connor to his swimming lessons. Joy often watched Thea on Saturdays for a few hours so Stacey and her little boy could have some one-on-one time. Although he was a truly tremendous kid with the patience of a saint and the most cheerful disposition, he was only four, and if Thea was demanding too much of Stacey, Connor started to act out. So she was trying her hardest to give her son the one-on-one mummy time he needed.

His hair was damp from swimming, his cheeks ruddy and eyes bright as she swung into the parking lot of the dollar store. Emma had told her about the mittens she'd bought for the twins there, so Stacey was going to go see if she could find Thea some. Up until now, she'd just been putting socks on Thea's hands when they were outdoors, but the baby would suck on them and her hands would get cold anyway.

"We're just going to pop in here quick, okay?" she said to Connor, as he took her hand and joyfully skipped beside her through the dollar store parking lot. "I have to see if they have something."

"Okay, Mama," Connor said happily. "Are we having dinner at Nana Joy's tonight?"

"That's the plan, Stan. Already dropped off my dip."

"Will Zoe and Zane be there?"

She opened the door to the store and let him go in ahead of her. "I think so. I texted Auntie Krista yesterday, and she said they're planning to go."

"Yay!" he cheered, motioning to her to pick up a wire basket.

Stacey shook her head. "We're not getting much. I don't think we'll need one."

Connor shrugged and took her hand again as they started wandering up and down the aisles.

Unlike when Joy had mentioned the dinner that first day when Chase returned and Stacey had thought of a million reasons and ways to cancel, now that she and Chase were "back together," she was actually really looking forward to a big Hart family dinner.

Eventually, they found the mittens, and because children were notorious for losing mittens, socks and anything with a *mate*, she bought five pairs. Not bad for a buck a pair. She also grabbed a couple of next-size-up mittens for Connor as well, and by the time they were in line for the checkout she was wishing she had gotten a basket.

"Are you helping Mommy shop?" a lady two people up in the queue asked, bending down to speak directly to Connor.

Connor nodded. "We need gloves. Some are for me. Some are for my sister."

"Well, aren't you a big helper." Her eyes were dark, which was quite the stark contrast to her fair complexion and light blonde hair.

Pride radiated off the little boy, and he nodded again.

The woman, who was probably not much older than Stacey's thirty-three, smiled and turned to the impulse buys that lined the checkout area. "Can you recommend some snacks?"

Connor's eyes lit up, and he pointed at the root veggie chips, the Cheetos and the popcorn. The woman threw all three in her basket.

"What else?" she asked.

Connor proceeded to point to some chocolate bars Stacey sure as hell hoped her kid had never tried, and then finally some apple juice in one of the fridges. The woman proceeded to grab everything he pointed at. She'd only had like three items—all kids' toys—in her basket, and now it was loaded. It struck Stacey as odd, but she didn't let the thought consume her. The woman probably had kids or nieces or nephews, maybe Connor's age, who she was buying for, so it made sense to seek the opinion of someone of a similar age.

She thanked Connor and stepped up to the checkout. Before long, she was gone, waving at Connor with a big smile.

Stacey and Connor waited their turn behind another customer before finally getting up to the checkout to pay.

It felt like a lot longer than it probably was, but by the time they emerged outside again, it was growing dark. She hated how it started to get dark so early. Spring could not come soon enough. Wracking her brain about whether she should stop and get more bread for her dip, she was startled by Connor's question.

"What's that?" He was pointing at the back window of her SUV.

"What's what, buddy?"

He pointed again. "That!"

Her brows scrunched as she took in the numbers and letters scrawled in white on the back window of her Santa Fe.

1 F

1 MC

What the hell did that mean?

Hitting the fob for her car, she plopped Connor in his car seat. He could get himself into the straps—she'd just have to double-check the tightness—so while he did that, she was going to go about trying to remove the weird writing.

Setting the dollar store bag on the floor of the back seat, she reached into her purse for her pack of baby wipes. She never left home without them.

She'd parked under a street lamp in the parking lot, so it would be easy enough to see what she was doing as she wiped it off. She took a picture of it first, planning to show Krista, the cop, and the Hart brothers the image when she got to Joy's. Maybe they would know what it meant.

Connor was singing some Disney song as he fought with his straps and she started to wipe the window. It was on there more than she thought, so she really had to scrub. She was using her nail to scrape it off when she felt a sharp prick on the side of her neck.

"What the?" She spun around just in time to see the woman from the dollar store holding her up from behind. Stacey's head began to feel fuzzy, and her limbs felt like overcooked spaghetti. She slumped into the woman's arms.

She wanted to scream, but she couldn't.

The woman dragged Stacey to the front seat of her SUV and pushed her in behind the steering wheel before shutting the door.

Her last thought before the world went black was about Connor and how much she loved him.

———

HER NECK ACHED, and her head pounded.

Her eyelids felt like cinder blocks, and her tongue felt too big and cumbersome in her mouth.

A ringing was off in the distance, growing more and more demanding, more and more intense.

Mumbling, she rolled her head side to side, and her hands

fumbled in the dark. She still hadn't opened her eyes, but based on what she was feeling, she wasn't at home in bed.

The ringing was getting louder.

"Gah!" she cried out, forcing her lids open only to find herself in the dark front seat of her Santa Fe and her phone going crazy in her pocket.

With movements that were slow and awkward, she retrieved the phone from her coat, somehow managed to unlock it and put it to her ear. "Hello?"

"Stacey!" It was Joy. "Where are you, sweetheart? We've all been so worried. It's nearly seven o'clock."

Seven o'clock?

She blinked a bunch of times and pinched the bridge of her nose with her thumb and forefinger.

And then it hit her.

Connor!

"Connor!"

She spun around in her seat but didn't see him.

She couldn't feel him in the vehicle.

Since the day she brought him home from the hospital, she'd always had an acute awareness of his presence. He was an old soul with a big heart, and she could feel those things in the air around her.

She didn't feel a damn thing.

"Connor!"

Flinging her door open, she scrambled out of the front seat on wobbly legs.

Her vision was still spotty and blurry, but even blind as a bat, she would know—because a mother always knows—that her little boy was not in his seat.

Every molecule of air fled her lungs. She struggled to breathe. Her body shook. Her eyes darted everywhere; her brain began to short-circuit. This was not happening.

How did this happen?

Where was her son?

Where was her child?

Where was her baby?

Someone had taken her baby!

"Honey, what's wrong?" Joy asked, concern coloring her tone. "Where are you guys?"

"I need to ... oh my God ... he's ... they took ... she took him."

"Who took who?" Joy asked. Whispers and murmurs in the background sounded more like white noise.

Bile rose up in Stacey's throat, and she cupped her hand to her mouth. "She took Connor! Oh my God! They took my son!"

She started to scream.

———

CHASE NODDED at the police officer, who he recognized as one of Krista's coworkers. The whole parking lot was a sea of blue and flashing lights as he, Brock, Rex and Heath all made their way toward Stacey.

When his mother told them that Connor had been taken, all Chase saw was red. He still saw it now, and it would be the only shade he would see until Stacey had her son back and the fuckers who took that little boy were six feet under.

"We've put out an AMBER Alert, stalled all ferry sailing and did a sweep of all the ones en route, both domestic and international. So far, nothing," a male cop Chase didn't recognize said as Chase and his brothers sidled up to where Stacey was sitting in the popped trunk of her SUV. She was being looked at by a paramedic as well, because apparently, she'd been injected with some kind of sedative.

Chances are they'd need to get her to a hospital for a tox screen.

"Why?" she asked, looking smaller and more scared than he'd ever seen her. "Why did they take my baby?"

Once the paramedic stepped away, Chase went to her, taking her in his arms immediately. Her fear and panic didn't transfer to him. He just absorbed it and felt it seep into his body. He kissed the top of her head. "We'll get him back. *I* will get him back."

"It's what a few child trafficking rings do," the male cop said. "That thing you showed us on your phone, it means *One Female, One Male Child.* You were marked, probably by whoever took your son or a bigger syndicate, we don't know."

"Child trafficking ..." Stacey began to shake, and Chase hugged her tighter, whispering things to her as she began to hyperventilate.

"I want access to the parking lot's surveillance," Chase said, his chest aching as he held Stacey and she began to sob against him. "Let's get a look at who we're dealing with. See if we can get some facial recognition, see where they're headed." He didn't want to say it out loud, but the first forty-eight hours of a child abduction—of any kind of abduction—were the most critical. After that, the chances of finding Connor reduced significantly almost by the hour.

"Who the hell are you?" the cop asked, giving Chase a look like he was just some random civilian coming in and demanding to be let in beyond the red tape. Which in some ways he was. But he was also a former Joint Task Force 2 operative with years of training in the Navy and a master's degree in computer science and programming. He could hack into just about anything. He didn't *need* to be given access to the security cameras to get access, but he'd found that asking for something rather than just taking it seemed to piss people off less.

"Harty Boys security and surveillance," Brock said, stepping forward with a card. "Ms. Saunders and her little boy are family. We are at her and the police department's disposal. Anything we can do to help, just let us know."

Chase knew this spiel from Brock was just a courtesy to the good men and women in blue. The Harty Boys weren't above the law, but they did what needed to get done, and sometimes that meant keeping the cops in the dark.

The male officer, whose nametag read Cowen, glanced at the card before stowing it in his pocket. "We've got it under control, guys, but it's good to know you're around if we need you."

Chase and his brothers exchanged looks.

An entire conversation without a word said.

They'd find Connor, and they'd do it without the help of the West Shore police.

Brock stepped back and whispered to Chase, "Need to get you home so you can hack into the footage."

Chase grunted.

"Look at all cameras for all ports. No harbor is too small."

Chase grunted again and this time added a nod.

Brock glanced at Heath. "Stay here, find out what you can from the cops." He turned back to Chase, who was still holding Stacey up while she unraveled. "You get her back to Mum's. We'll reconvene there in twenty." He glanced at one of the paramedics. "Unless you think she needs a tox screen?"

The paramedics were muttering with their heads together.

"Probably best, yeah," the male paramedic said.

Chase nodded and gently pried Stacey out of his arms and steered her toward his truck. Her SUV was a crime scene now, so she couldn't take it. They also had no idea what kind of a sedative she was given, and her son had just been abducted, so she was in absolutely no state to drive.

Rex and Brock were already talking more to the cop.

He helped her into the front seat of his truck and buckled her in.

She was shaking, and the tears streamed down her face

unchecked. The vacant expression on her face frightened the shit out of him.

He needed to get her out of there.

He needed to find her son.

———

THE DOCTOR DETERMINED that Stacey had been given a small but potent dose of ketamine to knock her out. The side effects would be minimal. They did more tests though, such as an HIV test, considering they'd used a needle they'd gotten from only God knows where, but those results wouldn't come back as quickly. She'd also have to get tested later as well, as HIV wasn't always detected in the initial test.

He helped her back into his truck in the hospital parking lot, only this time, she mumbled that she wanted to sit in the back seat.

He obliged, albeit reluctantly.

She was quiet on the drive.

He kept a close eye on her in the rearview mirror, worried that she was going to retreat inside herself completely and shut down.

Not that he could blame her.

She was worrying herself sick. As were the rest of them.

Chase was having a tough time keeping the rage shakes from sending him off the deep end. And if he did that, then he'd be of little use to anyone, particularly Stacey and Connor.

Who would take such a sweet, wonderful kid like Connor?

There was only one logical, disgusting answer to that question.

A dead man.

Or at least he or *she* would be dead when Chase finally got his hands on them.

People who stole children, who traded them like baseball cards, were the scum of the Earth and didn't deserve to breathe the same air as the children they traded.

And Chase would see to it that they weren't breathing for much longer.

He fought back the tears and the growing tightness in his throat as he drove through the dark city streets. It was closing in on nine thirty. According to Stacey, they'd taken Connor around four.

They could be just about anywhere by now.

He needed to get back to his mother's place and hack into the parking lot surveillance and all the ferry port surveillances. Victoria was located on the tip of Vancouver Island.

There were at least four ferry ports they could have used to get off the island within a twenty-mile radius. Or they could have driven further up the island and taken a more northern ferry, with the hopes of not being detected, since the abduction happened in Victoria.

All of these scenarios were plausible.

Airports were possible, too, but less so. They'd still send out notifications to all the airports on the island and Vancouver International, as well.

Another glance in the mirror at Stacey had his knuckles tightening on the steering wheel. She was staring vacantly out the window, tears still streaming down her face, body shaking.

Fuck!

Those motherfuckers would pay.

Chase thought back to the first time he'd met Connor and how the kid's enthusiasm and friendliness had won Chase over immediately.

Unfortunately, it was also what probably made him a prime target.

He retreated to his memories, since the present was just too painful.

It was the first day he'd met all of them.

Nearly ten months ago, Chase had let out a long, steady exhale as he made his way back up Stacey's driveway to his rented SUV.

He was going to crash on her couch for the next few days until they got all packed up and he could safely escort her; Daniella, the temporary nanny; and the children to Victoria. He snatched his duffle bag from the front seat, grabbed his phone charger from the lighter plug and re-locked the truck.

He wasn't a big fan of babysitting duty. He preferred to be finding the bad guys on his computer, hacking and tracking, hunting and sniffing out the scum of the world. But he also had to be flexible, and a job was a job.

He wasn't two steps down the driveway, his eyes scanning the street on either side for possible danger, when a blond tornado barely three feet high caught him at the shins and nearly sent him ass over teakettle.

"*Oof!*"

He caught his balance and peered down at the little boy clinging to his leg. "Hey, kid."

"I'm Connor."

"Cool."

"What your name?"

"Chase."

The kid's eyes went wider than anything Chase had ever seen before, and then the world's biggest smile erupted also. "Chase!"

Chase gently shook the kid off his leg and made his way up the path. There was an enemy out there. The little boy should not be outside, even with Chase right there.

"My favorite pup on Paw Patrol is named Chase," Connor went on, following Chase up the driveway like a puppy himself. "He's a German shepherd and the police dog. Are you a police officer? Do you have a badge? Can I see it? Do you arrest bad guys? Are you sleeping over? Did you bring a sleeping bag? I have a Paw Patrol sleeping bag. It has Chase on it. Do you know who Chase is, Chase?"

They reached the front door, which was wide open. "Jeez, little man, that's a lot of questions."

Connor smiled a big, toothy grin. "You want to watch Paw Patrol with me, Chase?"

"Uh ..."

"Mama said I could watch an extra episode of Paw Patrol after my snack. Do you like PB and J?"

Chase dropped his duffle bag just inside the front door. Ms. Saunders was nowhere to be found.

"Do you like PB and J?" Connor asked again. In the blink of an eye, the kid had dipped into the kitchen and come out seconds later waving a half-eaten triangle of a sandwich. "You want a bite?"

Chase breathed out a small laugh. This kid was something else. "I'm good, thanks. Maybe later."

"My mama can make you one."

Chase snorted. He was sure Ms. Saunders would *love* that. She didn't seem overly enthused to have him there to begin with.

The warble and coo of a baby drew his attention deeper into the townhouse. He knew from Freya that Stacey had a newborn daughter in addition to three-year-old Connor.

He also knew her *situation*.

Two-timing bastard husband.

Saddling her with two children while he had another wife in another city.

He was better off dead.

Wandering into the living room, he found Miss Saunders sitting on her couch and nursing the baby. Her entire breast was out, and the baby was reclined on a light blue U-shaped pillow, eating away.

"Oh, uh, sorry." He quickly averted his eyes.

"Haven't you ever seen a breast before?" she asked. "Or a person eat?"

Ah fuck, was she really going to hit him below the belt like that? Of course he was pro-breastfeeding and that women should feel comfortable to do it anywhere without having to cover up, particularly their own homes. Didn't mean when he came around the corner and saw a big, creamy breast he wasn't momentarily taken aback. He knew if his mother was there, she'd knock him in the back of the head and then give him a thirty-minute lecture.

Joy Hart was not only a therapist specializing in sexuality and relationships, but she was also a lactation consultant and was once the president of the La Leche League. He knew *all* about breast-feeding. Probably more than he would ever need to.

He scratched the back of his neck and lifted his head to meet her eyes. "Sorry, Ms. Saunders. Yes, of course. Feed your child."

"Stacey." She looked back down at her child. "Please call me Stacey."

He nodded. Fuck, they were not getting off on the right foot here.

"Right. Would you mind if I had a look around? Make sure the house isn't bugged or anything."

Her gentle, light brown eyes flew back up to him, and she tucked a strand of poker-straight strawberry-blonde hair behind her ear. "You think it might be?"

A dash of pink flooded her cheeks, making her freckles blend into her complexion.

He lifted one shoulder. "Might be."

She nodded fervently. "Yes, please. Go check." Her gaze dropped again to the baby, and she slid her knuckle over the infant's cheek.

Chase took off in the direction of the staircase leading to the second floor, but he didn't make it far before he had a shadow. "Whatcha doin', Chase?" Connor asked. "Where ya going? Can I give you a tour? We can start with my room. You can sleep on my floor if you want. I can be brave and turn off my nightlight if you want."

Careful not to knock any of the family photos lining the stairwell, he moved against the other wall. "Going upstairs."

"Why?" Connor squeezed next to him, making him lift his arm so his elbow didn't bop the tyke in the head. "Why you going upstairs? You wanna see my room?"

No. But he did need to sweep for bugs, and there could be one planted in Connor's room, plus the kid was pretty cool. He was also probably starved for attention, not only because of the new baby but also because of the whole dead dad thing.

He needed to throw the kid a bone.

They reached the top of the stairs, and he glanced down at the mop-top kid. "Sure, show me your room."

CHAPTER TWELVE

By the time they arrived back at Chase's mother's house, all the children—Zoe, Zane and Thea—were asleep in the spare bedrooms.

God.

All the children.

No, not all the children were asleep. One was missing.

Connor should be tucked in bed in a room with his sister, not God-only-knew-where with soulless child snatchers preparing to sell him like cattle.

Chase asked Heath to swing by his apartment and grab his laptop and shit, since Chase had Stacey and didn't want to drive all the way back downtown from the hospital.

Chase and Stacey were the last to arrive at his mother's house, since everything at the hospital seemed to move at the speed of a snail.

All three of his brothers were either texting on their phones or had their phones to their ears and were making plans.

Joy and Krista immediately went to Stacey and pulled her into a hug.

Not that it wasn't comforting, he was sure, but his mother and sister-in-law's attentions only seemed to bring on a new wave of tears and fear in Stacey, and her sobbing grew louder again, her trembling more intense.

She was in good, capable hands though. His mother and Krista would look after Stacey while Chase did what he did best.

He set his laptop up on the table and logged on.

"They're searching every vehicle at every ferry terminal on the island," Heath said. "Cops are out everywhere, not just here in Vic but all along the island in case they're being sneaky and heading north to cross over to Prince Rupert from Port Hardy."

"You can never be too careful or underestimate lowlifes who take kids," Rex murmured, rubbing his hand over Diesel's blocky head when the pup came up to his owner for attention.

Brock ended the call he was on just as Chase worked on tapping into the dollar store parking lot surveillance. Krista had used her cop skills and connections and gained him access to the surveillance, so he didn't have to pick the lock on the backdoor and hack his way into the footage. He had the video up on his computer in no time.

The store was located in a strip mall complex, next to a liquor store, a thrift store and pet store. And thankfully, Stacey had been smart and parked under a street lamp.

He was busy scanning through footage, so he barely heard her push up from her seat and come to stand behind him. He felt her though. Felt her presence, felt her fear, felt her ache.

"Stop there," Brock said abruptly, pointing at the screen. "There they are."

Yep. There they were.

Mother and son happily leaving the store. Connor was skipping and chatting away, his smile radiant even in the shitty surveillance footage.

They saw Connor point at the back window of her Santa Fe.

Saw Stacey glance at the markings, too, then she put Connor in his seat. They watched as she brought out the wipes from her purse and began scrubbing off the marks. What happened next made his insides turn to ice. A woman got out of the passenger door of a black SUV parked two stalls over, crept up behind Stacey and stuck something in her neck.

The sharp snag of breath behind him made the red in his vision turn dark and closer to the color of fresh blood.

People would bleed for taking Connor.

They continued to watch as the woman dragged Stacey into the front seat of her vehicle. A man wearing a dark hoodie, making sure to keep his face hidden, came out from around the dark SUV and went toward the back passenger seat, retrieving Connor.

You could see the little boy fighting the man. You could see his mouth open as he screamed. Why wasn't anybody going to help him?

Why wasn't anybody helping *them*?

"Oh God," Chase's mother whispered.

There was some fumbling as the man from the SUV struggled to get Connor into his seat. Then they watched as the woman finished with Stacey, went to the passenger side of her vehicle, retrieved something, went to Connor, and suddenly the little boy's body went limp.

"Oh my God." He had to resist turning around to see Stacey, but he could see in the reflection on his screen that she had turned into Heath's chest, and soft sobs echoed around the silent room.

"Holy fuck," Rex breathed.

The SUV sped away, and it was a while—hours on the recording—before they saw Stacey emerge from her vehicle looking disoriented. She went to open Connor's door, and when she collapsed to the ground, Chase felt his own soul get ripped clean from his body.

Good. He would need no soul when he finally came face-to-face with the people who took Connor. When he did what needed to be done.

"We'll find him," Heath said, venom and bloodlust in his tone. "I'm on this job. Nobody can tell me I'm not."

"I am, too," Chase said softly, rewinding the footage and zooming in on the license plate of the black SUV. It had Washington plates. Not that that meant it was heading back to Washington, but it would make it easier to spot in a line of cars, rather than the thousands of Beautiful British Columbia plates.

"It was the same woman from the store," Stacey said just above a whisper. "She was super friendly with Connor. Asked him to help her pick out snacks." She gasped. "Oh God, was she getting him to help her pick out snacks for *him?*"

Chase went further back on the recording until the woman exited the dollar store. He zoomed in on her face, which, thankfully, wasn't covered by a hat, glasses or anything else. He snapped a clear shot of her.

"We need to blast this face out everywhere," Brock said. "Stacey, you need to describe what Connor was wearing."

"I already did to the cops."

"Yeah, but we're working faster," Brock said. "Again ..." He grunted, which probably meant Krista elbowed him. "Please."

"I'll get her statement," Krista said.

"I'll get in touch with our contacts in Seattle," Heath said. "Aaron Steele and Colton Hastings are down there. Aaron can reach out to his contacts, too. The more people who know the better."

While his brothers took care of what they did best, Chase got to work on what he did best, which was all things technological. He'd already hacked and installed a backdoor into all the island ferries' surveillance systems years ago for another job, so it was easy peasy to get back in. He brought up all the BC Ferries' surveillance footage, then the footage from the ferries that connected Victoria to the States. The Anacortes Ferry from Sidney to Anacortes, Washington, and the Clipper, which was a passenger ferry that linked downtown Victoria to downtown Seattle. Maybe they were cunning and put a sedated Connor in a stroller and walked on. It wasn't a stupid idea, particularly if they'd gone far enough to get him a fake passport.

The worst thing you could do was underestimate the bad guy.

Finally, he brought up the footage for the Coho ferry, which linked Victoria to Port Angeles, Washington. There wasn't anything on the Victoria side, but—

"Here!"

Shadows formed on the screen as people crowded in behind him again, blocking out the light from the living room.

"That's her!" Stacey practically shouted, hanging over his shoulder and pointing at the screen. "That's the bitch."

"They're in Washington," Brock said. "At least we know that now."

"But for how long?" Heath whispered. That was the thought that was on all of their minds. At least on the island, the traffickers only had so many places to hide. Now that they were back on the mainland, their possibilities were endless.

Finding Connor just got a whole hell of a lot harder.

Time was of the essence now more than ever.

They watched on the screen as the woman from the dollar store got out of the dark SUV and opened up the back hatch. She pulled a blanket free and then proceeded to spread it.

Nobody had to say anything. They all knew Connor was in the back under the blanket.

"My baby," Stacey whimpered.

"We need to move," Brock said at the same time the SUV pulled away from the curb on the screen. "They're not going to stay in Port Angeles. We need to put out an AMBER Alert in Washington, Oregon, Montana and Idaho, even as far south as California.

Get that license plate and her face circulating everywhere. I'll order us a chopper, and we can head out tonight."

"I'm coming," Stacey said.

"Not a good idea," Krista said gently. "Thea needs you here."

"Connor needs me," Stacey said defensively. "Thea has a family here that loves her. Here she's safe. She trusts you. She trusts Joy. She will be fine. Connor is *not* safe, and when we get him back, he's going to need his mother right away. I'm coming."

Thank God she said *when* they get him back and not *if*.

Had Chase heard those words out of her mouth, he wasn't sure what he would have done. His heart was already threatening to shatter. His control was hanging on by a frayed thread.

Brock was murmuring on his phone in the background again, while Chase hacked into more surveillance systems along the highway he assumed the traffickers would take. They stopped at a gas station just outside of Port Angeles. The driver got out this time, and they managed to get a clean shot of his face. He was a big guy. Mean-looking. Muscles were packed thick beneath his black leather jacket; he wore a dark wool cap, and his scowl seemed to be permanently stuck on his face. The man's smile muscles probably stopped functioning the moment he sold his soul to the devil and started stealing children.

He zoomed in on the guy's face and enhanced the clarity.

"Seen him before?" he asked, directing his question to Stacey but not bothering to look at her.

"No. She was the only one in the store."

He cleared up the images of the man, woman and their license plate even more, then compiled them into a file along with a photo of Connor that Stacey had taken earlier that week. He was smiling and holding a ginger snap cookie.

"Same outfit as today," Joy said. "He loves those camo pants."

"Blue boots, too?" Chase asked.

"Yes," Stacey confirmed.

"Black shirt?"

"Yes."

"Coat?"

"He knows better than to be strapped into his car seat wearing his big puffy winter coat—it's not safe. He took it off, and they didn't grab it. He's probably freezing."

Children's health and safety was the least of these fuckers' concerns. After all, it looked like they'd put Connor in the back of their vehicle under a blanket and without a seat belt to avoid border detection when crossing back into the states. The bottom dollar and saving their own hide were all these assholes cared about.

And that was what terrified Chase the most.

If things got *too* dicey, they could just ditch Connor to get the authorities off their scent. They wouldn't run the risk of disposing of him, because murder charges—particularly that of a child—carried a greater prison sentence than human trafficking—though in his opinion, both deserved the fucking death penalty. And nothing cushy like lethal injection. Hang them. Quarter them and light their insides on fire.

He really shouldn't have watched that documentary on Henry VIII while in Georgia. It was only giving him more creative and gruesome ideas on how best to punish those who hurt innocents, who hurt the people he cared about.

"Chopper is ready to leave in an hour," Brock said, returning to where they all remained in the dining room.

"I'll take Stacey home to grab some clothes," Heath said. "Her house is on the way to mine."

Chase heard Stacey murmur, "Thank you."

Chase needed to run to his place and grab the rest of his supplies, too.

They wouldn't be able to take the weapons they needed, which was why Heath was touching base with his contacts in Seattle.

"Rex and I will stay here for now," Brock said, earning a grunt of disagreement from Rex. "We're a flight away if you need us. But you've got men on the ground in Washington who can help."

Once he knew everyone had stepped away from his computer, he gave one more glance behind him to double-check Stacey wasn't looking over his shoulder. She was speaking softly with Krista in the kitchen, each of them cradling a mug of tea, worried expressions creasing their features.

His brothers were making various arrangements, and his mother was doing what she always did when she was worried— cleaning. When his father was alive and a police officer, their house had been the cleanest home on the block. It always smelled like lemon Pledge, and his mother's hands were often raw from so much scrubbing.

"The hutch is dust-free, Mum," he said gently, grabbing her elbow.

She glanced back at him, nostrils flaring, blue eyes filled with worry. "Don't you think I know that?"

Yeah, he knew she knew that. He also knew how helpless she felt. Nearly as helpless as he did, and there was a lot more that he could do than his mother could.

Taking a deep breath, he cracked his knuckles and tilted his neck side to side.

He hated doing what he was about to do.

Hated it more than he hated small spaces or closing his eyes to sleep.

This was where the real evil lurked. Where the true plague of humankind hung out and did their dirty work.

He logged onto the dark web and went in search of people.

People who bought and sold children.

People without souls.

People who would pay dearly for what they'd done.

CHAPTER THIRTEEN

By the time the chopper set down in Seattle, it was well past midnight. Aaron had booked them all a suite at The Windward Pacific, and as luck would have it, the co-owners of the hotel— Aaron's buddy Roberto "Rob" Cahill and his wife, Skyler McAllister Cahill, were down in San Diego and planned to fly up to Seattle later that day.

The hotel had a helicopter pad, so they just landed there, and Aaron met them in the hotel lobby, his dark red hair, muscular build and icy-blue eyes telling anyone within twenty yards he was a death machine and not to be messed with. Colton was no slouch either, with short-cropped military-style hair and alert hazel eyes that had an intense, almost alarming focus to them.

Chase and Heath shook hands with Aaron and Colton.

"Thanks for meeting us," Chase said, taking in the tired and worried expression on Stacey's face as she scanned the lobby. He'd kept her tight against him on the flight over and hadn't released her hand until just that moment to shake the other men's hands.

"Absolutely," Colton said. "Even if we didn't have kids of our own, we'd be here."

"That's right," Heath said. "How are the families?"

"Mercedes has her hands full with Portia and baby Ford," Colton said on a deep exhale, rubbing his hand over his dark hair.

"Iz, Soph and Weston are good, too," Aaron said with far less enthusiasm than his friend.

"Should we leave you guys to get some sleep, and we can debrief and set up a plan first thing in the morning?" Colton asked, his gaze settling on Stacey.

"I won't be able to sleep," she muttered, her eyes continuing to dart around the lobby. Tears stained her face, and beneath her eyes were dark, deep circles.

Heath's phone buzzed in his pocket, and he stepped away for a moment to answer it.

"Fair enough," Colton said. "I wouldn't be able to sleep, either."

"Rob said to order whatever you want from room service. It's covered," Aaron said, jerking his chin toward the elevator to indicate they should all head up to their room.

Heath joined them again, stowing his phone in his back pocket. "That was Brock. Highway patrol found the SUV from the surveillance footage abandoned in a parking lot in Silverdale. It's safe to assume they switched vehicles and are on their way to Seattle. We just don't know what they're driving."

Chase hadn't told them what he'd uncovered on the dark web. He wasn't ready to share that information with Stacey, so he wanted to wait until she was out of earshot before he divulged the information to Heath, Aaron, Colton and his brothers.

They stepped onto the elevator, and when the door closed, the panic hit him instantly. Fuck, he hated elevators. He should have taken the stairs.

But Aaron said they were on the eighth floor, and even though he could climb those without breaking a sweat, he was reluctant to leave Stacey for even a second.

His mother told him to close his eyes and take deep breaths

when the claustrophobia got overwhelming, but what she didn't know was what he saw when he closed his eyes. That was worse.

So instead, he stared straight ahead at the seam where the two doors met, counting in his head.

One ... two ... three ... four ... five ...

He didn't blink. He didn't breathe.

Six ... seven ... eight ... nine ... ten ... eleven ...

Spots started to cloud his vision. His stomach was a tight knot, and bile began to rise up his throat.

Twelve ... thirteen ... fourteen ... fifteen ...

Stacey's fingers laced with his.

The spots in his vision receded.

The knot in his belly loosened.

Sixteen ... seventeen ... eighteen ... nineteen ... twenty.

Ding.

Thank fuck.

The doors slid open, and when he took that luscious gulp of fresh air and finally let himself blink, it was nearly as good as a fucking orgasm.

"Just down here," Aaron said, leading them down the hallway. He pulled a key card from his pocket and waved it in front of the pad until it clicked and turned green.

It was a nice suite. Complete with a kitchenette, dining space, two bedrooms and a living room.

"This was all Skyler could arrange on short notice," Aaron said. "The couch pulls out though."

"I can take that," Chase said quickly, preferring the wide-open space of the entire suite than a small bedroom where he'd have to shut the door. Heath gave him a strange look but then shrugged.

Setting his bags down on the coffee table, he glanced around the cold, dark suite. There was even a gas fireplace beneath the flat-screen television. If the situation were different, he could see himself enjoying staying here.

Turning around, he found Heath and Stacey speaking in low voices in front of one of the bedrooms. His brother's hand rested on her shoulder and she was nodding.

She nodded again before disappearing into one of the bedrooms.

Heath joined Chase in the living room, where Aaron and Colton had grabbed spots on opposite ends of one of the couches. "Figured you wanted her out of the room when you told us what you found when you went 'hunting.'"

Chase grunted and took a seat at the dining room table, booting up his laptop and glancing at the door Stacey had retreated through.

"She's going to have a shower," Heath said. "You got some time."

"You went onto the dark web?" Aaron asked.

Chase nodded. "There's a 'buyer' here in Seattle. Goes by the handle Impervious."

That name earned him the eye rolls and *"for fuck's sake"* he figured he would get.

What a fucking ego. To call yourself *Impervious* was reason enough to get your head smashed in by a cinder block.

"He has clients in Asia, South America, Eastern Europe and the Middle East. Mainly deals in little boys. Caters to *that* clientele."

All three men turned stone-faced, and he could feel the atmosphere in the room shift. They were all feeling what Chase had been feeling since he entered the dark web, since he heard Stacey screaming on the phone that someone had taken Connor— pure, unadulterated, white-hot rage. The need to hunt was rampant and feral inside of him. He had the scent of blood, and it made him crazy.

"I'm posing as an interested 'buyer' here in Seattle, saying I just moved to the area and haven't been able to get my 'cravings' met.

Impervious said he's getting a new shipment of—" He had to push the bile down as it started to rise up his throat. A hard swallow barely helped. "A new shipment of *dolls*."

"Jesus Christ." Colton glanced away, his face pale, a thick muscle in his jaw jiggling.

Aaron made a predatory noise in his throat. "Fuck me."

Heath was quiet, but Chase knew that look on his brother's face well. They'd been on a lot of missions together, and when Heath was reaching the point of bubbling over with fury, he went dead quiet. He was as silent as a void now.

"Won't believe you're a buyer though, man," Colton said, facing Chase again. He stood up and located the remote for the fireplace by the television and turned it on. Orange flames danced behind the glass. "You scream military and undercover."

"Need someone who looks like a perv," Heath said.

"Or someone who's willing to *pretend* to look like a pedophile pervert," Aaron said. "We can make them look the part." He glanced at Heath and then Colton. "Think Liam would do it?"

Colton shrugged. "Never hurts to ask. I'm sure he'll take offense to being likened to a pedophile pervert, but the man is always willing to help. Plus, he and Richelle went through something similar with Mallory, so ..."

Aaron dug his phone out of his back pocket, stood up and wandered into the kitchen.

"Did Impervious say when the new shipment was coming in?" Heath asked.

Chase's head shook. "Next few days was all I got. He also said the window to find my *doll* was small, as he was sending them to buyers abroad by the end of next week."

"These organizations are slick. They know how to keep the kids hidden and move them around from place to place until they're shipped out to keep off the authorities' radar." Colton tugged at his chin. "Did a few busts of child brothels and trafficking rings in

South America. They keep 'em in slums. Dirty pay-by-the-hour hotels, cold warehouses, dark, dank basements and back rooms of sketchy businesses. Anywhere they can hide 'em, they will. Barely feed the kids. A lot of them don't have bathroom facilities, just a bucket in the corner they're all expected to use."

Heath pushed his fingers through his hair. "Christ almighty."

"They could also be keeping him here in the States and not shipping him abroad. There are some sick fuckers right here in our own backyard, too. Keep kids as pets for their own twisted pleasures." Colton's nostrils flared. "Thought about starting up a bit of an underground *hunting* party, if you get my meaning. Take 'em out, quick and quiet like."

Colton could count Chase in on that *party*.

Chase felt the bile begin to lift up toward his mouth again. If there was a hair out of place on Connor's body, if that kid so much as had the sniffles or a grumbling, hungry belly, Chase wouldn't stop until every last person involved in this ring of evil was dead. Sure, prison a second time around would probably kill him—or make him go insane—but knowing Connor was safe would be worth it.

They heard the water for the shower turn off at the same time Aaron rejoined them. "Wasn't happy about being woken up after midnight, but Liam is in. Said whatever we need, he's available. Richelle wants to meet Stacey, too. Since Mallory was kidnapped, too, she feels she's got a bit more of an understanding of what Stacey's going through than most women."

All the men nodded.

"Okay, so what we need from you, Chase, is a time and location for the meetup. Push for sooner rather than later. My guess is, they're driving through the night to get to Seattle and hide the kid. The sooner they're off the road and the kid is out of sight, the better off they are. Will be harder to find him since the AMBER Alerts will be seen mostly later this morning." Aaron didn't bother to sit down again and stood next to Chase at the dining room table. "Colton and I will head home now, and we'll meet back here at eight tomorrow morning."

Stacey emerged from the bedroom, all bundled up in a fluffy white bathrobe. Her hair was damp, her face flushed, eyes red-rimmed like she'd spent the entire shower crying.

Understandable.

Aaron's face turned gentle. "We'll be back in the morning with reinforcements, okay?"

At that, Colton stood up, too, and he and Aaron headed toward the door. Heath and Chase stood up, as well, and followed them. Stacey hung back but followed.

"Might be a good idea to bring in *all* our manpower on this one," Aaron said. "Your brothers busy?"

Heath shook his head. "They're on standby. Can be here by morning."

"Probably best," Aaron said. "We don't know what we're going into, and being overprepared, overmanned is better than being under."

"Assuming you're going to need weapons?" Colton asked with a small but wicked smile.

"Brought what we have," Heath said, earning a surprised glance from Chase. "But more is always better."

Colton nodded. "I'll bring what I got."

They said their goodbyes and closed the door behind the two retired SEALs.

"You brought weapons?" Chase asked Heath as they reentered the living room.

"Never leave home without at least something. But yeah, you think I need a duffle bag *that* big full of clothes?" He went to the big black bag he'd brought with him that was sitting on the kitchen counter and unzipped it.

Chase leaned forward and saw knives, automatic rifles, hand-guns, grenades, enough explosives to blow up a city block.

"Jesus, how'd you get that past customs?"

"Customs?" He shrugged, a devious twinkle in his eye. "Not sure *what* you're talking about."

Chase just rolled his eyes. "Zip that back up. You don't want housekeeping finding it." He pivoted in the room to find Stacey standing in front of the big picture window that lent them a view of the entire city. She looked so small and fragile in the enormous robe.

"Gonna have a shower and try to sleep," Heath said, slinging his bag over his shoulder. "Is it wrong that I want to spoon this bag?"

Chase gave his youngest brother a disturbed look. "Yes."

Heath shrugged again. "Too bad, I'm gonna."

And then it was just them.

CHAPTER FOURTEEN

SHE SAW him approach behind her in the reflection of the window. He stopped before they could touch, but that didn't mean she didn't feel him there, didn't take comfort from his heat, his scent, his presence.

The ache in her chest was beyond overflowing.

Her son was missing.

No, not missing.

Her son had been abducted.

He'd been taken right from under her nose. Hauled away in a van by people he didn't know, who saw him as no more than a commodity.

She'd failed him.

A mother was supposed to protect her child, and she hadn't.

She failed to do the most basic thing a parent can do for their child, and that is keep them safe.

Now, Connor was only God knew where, probably scared, hungry and crying out for her, and there wasn't a damn thing she could do to help him.

She'd never felt so helpless, so utterly useless in all her life.

She didn't think she had any more tears left, but somehow more fell, and her throat grew tight as the sobs clutched her body and she began to tremble uncontrollably.

"Shh." Chase's arms wrapped around her, and he spun her around. She clung to him, buried her face in his chest and gripped the front of his shirt like the lifeline she desperately needed.

Right now, she wanted to die.

She wanted to crumple into a ball on the floor and not eat or sleep ever again until she withered away to nothing.

"We'll find him," Chase said, running his hand over her back. "I will bring him back to you."

"You can't make that promise," she said, lifting her head to look at him. "He could be anywhere." That last bit was forced out like someone was giving her the Heimlich, but she said it. It needed to be said. They all knew it to be true. Even if they *thought* they had a lead, it could just as easily be a dead end or a trap.

Connor could be halfway to San Francisco for all they knew.

"You eaten?" he asked, taking a step toward her.

She hadn't had anything since breakfast, but she also wasn't hungry. She shook her head, and tightened the cord on her robe. "I can't eat right now. I'm going to lie down for a bit." She already knew she wouldn't be able to sleep, but maybe if she closed her eyes, she could connect on another level with her son.

In their dreams.

Maybe if they were both sleeping, or had their eyes closed and thought hard about the other person, they could meet in another world, in the spirit world. She could tell him she loved him and they were going to find him. She could let her baby know that his mama was coming and wouldn't stop looking until he was back in her arms.

Her entire body was just a throbbing, dull ache. She made to pull away, to go to her room, but he didn't relinquish his hold.

His finger came up beneath her chin. "I can't stay in the bedroom with you, but you can stay out here with me."

Her brows pinched.

She wanted to ask why he couldn't stay in the bedroom with her but was also too tired and had too many other things on her mind to start digging.

All she did was nod.

He pulled away and immediately went about setting up the pull-out couch. Then he shucked his pants and shirt, remaining in just his boxers, and he climbed into bed, welcoming her with him.

"I need to leave the light on," he said.

Another thing she wanted to ask about but just didn't have the energy.

Ditching the fluffy robe and draping it over the back of a chair, she wiped the tears from her cheek and slid into the bed beside him.

He tugged her close, so she was the little spoon.

"Tell me about your childhood," he murmured, kissing her neck. The heat of Chase's body and the strength of his arms was a welcome boon of comfort. It didn't take away the empty hole she felt in her chest, but it soothed the ache just a touch.

She shook her head. "Wasn't great."

"I'm sorry," he whispered.

"Not your fault."

"Are your parents still alive?"

"Yeah. But they couldn't give two shits about me. About any of us."

"I'm sorry."

"Again, not your fault."

"Siblings?"

She knew what he was doing, trying to distract her from the spiral of despair she was currently trapped in. It was like when Connor had to get his vaccinations. She let him watch a Paw Patrol episode on her phone to distract him. Chase was trying to do that now. Little did he know, her childhood and her parents weren't a happy distraction. They were just a long, scarred-over wound that if picked at long enough would open up and bleed.

"Brothers," she finally said. "My parents divorced when I was five, and both of them—on separate occasions—told me they wanted a son, not a daughter—that *I* was the reason for their divorce."

"Holy shit." His arms around her loosened, and he encouraged her to spin around and face him. She did.

"I was seven when they told me this. They got their sons. Mom remarried and had two boys. Dad remarried a woman with sons and then had another one. I'm not close with any of my brothers."

The pain in his eyes was tangible. He was close with his brothers, and she knew that it would gut him not to have his family all happy, bright and full of rainbows.

He'd texted her last night to say that he'd reconciled with Rex over beer and hockey and once again apologized for his assumptions and behaving like an ass.

She'd texted him a slew of hearts and said she loved him and was happy that he was back on good terms with his brother.

"Have you tried getting closer with them?" he asked. He cupped her face with his big palm and swept a tear off her cheek, his thumb warm and strong as it brushed back and forth across her heated skin.

She shrugged and sniffled. "Not exactly easy. Dad's in Lodi; Mom's in Toronto. Dad moved after the divorce. Mom moved when I was sixteen, didn't even ask me if I wanted to come with. Just told me that I was an adult and needed to find a place to live to finish out high school."

"What the fuck?"

All she did was nod and purse her lips. All this had happened ages ago and had only made her into the strong, independent person she was today. Sure, she resented her parents—and her brothers, for that matter—but those wounds had thick, ugly scar tissue over them. She had her own family to take care of and focus on now.

"So what did you do?" he asked, finding her hand beneath the covers with his other hand and linking their fingers together.

"A friend's family took me in for the last two years, and I paid them rent by working after school and weekends at a restaurant. I put myself through nursing school, too. Parents didn't pay for a damn thing. Haven't seen or spoken to either of them in over five years. They have no interest in their daughter or their grandchildren. They have their own *new,* better families. My brothers are adults now and have nothing to do with me. *Want* nothing to do with me. I don't know what my parents said to them to taint them about me, but I can't spend my energy worrying about it. I know I did nothing wrong."

"How old were you when they were born?"

She sucked in a deep breath through her nose. "Felix was born when I was ten. That's my dad's son, so I've never really known him, as I stayed in Edmonton with my mom and only saw my dad a couple of times a year. And Daniel and David were born when I was twelve and fourteen. They were babies when my mom and stepdad moved to Toronto, leaving me in Edmonton to figure things out on my own."

He squeezed his eyes shut and kept them closed for a long moment before finally opening them again and shaking his head. "I just can't understand people like that. Your parents abandoned you."

And so began her abandonment issues.

Then came Ted and his lies and betrayal, and Chase leaving without a word was the cherry on top of that horrible fucking strawberry sundae.

"I don't even think the fact that Ted left us over a million dollars in his life insurance policy and that the kids and I are financially set would even make my family take interest. I was never what they wanted, and they've made that very clear."

She roughly wiped away a tear that had sprinted down her cheek. Her words were growing more and more strangled, her nose was getting stuffy, and her throat felt tight.

She untangled their fingers and turned back around, resuming their spoon position. As much as she appreciated what Chase was trying to do, it had felt more like a dull saw working back and forth to further open up the hole in her chest.

Talking about her parents and brothers was just another reminder of how alone she and the kids were in the world.

Her entire life and marriage with Ted had been a sham from day one, and then he'd left them with abundant loose ends to clean up.

Even after nearly a year of him being dead, she still found herself shedding tears of hurt and anger when she was alone at night folding laundry or doing the dishes. The kids were asleep in their beds, happy and well-adjusted to their new life. And she was left feeling lost and still scrambling to right her world on its axis once again.

She felt like a dog chasing its tail. Spinning around in circles until she was too dizzy to stay upright and just collapsed to the ground a muddled, teary mess, alone on her kitchen floor, creating a puddle of her tears on the linoleum.

But she couldn't live on her kitchen floor forever.

She had children who counted on her. Children who needed her.

So after an acceptable amount of time wallowing in self-pity and wondering what kind of horrible things she'd done in past lives to deserve this life now, she picked herself up, dusted herself off and put on the brave mask for her kids.

They needed her to be strong, to be present, to persevere through the darkness and lead them through into the light.

The first time she'd been forced to don the brave mask was when she was five and her parents divorced. It was an ugly separation, and she was used as a pawn between them. They negotiated for her like they did the lake cottage and her father's boat. And her mother made no effort to hide her disappointment in "ending up" with Stacey and losing out on the ski boat.

Then her world seemed to find its stability again for a few years when it was just her and her mom. Her stepfather wasn't a mean man, but he certainly made sure she knew that she *wasn't* his and never would be. He married her mother; she was just an unfortunate addendum.

Her world fell off into a black hole again when her mom, brothers and stepdad moved to Toronto and didn't invite her to join them. Her father hadn't said a word, didn't invite her to move in with his family and had even tried to get out of paying child support to the family she lived with for those last two years.

The family she'd moved in with had been lovely and welcoming, but she still felt like an outsider. She felt like an interloper at Christmas and other important family gatherings. She was left to take the family photo in front of the Christmas tree or at Great Aunt Stella's ninetieth birthday party but was never invited to be *in* the picture.

The moment she turned eighteen, she was out on her own.

Which was how she preferred it.

The world started to make sense again after that. She worked her ass off and put herself through nursing school.

Then it really started to make sense when she met Ted.

He understood her. He made her feel loved and beautiful—unlike anyone ever had. He was complimentary and protective. She thought he genuinely wanted her and only her.

Until the day Freya answered his phone and the world crashed off its axis and shattered into a million pieces.

Chase's voice sounded distant even though he was right behind her. He kissed her neck and tugged her tighter against him. "I'm sorry your family was so terrible. But you have a new family, and we won't cast you out. None of you. Not ever."

Fresh tears sprang into her eyes and she hiccupped in his arms, a shudder stuttering through her.

"I love you, Stacey, and we will find Connor and figure it out."

She shut her eyes, but the tears continued to fall, dripping into the pillow beneath her head.

"Sleep now. Rest," he said. "Connor's going to need his mama to be strong for him. There's nothing you can do right now."

To wear the brave mask.

The mask she'd been wearing her whole life, but even more so since her children were born and their father died.

That mask had seen better days, though. She wasn't sure how much of it was left or how effective it would be.

Her throat was full of razor blades as she tried to swallow. But she kept her eyes closed, nestled into Chase's warmth and did the best she could to not let the grief and fear consume her.

If they didn't find her son, this was one black hole she wasn't sure she'd ever be able to escape from.

———

CHASE COULDN'T SLEEP.

It wasn't because of the room or the lighting.

All that was bearable.

It also had nothing to do with the woman curled up into his body, finally asleep.

It was because there was more he could be doing to look for Connor. More he *should* be doing to look for Connor.

Her even breathing and lax body told him she was finally out, so gently, slowly, he extracted himself from around her and slid out of the pull-out bed.

He stood there for a moment and watched the woman he loved sleep.

He'd never met a stronger person in his fucking life.

She'd been through so much and still, through it all, was raising her children to be good people.

Her parents didn't deserve her. Her brothers didn't deserve her.

But Thea and Connor did deserve her. She was a good person. A good woman and a good mother.

She deserved nothing but happiness and calm seas for the rest of her days.

And even though she hadn't been to prison like he had, or seen the sludge-covered bottom of the barrel scrapings of humanity, she still had a lot of trauma in her life.

Her trauma was different than his, but it was no less gut-wrenching. It still had the capacity to fuck a person up.

And he knew better than most how trauma could fuck you up. Even if you tried not to let it, it usually found a way to do it anyway.

One final glance had his conviction only growing more deep-seated and his anger hotter, so he sat down at his computer again.

Brock was in charge of making contact with the police departments in Washington, while Krista took care of the Canadian ones. AMBER alerts were already out, and now that they had the kidnapper's faces, those two had been broadcasted everywhere.

Their vehicles had fake plates, so that was a dead end.

But he knew there was still more he could be doing. Still more he *should* be doing. With a neck crack and a deep breath, he went back onto the dark web. The troglodytes came out at night. They were nocturnal creatures from the deepest, most depraved crevasses of hell, and they did their worst when the rest of the world slept.

He connected again with Impervious and teed up a time to meet. Apparently, the new shipment of *dolls* was set to arrive tomorrow afternoon. Impervious said Chase—who was using the alias Chimbo—could meet his associates at the Satin Lounge at midnight tomorrow to peruse the "new stock." Every word, every syllable made Chase gag and had him seeing red. He really needed to get to Impervious though. Taking out his associates would be great, particularly that bitch who had stuck a needle in Stacey's neck, but in order to kill the monster, you needed to cut off its head.

He only hoped Impervious *was* the monster's head.

He finished up his arrangements with Impervious, left his laptop on but turned it away from him so the light wouldn't bother him, then he opened up all the blinds. Hopefully none of this bothered Stacey. But he couldn't close the blinds or turn off the light and expect to get any sleep.

He could hear Heath snoring in the other room—his brother had always been able to pass out anywhere at any time. He slid back into the bed next to Stacey, and she stirred, curling back into him without waking up.

He buried his nose in her hair and drew in a deep breath.

During those months he was in Georgia, if he concentrated hard enough and turned on his side, he could still remember the way her hair smelled as they spooned after their one night together. Still remember the way she felt in his arms, the softness of her skin, the gentle swell of her lower belly from having only recently had Thea.

She was perfect then, and she was perfect now.

That first day when he walked back into her home for dinner and sat at the table with Stacey and the kids, the feeling of *coming home* had never been stronger.

With Stacey, with the kids, he was home.

CHAPTER FIFTEEN

WITH THE LIGHTS ON, the blinds open and Stacey in his arms, Chase was able to get a couple of hours of light sleep. He still heard the comings and goings of the hotel and traffic outside. He heard when Heath got up, used the bathroom and headed down to the hotel fitness center at five o'clock.

But the woman in his arms, who was snuggled up tight against him with her head on his chest, her hair wildly strewn across his shoulders, was fast asleep, so even though he could get up—he wouldn't. It'd been roughly two thirty when she finally fell asleep—closer to four thirty for him—so he would let her rest. She needed it.

At six thirty, the hotel door clicked and opened again—Heath coming back—which caused Stacey to stir. Her eyes flew open and she bolted upright, panic streaking across her face. "Connor!"

Chase sat up beside her and rested his hand on her back. "What?"

Tears welled up in her eyes, and her bottom lip jutted out and wobbled. "I just ... I'd hoped it was all a nightmare and that I'd wake up in my own bed and he'd be down the hall." She pinched her eyes closed and tossed her face into her hands, her body shaking. "I'd thought it was all just a dream."

Heath came over to stand beside the pull-out couch. He was all sweaty and wore tape around his hands. He'd probably gone a few rounds with a punching bag, which was what Chase should be doing, too. They often sparred together, but when the anger creeped in, either over a job gone wrong or something else, they hit the bag and they hit the bag hard.

He pulled his shaggy mop free from a manbun—gross—and the damp strands fell to his shoulders. "Not a dream," he said with sorrow, glancing at Stacey. "But we'll get him back." Heath's face was a hard mask, and when he tipped his midnight-blue gaze to Chase, all Chase saw was the stone-cold killer Chase knew lurked beneath the easy-breezy surfer bum exterior.

Chase would actually go as far as to say that out of all four of them, Heath was the most ruthless—at least when it came to doling out punishments to those who deserved them.

Stacey removed her hands and glanced up at both of them with her sad, red-rimmed eyes. "I feel so helpless. Like I've failed him and just continue to fail him because I'm not out there actively looking for him. I'm not knocking on doors, putting up flyers or sitting at the police station giving an endless stream of statements."

Chase rubbed her back and leaned over and kissed her bare shoulder. "You didn't fail him. And we're doing everything we can to get him back."

"It's not like he ran away from home and could be just hiding at the playground or under a bridge," Heath said. "He was abducted. By professionals, no less. We have to go about this the right way, and we are."

The *right* way didn't necessarily mean the *legal* way, but this was the way they knew, and the way they knew usually got results a hell of a lot faster and cleaner than if the local authorities or feds were sent in.

With more tears spilling down her cheeks, Stacey swung her legs over the side of the bed and stood up. "I need to use the bathroom."

Chase watched her walk away, his own feelings of helplessness tripling in size the farther she got away.

He knew he was doing everything he could, but that still didn't feel like enough. Particularly not when it came to comforting Stacey.

The bathroom door gently clicked closed, and the sound of muffled sobs echoed out into the suite.

Heath and Chase exchanged looks.

"Need to make the fuckers pay for what they're doing to Stacey," Heath said, mopping his face with a white hand towel.

Nodding, Chase double-checked he wasn't sporting a half chub or anything before tossing his legs over the side of the bed and standing up. He scratched his crotch over his boxers and went rooting around in his duffle bag for his toiletry bag and fresh clothes.

"Ordered room service on my way past the front desk," Heath said, squirting water from his water bottle into his open mouth.

"Not hungry," Chase grunted.

Chase sensed his brother moving closer toward him, and Heath's big frame created a shadow over where Chase was rummaging around in his duffle bag. "You think we got a chance at getting him back?" Heath asked.

Blinking slowly, he lifted his head to face his brother. Real worry and fear stared back at him. "We fucking have to," he said. They fucking had to, otherwise he would never be able to look Stacey in the eyes again. Fuck, he wouldn't be able to look his family in the eyes again if he didn't get Connor back.

Heath merely nodded. He understood what Chase was feeling and knew better than to push any further. "I called Brock and Rex. They'll be here before noon."

Chase's head bobbed, and he grabbed his toiletry bag. "Gonna use your bathroom."

He didn't wait for Heath to squawk and simply walked over to Heath's room and headed into the bathroom. He needed to shower. To get his head back in the game.

He kind of hoped Stacey would stay in her room so he could do some more digging on the dark web. He didn't really want to do that with her just pacing the suite, glancing over his shoulder.

If she knew just what could be happening to her son, she might not ever recover.

That was something Chase was struggling to deal with himself. He didn't need both of them with those thoughts. She needed to stay positive and hopeful, leave the grimness and despair to him.

"You want me to come wash your back for you, big brother?" Heath called after him just before he closed the bathroom door. He could hear his brother snickering even as he turned on the hot water.

A goof he might be, but when push came to shove and they were at war, there wasn't anyone he'd rather have in his corner or on his six than Heath.

———

THE KNOCK on the hotel room door made Stacey jump where she sat on the couch. She'd been on edge all morning.

Goosebumps raced along her arms beneath her hoodie. She grabbed the folded blanket from where Chase had cleaned up the pullout bed, and she draped it over her legs.

Heath had ordered room service, but Stacey couldn't stomach

the thought of food. Not with her little boy out there somewhere probably cold, starving and afraid.

Chase placed a mug of coffee in her hands, but she'd only held on to it, absorbing the heat. It'd gone cold before she took a sip. She was too busy staring out the window, watching the raindrops dribble down the glass.

Her baby was out there somewhere, and she had no idea how to find him.

Heath was up from his spot at the dining table and opening the door. Several male voices and a female voice grew louder as they all entered the room.

She recognized Aaron and Colton from last night, but the woman and the other man, she had no clue who they were. The woman regarding her with sympathy was short—like possibly not even five feet tall. She had a blonde pixie cut and hawk-like amber eyes. She also had an edge to her that even the astronauts on the space station could probably see.

Aaron was the first to speak. "We brought reinforcements."

"I'm Richelle," the blonde said, walking over to where Stacey remained on the couch. She sat down beside her.

The men had already wandered over to where Chase had taken root at the dining room table on his laptop.

What was he doing on his laptop?

They'd mentioned the dark web.

What was he looking for?

Did he know more about Connor's whereabouts than he was letting on?

"A couple of years back, my daughter, Mallory, was kidnapped," Richelle said, drawing Stacey's attention away from Chase. "It was right under our noses, too. She was thirteen, and we were all at a music festival at a community park for Independence Day." Richelle's hands knit together in her lap, and she stared straight ahead as she spoke.

Richelle seemed to keep her emotions and feelings close to her chest. It was probably easier to keep her gaze focused on the centerpiece of fake flowers on the coffee table than on Stacey's tired, terrified eyes and be forced to show her vulnerabilities to a stranger.

Richelle cleared her throat and continued. "I had rebuffed a man who turned out to be a very dangerous person. He was also the ex of a client I was trying to help with her divorce. I had no idea he was the same man who'd attacked me in the elevator. He found out I was his wife's attorney, and he went after my daughter in retaliation. I mean, there's more to the story, but that's for another day." She waved her hand dismissively. "They got her back, though. Heath, Rex, Aaron, Colton—they got Mallory back. She's safe. She's happy. She's ... alive." She reached for Stacey's hand and took it in hers, though Stacey could tell the act of touching a stranger wasn't in Richelle's comfort zone. "She needed some therapy afterward and still doesn't like to go anywhere alone, even during the day, but she's okay. And your son will be, too. I know what you're feeling right now. The helplessness, the fury, the terror. I know it all."

"He's only four," Stacey said, her throat painfully tight and the words a beast to get out. "He's so little. So sweet. He makes friends with everyone."

God, would things have gone differently if she'd taught her son to be more afraid of strangers? Should she instill the fear of God in her kids to be wary of anyone that speaks to them? Even if she was right there.

Stranger danger was real. And Connor knew about it. But it all seemed so harmless at the time.

It'd been a woman and not a man, which disarmed Stacey.

Stacey had been right there. She'd been with Connor the entire time, which made her think nobody would dare take her child while she was right there, too. So her defenses were down.

He was in the vehicle and it was broad daylight with other people around. Of course she didn't think anyone would be ballsy enough to try and take her child.

How naïve and ignorant could she be?

She'd gone over that afternoon a trillion times in her head, and even though she'd been ambushed and drugged, she still couldn't stop haranguing herself. Somehow Connor being taken was her fault. He was with her. She was his mother, and she was supposed to protect him, and she'd failed.

Would he ever trust her again?

Would he run to her with his booboos? Would her kiss on a scraped knee continue to numb the pain like it had yesterday? Or would he look at her differently? Not see her as the protector, the fixer, the safety net of love, warmth and security that she'd worked her whole damn life as a mother to build for her children.

After all, she was mother *and* father to them, so she'd been extra vigilant in making sure her children knew she would go to the ends of the earth to take care of them. She would take a bullet, run into a burning building and jump in front of a bus for her kids.

Richelle dropped her voice down low. "Whatever you need, we're here."

Need?

She needed her son.

She needed her baby back.

She needed Connor in her arms, with his dirty fingernails, rocks in his pockets and unruly mop-top.

She needed the missing piece of her heart.

A man clearing his throat had all the women lifting their heads.

"So we've made contact again with Impervious," Chase said. "Guy isn't stupid though. He's going to be wondering if I'm five-oh."

"Which is where I come in," the man Stacey didn't recognize

said. He stepped forward and offered Stacey his hand. "I'm Liam, Richelle's husband." Chocolate-brown eyes sparkled at her as he squeezed her hand. His smile was heartfelt and genuine, but she could also sense his sympathy for her, as well.

Until her horrible choice in husbands, Stacey liked to think of herself as a good judge of character, and she could tell Liam had a lot of character and a big heart.

Chase nodded and grunted. "We're going to deck Liam out in—"

"Perv attire," Liam said with a goofy smile. "Have to go shopping though. Nothing in my closet is pervy."

"There are no *stereotypical* pervs," Colton said. "People you least expect to be molesters can be. CEOs, cops, doctors, mailmen."

Stacey's stomach twisted into a tight knot, and all the heat left her face.

"Shit," Colton said, taking in Stacey's reaction. "What I mean is ... we're using Liam as a stand-in perv because he's—"

"Less obvious and threatening," Richelle finished. "He doesn't scream muscles, military and mayhem." She rolled her eyes. "I'm sure we can find something."

Liam's expression of mock irritation only lasted for a second before he shrugged. "If you think so, dear."

"Aaron and Colton are going to go do a bit of recon," Heath said.

Chase nodded again. "That's right. I was able to find a back door that provided me with Impervious's IP address. Not that that means he is where the IP address says he is. He's undoubtedly using an anonymous VPN and has it rerouted a hundred times. But it's a start. Couldn't sleep last night, so I hacked into his emails."

Stacey whipped her gaze to Chase. He didn't sleep?

Had he climbed out of bed while she slept and gone back onto his computer? He must have.

He was doing everything he could to help get her son back.

Chase shook his head slightly at her and then continued. "There was mention of The Glossy Gem Motel, which is on the edge of the industrial park, right by the water."

"Colton and I will go scope the hotel out, pretend we need a room or something," Aaron said, tugging on his short, rusty scruff. "Can't do a ton in the daylight."

Liam glanced out the window, which was covered in raindrops. "Good thing it's February and the weather is disgusting. Won't be daylight for long. Won't be a lot of lookie-loos either."

"So you guys don't need us for anything specific," Richelle asked.

Aaron shook his head. "No. Not until tonight."

"That's right," Chase said. "With Liam posing as Chimbo the pedophile, we'll send two teams, one with Liam to the Satin Lounge and another to the motel. They're like four blocks from each other, so we'll park the vehicles in between the two and leave Stacey and Richelle in the truck. You'll stay in the vehicle and be ready to drive when we bring Connor to you. He may need medical attention; we don't know."

Dread swirled like a whirlpool in her stomach.

"Should we bring Mark or Emmett?" Liam asked. "Or Riley or Will? They're all doctors."

Aaron shook his head again. "No. Colton was an army medic. He'll be enough until we assess the kid and decide if he needs to be taken to a hospital. But he'll want to see his mother, which is why we'll bring you both."

Shuddering at the idea of her baby needing medical attention because of what these monsters may or may not have done to him, Stacey released herself from Richelle, wrapped her arms around her knees and began to rock back and forth.

"Hey, hey," Richelle said, wrapping her arms around Stacey's shoulders. "We're going to get him back. It's going to be okay." An idea seemed to spark inside her, and she sat up straight, untangled herself from Stacey and stood up. She approached Chase. "Can I speak with you for a moment?"

Stacey wasn't paying attention to Chase and Richelle, but she knew they ducked into the corner kitchenette and were murmuring.

Stacey just continued to rock back and forth, watching the rain fall and a few seagulls get caught on a gust of wind.

Richelle returned and sat back down beside her. "I'd like you to come with me for a little bit. I think you could use the distraction and something to channel all these fears and the anger." Her voice was low but not low enough, and Heath perked up from where he stood talking to Colton and Aaron.

"Are you going to The Rage Room?"

Richelle glanced at him. "Moms only."

Stacey didn't want to go anywhere right now. She just wanted her little boy back. She didn't care about anything else. Her feelings, her heart, they didn't matter. All that mattered was Connor and getting him back in one piece.

"I can't," Stacey said with a head shake. "I can't go anywhere."

Richelle squeezed her hand. "It will help."

Nothing would help.

Connor was out there somewhere in the city, scared, hungry and cold. Every minute they spent doing something else, besides looking for him, was a minute her son could be getting hurt or abused. Was another minute for the traffickers to move him farther away, off their radar and possibly gone for good.

Chase stepped around the chair and Heath and held out his hand for her, not saying a word.

She took his hand, and he pulled her to standing, allowing him to lead her to her bedroom.

"I can't go," she said. "Not when my son is out there somewhere. I should be knocking on doors, putting up posters or something."

He pulled her into his arms and kissed her forehead, his hard body a welcome comfort and one she sorely needed. A chill had sunk into her bones from the moment she woke up, and she hadn't been able to get rid of it. Chase's warmth was helping.

She wrapped her arms around his waist.

"There's nothing you can do but wait and let us do our jobs. It will help. Richelle has been through something similar with her daughter, so lean on her. She asked to come when she heard what happened," he said.

She gripped the back of his shirt and held on. "I can't."

"You need to do something, Stacey. I have more to do here, and the guys are going to go and do more recon. We need to know more. How much security are we dealing with? How smart are these guys? How heavily armed are they? How many other kids there might be."

She gasped and pulled away to look at him.

His pressed-together lips and the darkness behind his eyes said that the chances of Connor being alone were slim. After all, Impervious had said *dolls*. As in plural.

She hadn't even thought of the possibility of there being other kids.

Dear God. There were other parents out there going through what she was going through. Feeling what she was feeling.

Helpless. Hopeless. Useless.

Like their heart had been ripped from their chest. Their lungs sawed out with a rusty blade, making a deep breath damn near impossible.

"Go with Richelle and Heath," he encouraged, gazing down at her. "I'll have more news and a better idea of the next step by then."

With dread swirling inside her and very little hope left to cling to, she tightened her grasp on his shirt and fought back the rush of tears that made her throat ache and the back of her eyes burn. "Promise me you'll bring him back—and the other children, too. Promise me, Chase. I couldn't go on knowing my son was out there and what might be happening to him. I couldn't live."

"I promise," he said, brushing her hair off her face. "I will get you back your son."

CHAPTER SIXTEEN

"So you put the gear on, pick your weapon and smash the shit out of stuff," Richelle said, handing Stacey a pair of safety goggles. "Best way to get the rage, the hurt, the pent-up energy and aggression out without maiming anyone.

"Plus, Luna makes art and mosaics and stuff out of the broken dishes, so you're helping contribute to her medium," Richelle added. She held out the protective gloves.

Stacey glanced at Heath. "You've been here before?"

"When I was working for Richelle's client. Came here with Richelle's daughter." He turned to Richelle. "How is Mallory?"

"Still stubborn as hell, but she's doing well, thanks. Asks about you."

Stacey wasn't sure she'd ever seen the surfer-haired beefcake blush before, but he did, adding in a cheesy grin just for good measure. "She's a good kid."

"With a major crush on a man nearly twice her age," Richelle said with an eye roll.

"Perhaps in another lifetime," Heath said, raking his fingers through his tresses. His whole demeanor had shifted since Richelle had told him he wasn't invited to The Rage Room. He'd been quieter. More serious. She knew Heath loved Connor, and Connor loved Heath, so it had to be taking its toll on the blond teddy bear just like it was on the rest of them. His lips lifted up briefly on one side. "Tell her that any man lucky enough to date her will have to deal with me if he breaks her heart."

Richelle's smile was knowing and almost coy. "You and an army of her father's friends."

A woman with a shock of pink hair, tattoos on her arms and piercings came out of the room behind the Plexiglas. "All set."

"Thanks, Luna," Richelle said with a smile. She turned to Stacey. "What's your weapon of choice? I highly recommend the crowbar. Packs one hell of a wallop."

"I'm partial to the metal baseball bat myself," Luna chimed in. "Can't go wrong with the nine iron either."

Stacey let her eyes roam the wall of weapons. They all looked like they would effectively torture a microwave into giving up all its plans for world domination. But her gaze kept falling on the long, black, L-shaped tire iron.

"Sometimes one just speaks to you," Luna said gently.

The tire iron was speaking to Stacey. Images of her taking the iron to the face of the woman from the dollar store flashed into her mind. Of shattering the kneecaps, then skull of the man who was driving the getaway car. She picked the weapon off the wall, pulled the goggles down over her eyes, the gloves onto her hands and stepped into the room.

Before she closed the door behind her, Luna said, "Nothing is off limits. Just get it all out. This is meant to be cathartic."

"How long do we have?" Richelle asked Luna quietly.

"Long as you need," Luna said. "I put a *closed for private event* sign on the door, so nobody will bother you. Take all the time you need." She rested a cool, delicate hand on Stacey's shoulder before heading back down the hallway.

Richelle appeared beside Stacey. "I know you didn't want to come. I understand. I get it. But you're not doing any of them any good being there right now. Particularly Chase, who needs to focus on getting more information."

Stacey swallowed past the harsh lump at the back of her throat and nodded, her fingers gripping the tire iron until her knuckles ached.

Heath held the heavy acrylic glass door open for her, and she stepped into the room filled with small appliances, dishes, lamps, vases and various office electronics.

A squat mustard yellow vase in the corner, not more than a few inches high, drew her eye, and she slowly wandered over to it.

It was the same color as the hair on the woman from the dollar store. Fake. Like from a box and the dye had been left on for too long. It was also roughly the same shape as her face. Round and seemingly unremarkable.

But oh, there was more to this vase than met the eye.

There was a long crack up the front, which meant if you filled it with water, it would leak.

The bottom was also raised inside significantly, so putting flowers in it wouldn't work either. You'd have to cut off stems so much, the flower would wither and die in a day or so.

Sure, the vase *looked* harmless, and it would probably spruce up a dull living room, but the secret this vase was keeping was that it would secretly ruin anything it touched.

If you filled the vase with water and put it on the mantle, not only would it leak and damage the wood, but the flowers would lose all their water and with no stems, die in no time.

This vase took life.

This vase needed to be destroyed so it didn't inflict any more harm.

Stacey closed her eyes for a moment and pictured Connor.

Sweet, happy, smart, beautiful Connor.

He was on the swing at the park with a huge smile on his face. He'd just learned how to pump and get moving on his own, and the pride that shone off him at his *big kid success* melted Stacey's heart.

Her son was pure joy, and he had been since the day he was born.

And this vase had taken away that joy. It had stolen that joy from Stacey, from the rest of the world.

And now, even when they did get him back, she worried if that joy, that happiness and his good-natured spirt would be quelled and unsalvageable.

With a scream she pulled from the tips of her toes and all the anger, pain and helplessness she felt, she lifted the tire iron and swung it as hard as she could at the vase.

It fell to the ground from where it was on the shelf, shattering into probably a dozen pieces.

That wasn't enough.

She still knew what it was.

Changing her grip on the iron, she stood over the vase and began to beat it into the ground. The satisfying sound of destruction only fueled her bloodlust, and she kept going.

Then she spun around and went after more.

The black toaster oven. Ted always loved toast.

White Wonder Bread just barely toasted with unsalted butter.

How. Fucking. Boring.

She swung at the toaster and sent it flying into the wall. It fell to the ground, but only one side of it came off.

Ted was dead. His children were fatherless, and now she wasn't sure if she'd ever see her little boy again.

How could he do this to her? To them?

Never again would she believe people were inherently good. That people were innocent until proven guilty.

Everyone was guilty now. Until they proved her otherwise.

A small dollhouse reminded her of the lake cottage her

parents fought over. Prized more in their divorce than she was. She didn't stop on that until even the tiny wooden front door was in pieces.

After thirty minutes, not one thing in the room was recognizable. Electronics and appliances were no more than metal hunks and chunks of plastic. Dishes were reduced to slivers and chips, and that poor old bookcase, it didn't know what hit it—and it still probably didn't, rendered nearly to sawdust. Stacey had taken every last ounce of pain she had inside of her and channeled it into the tire iron and taken it out on the old wooden bookcase.

Anger she'd buried so deep down, resentment toward her parents, her brothers—it all came out with each mighty swing. She imagined the #1 *Dad* and matching #1 *Mom* mugs were her parents, and she wound up like she was at home plate and took a swing right dead center between each of their cold, compassionless eyes. Her father flew against the wall and fell with a loud smash first, then her mother joined him. But she wasn't going to let either of them get off that easily. Not after the way they'd discarded her like an unwanted puppy after Christmas.

She went up to where they both lay shattered in five or so large chunks each, and like she had with the vase, she just started to wail on those remaining pieces.

When she finished with her parents, she lifted her head and brushed the strands of hair that had escaped her bun off her face.

She was dripping with sweat, and tears marred the inside lenses and pooled along the bottom of her goggles.

She took in the room.

Nothing smashable remained.

She'd destroyed everything.

Just like her world, just like her heart, everything in front of her was shattered.

A flash of red beneath a broken lampshade drew her eye, and she stepped forward and pulled it free.

Untouched and intact, a small red children's toy fire truck sat in her palm.

Connor had one just like it.

She hadn't checked to see if he'd left it behind in her SUV or if he'd taken it with him when the traffickers snatched him.

This truck very well could have been his. It was identical.

She knew better than to think that it actually was Connor's exact toy. It didn't have the C in black Sharpie that he'd insisted she put on the bottom just in case a kid at the park mistook it for their own.

But out there, another child was missing his or her toy.

Just like she was missing her son.

The tire iron slipped from her grasp and hit the floor with a *clunk*. She wrapped her fingers around the small fire truck, and when the emotion rushed forward, being propelled by a tidal wave of tears, she crumpled to the floor on her knees and wept for her child.

Connor.

Where was he?

Why him?

Why any child?

Children were the beacon of hope for the future, the bright spot in a dark and confusing world. Her children were the only thing she was grateful for in her sham of a marriage to Ted. They were the reason she awoke every morning. Even on the days she'd rather just stay in bed with her dreary thoughts and let the depression coil around her like a snake and drain the last of her breath, she got up and kept going—for her kids.

Her parents had made it very clear that they never wanted her. They proved that time and time again and even made a point of letting her know now, since they had no desire to reach out or get to know their grandchildren.

So when she found out she was pregnant with Connor, she

made a point of telling him every day he was inside of her and every day since that he was wanted. That he *is* wanted.

He and Thea were her chance to *not* rewrite history. She couldn't live with herself if they ever felt the way her parents made her feel.

Unloved.

Unwanted.

A burden.

Because for Stacey, she no longer felt whole without her children. And perhaps some might say that wasn't healthy and that she should still be a complete person even without her children. But fuck those people.

She was all her kids had, and they were all she had.

It was them against the world.

They *were* her world.

And now a piece of her world was missing.

A bright, shiny piece. With beautiful blue eyes, unruly blond hair and a smile that could make even a member of the Queen's Guard crack a grin.

The sobs came out thick and choppy. Her lungs burned, her chest ached and her nose was plugged. She wasn't sure how long she sat there on her knees, clutching the fire truck like it might disappear, but big hands coming up under her knees and around her back had her blinking through the tears.

She thought it was Heath picking her up, but when she glanced up, she saw it was Chase.

"I got you," he said, carrying her out of the room.

Richelle and Heath were standing against the wall, worry etched clear across their faces.

Stacey's sobs had ebbed a bit, and she curled into Chase as he carried her to the front door.

"I'll bring the gear back to you later," Richelle whispered to

Luna before she and Heath joined Stacey and Chase on the sidewalk.

Chase hit the fob in his pocket, and the lights for a black truck similar to his flashed. Opening the door, he gently placed her into the passenger seat. "It's okay, baby," he said, brushing the hair off her face. "I got you."

———

WHEN CHASE RETURNED to the hotel with Stacey, Heath and Richelle, he took Stacey to her bedroom and laid her on the bed. She was a total mess, and he knew she needed a break. All she'd done when he laid her on the bed was curl into a ball, the tears still flowing unchecked down her cheeks as she sobbed into the pillow.

Richelle went to her, but Chase shook his head and closed the door.

Stacey needed time.

She needed space.

He'd been reluctant about letting her go to The Rage Room with Richelle. He wasn't sure if she'd be able to handle it. Especially the surge of emotions when she finally let out everything bottled up inside her. It was probably like dropping a Mentos into a Coke bottle and being shaken up. She didn't stand a chance when things finally blew up.

Heath left with Aaron and Colton to go do a bit of recon around The Glossy Gem Motel while Liam and Richelle headed home. Chase was now in the hotel room alone.

Brock had called to say he and Rex would be at the hotel by one o'clock, and before he left, Aaron said that Rob Cahill—whose family owned the hotel they were staying in—would be at the hotel by five that night so they could nail down the specifics for the plan.

But for now, besides Stacey in her room, the suite was empty. He could get down to real business and go deeper into the dark web than he'd ever been before. To the places and rooms where only the most depraved and sadistic lurked: child molesters, human traffickers, terrorists. He needed to know more about the man and the operation they were dealing with. He wanted to know more about Impervious than the people closest to him did, and the best way to do that was hunt.

Chase loved hunting. Though not in the current setting with the creeps and weirdos around every turn.

But he enjoyed researching things. Finding people, things and places. He'd become freakishly good at hacking into restricted servers and the emails of top government officials.

He was one of the reasons why a certain senator of a certain state suddenly decided *not* to run for office again. Just a little side project Chase took on while babysitting Charlene and Bobby-June down in Georgia. Turns out Senator Crane had a penchant for underage girls and private parties on billionaires' yachts. Now the motherfucker was doing time and lots of it.

Score one for the good guys!

He cracked his neck side to side and cleared his throat. The deeper he went, the more he felt like he was going to puke.

Parents trading their children. Making deals for cash with perverts. Men talking about trying to adopt children to keep as sex slaves. One guy, and this guy Chase intended to find later and end in the most finite way, said in a forum how he'd love to have daughters, rape them, get them pregnant and then rape his granddaughters. People who thought like this didn't deserve to breathe. And once he found Connor and the little boy was safe once more with Stacey, Chase would start his hunt all over again.

He sifted through forums, narrowing his search to the Pacific Northwest, then Washington state. He'd set up a flag for the name Impervious and nearly jumped where he sat when his computer dinged and a message popped up.

From the devil himself.

Change of plans.

Change of plans? What the fuck did that mean?

He didn't want to sound too eager or pushy for info, so he sat back and watched those three little dots dance as Impervious typed more information.

Meet at Velour at midnight. Just you.

Velour? What and where was *Velour?*

He did a rapid Google search and found that Velour was a seedy speakeasy-style bar behind a strip club in the Industrial District West. It was a ways away from The Glossy Gem and the Satin Lounge.

Shit. Did this mean they needed three teams? That would tighten their manpower significantly.

Knock, knock.

He glanced at his phone. It was already one o'clock. How the fuck did that happen? It was eleven when he set Stacey on her bed and sat down at his laptop. Had he really been hunting cretins for two hours?

He got up and unlocked the door so that his brothers could open it but didn't wait around the foyer to exchange pleasantries. He had to get back to Impervious.

I can be there at midnight, he typed. *How much?*

Bring 10K.

Better be getting two dolls for that price.

I have buyers in Asia who will pay double for one. Take it or leave it.

Shit. He figured if he was too agreeable and didn't try to barter a bit, Impervious would think he was being catfished. But now he was worried Impervious was going to break the deal entirely.

10K. Got it.

We wait ten minutes, then we go. Don't waste my time.

Chase wasn't able to reply because Impervious had signed off.

"That the scum?" Brock asked, his voice now right behind Chase.

"Yeah. Just finalizing a drop point. He changed it from where he said to meet last night. Gonna need three teams now." Chase double-checked that Impervious had logged off before standing up to face Brock. Rex was behind him.

Chase cleared his throat and nodded. "Thanks for coming."

"Of course," Rex said, giving Chase a curious look. "Love Connor and Stacey, too. Even if I didn't, this is a missing kid, for Christ's sake."

Chase nodded.

Not just any missing kid though. It was Connor who was missing.

Stacey's son and a little boy he'd quickly grown to love like his own.

"What's the plan?" Rex asked.

Brock grunted and plopped his hands on his hips. His green eyes, the same shade as Chase's, narrowed as he waited for Chase to explain.

Brock was waiting to talk, too. Chase knew it.

He was also probably waiting for the right time to step in and take over.

As was the Brock Hart way.

Well, not this time.

"I'm running point on this," Chase said, glancing at Brock. "Just because you showed up doesn't mean you're taking over."

All Brock did was lift a brow, which—for the broad-shouldered man with a military crew cut who wore a leather jacket even in summer—was the equivalent to "We'll see about that."

Normally, Brock was the leader. He ran the business, and when he went on a job, he ran point. But when Chase was sent on the job without Brock, he ran point. He wasn't about to hand over the reins now just because they needed backup.

Rex cleared his throat at the same time he tugged a brown knit cap off his head to reveal his shiny, hairless scalp. "You sure you're not too close to this to be running point?" Rex asked, gauging Chase cautiously. "It's not too personal?"

"Personal for all of us," Chase said. "We all love him."

"And we're all going to get him back," Brock said, resting a meaty hand on Chase's shoulder and squeezing. "With Chase running point."

———

STILL A FRACTURED VERSION of her formal self, with a heavy heart, tired and sore eyes and a throat that was raw from all the crying, Stacey emerged from her room. The sky outside was dark, and the hotel suite was quite a bit fuller than before.

It didn't help that all the men that occupied the room were larger than life to begin with. Stacey felt like a sapling among a forest of star-reaching redwoods.

She quietly slipped through all the big bodies and found Chase, who was sitting at the table, a map of the city and the areas they were going to hit in front of him.

Rex and Brock were at the table, too, but Heath had found a comfortable spot on the couch, and the newcomer, Roberto or "Rob," as he'd been introduced, was on the phone, apparently procuring some black SUVs for them to use.

Aaron, Colton and Liam were back, too, and they were scattered around the living room in chairs and the other couch.

"I've got us three Escalades for tonight," Rob said, stowing his phone into his back pocket. "I've been in situations like this before. There are going to be more children, and we're going to want to save them all, so we need vehicles to do that."

"I'm going to look into recently reported missing children in the Pacific Northwest and what the status is on them. Ambushing

Stacey was done with too much finesse for it to be their first attempt to abduct like that. I'll see if something similar has been done and maybe reach out to the parents," Rob went on. His passion for this case struck Stacey as almost personal.

She knew from the few things Chase and Heath had said that Rob had kids and he used to be a SEAL with Aaron and Colton. And based off what he just said about having been in a situation like this before, something told her—or at least she hoped—that he'd done his fair share of successful rescues.

"New plan," Chase said, reaching for his Subway sandwich from the bag on the table and taking out one half. "We're going to get Stacey to stay at Liam's with Richelle. Since we have three locations to stake out now, the teams will be reduced. The Glossy Gem is close to the Satin Lounge, but Velour is too far away to put a vehicle in the middle. I also don't want to have to worry about you guys sitting in a dark vehicle in a sketchy part of town."

Stacey opened her mouth to protest, but Chase hit her with a look.

It wasn't an alpha-hole, *do-as-I-say-woman* look. It was a look of pleading. He was putting himself and a lot of other men in possibly grave danger to save her son. The last thing he needed was to have to worry about her, too.

She got that. She got that he took his job seriously, and because it was her kid—because it was *her*—he was personally invested, too, so he was giving this one hundred and ten percent—probably more. She didn't want to worry him or compromise the mission, so she shut her trap and nodded.

"Colton will assess him, and then we'll bring him to you. If we need to go straight to the hospital, we'll call you and you can meet us there. Deal?" He took a bite of his sandwich, and she could see him instantly relax—well, kind of. She'd heard his stomach grumbling when she first approached.

She nodded. "Okay."

"Richelle will be here in bit," Liam added.

"Time to debrief what we found at The Glossy Gem," Aaron said, adjusting his position on the chair.

The Hart brothers nodded, and the room went quiet.

"Talked to the motel manager. Shady guy. On something for sure. Only took fifty bucks for him to spill his guts though."

"Guy hasn't *seen* any kids, but he's heard a lot of crying—kid crying," Colton said, his tone laced with a hefty dose of not only anger but regret. "We didn't really hear anything, though, and we wandered past every door. All the blinds were drawn. Same woman that stuck that needle in your neck is staying at the hotel. Room four. Nothing suspicious around her room when we checked it out. Even waited for her to leave and then we snuck in, but there wasn't anything to lead us to believe she's with the kids."

Stacey's hope deflated.

"We checked out the Satin Lounge, too," Aaron went on. "Real shady shit going down there. Poked around the back. Found kid-size socks, a kid's glove. Child-size shoe prints in the mud—a lot of them. They're either in the club now or they were."

"Impervious messaged me and wants to do the drop at Velour, some seedy speakeasy behind a strip club," Chase said.

Colton and Aaron both made cringey faces, but it was Liam that spoke. "That strip joint is nasty. Wouldn't be surprised if you could catch the clap from the door handle. Heard the speakeasy isn't much better."

A chill slid down Stacey's spine, and she wrapped her arms around her body tight. And they were going to bring her child to this hellhole?

"Once we hear Chase's plan, we'll head to Velour and do some recon before we go there tonight," Aaron said. "Will have to run home and have a shower in ethanol after going in there though."

A few of the men snorted and laughed. Not Chase though. He was watching Stacey.

"You think he's got the kids at Velour already?" Rex asked.

Aaron shrugged. "Maybe. Who the fuck knows? But we'll snoop around a bit, ask some questions."

Chase nodded, chewed more and swallowed before starting to speak. "So the plan as it stands right now is for Aaron, myself and Colton to go to Velour with Liam for the drop. We're hoping he has Connor and the other kids there. Brock and Rob will go to the Satin Lounge, and Rex and Heath can go to the motel. *If* the motel is empty, run to the lounge and back them up there. *If* the lounge is empty, then jump in the Escalade and get over here. It will mean Impervious will have *all* of his men here, and we'll need backup. Got it?"

Heath opened up a bottle of chocolate milk and took a long sip before asking, "When did Impervious say he wanted to meet?"

"Midnight. Said I had ten minutes before he took off." Chase glanced at Stacey again. She wasn't feeling so hot. All this talk about a sketchy motel, a seedy strip club and catching the clap from a door handle had her swaying where she sat. She had to grip the edge of the table like it was a cliff ledge to keep herself from falling over.

"Whoa!" Rex said, his arm shooting out and his long fingers wrapping around her bicep. "You okay?"

She shook her head and blinked. "All this talk about ..." She swallowed hard. "I can't ..." Struggling to stand up and not keel over, she held on to the table, but Chase was around to her side of the table before she could take another breath, his hands on her arms as he guided her around.

"I got you," he murmured, ushering her toward her bedroom. "I think you should lie down for a bit."

"I'm not—"

"You barely slept," he whispered into her ear as they entered her room. "I know you weren't sleeping when I brought you back here from The Rage Room. Heard you crying. You need to rest.

This is stressful and frightening. You could go into shock if you don't rest." He helped her climb onto her bed and pulled a blanket over her as she settled down into the pillows.

He was right. Damn him. She was tired. Worried. Scared. Angry.

The Rage Room had been helpful, but it was a Band-Aid, not a cure.

He leaned down and pressed a kiss to her head. "Close your eyes. You don't need to hear what we're talking about. I know you're tough as nails, but he's your child—so just be the mom here, okay?"

She nodded, and a hot tear slid down onto the pillow. "Okay."

"We'll get him back, Stace, I promise." He kissed her head once more, ran his hand over her hair and left.

She was asleep within seconds.

CHAPTER SEVENTEEN

THEY SPENT another half an hour going over the plan for that night.

Chase brought up maps of the area, satellite images and blueprints of the three locations. By the time they headed out, he expected every man to know the layout of all three buildings, the side streets and alleyways like the backs of their damn hands.

When Aaron and Colton left to go check out Velour and eventually go see their families for a bit, Brock and Rex decided to go do a bit of snooping of their own. They brought out their rattiest wife-beaters, their grossest jeans and their trucker hats, then they went *into* the strip club with fists full of dollar bills and toothpicks in their teeth.

Chase wasn't sure what schtick they were going for, but they looked ridiculous enough, Heath took a few pictures of them before they left the hotel.

Heath decided he needed a nap after his big lunch, so he retired to his room. Stacey was asleep in her room, and Chase was once again alone.

Back into the hell pit of philistines he went.

By the time the dinner hour rolled around, he'd managed to get a last known address, a real name, Social Security number, criminal record and birthdate for Impervious, or should he say Dakota Creed, born December 4, 1981. He was wanted for human trafficking, drug trafficking, racketeering, embezzlement, fraud and a whole other laundry list of redeeming felonies that would make any parent proud. There was a warrant out for his arrest, but if Chase had anything to say in the matter, the cops wouldn't be getting their hands on the man who traded children like cattle.

Dakota Creed didn't deserve prison.

Dakota Creed didn't deserve oxygen.

Dakota Creed didn't deserve mercy.

Dakota Creed was going to wish his mother had kept her legs closed by the time Chase was finished with him.

When he finally lifted his head up from the screen to the sound of Stacey's door opening, the clock on his computer said it was nine o'clock. His eyes hurt, his gut churned, and he had such a strong, consuming thirst for blood, a thirst he hadn't felt in a long time, that it actually scared him a little.

Stacey's hand slid across his back and rested on his shoulder just as he was closing all the windows on his laptop. He shut out the world of the depraved and disgusting. "This stuff doesn't mess with your sleep?" she asked groggily.

Oh, it did.

But a fuck-ton of other things messed with his sleep, too, so this was just one more monster to add to the stack that forced him to keep one eye open while he struggled to get some REM.

She took a seat next to him and reached for his hands. He turned to face her, their knees touching. Even though she'd been asleep for a few hours, she still looked exhausted. Maybe she hadn't slept. Maybe she'd been in her room crying all this time.

Now he felt like an ass for not going to check on her.

He tended to develop blinders when he was hunting. Nothing

but the target, the prey, was on his mind, and he'd often forget to piss, eat or sleep until he found what—or in most cases *who*—he was looking for.

Her soft, petite thumb rubbed the back of his hand. "Hmm?"

He nodded. "Yeah, this stuff messes with my head, but it's all part of the job." He glanced up at her. "I'll sleep better with you next to me."

A sexy pink flushed her cheeks.

Heath's door opened to reveal a big goof with bedhead and tired blue eyes. He yawned and reached up to touch the doorjamb around the same time there was a knock at the main door.

"I'll get it," Heath said with another yawn.

He opened the door for Brock and Rex, who had takeout bags with them.

"Grabbed dinner," Rex said.

"Hold the door!" Heavy footsteps drew near in the hallway until Colton appeared, followed by Liam, Richelle, Aaron and Rob.

"Gang's all here," Heath said, using his fingers to comb his hair into a bit less of a mess. "Hope you brought enough food."

"We came with more," Richelle said, giving Stacey and Chase a welcoming smile and plopping a big insulated flexible cooler bag on the dining table.

"I'm starving," Heath said, digging into the bag Rex hadn't even completely put down on the table. "What'd you get?"

Brock shot his youngest, biggest brother a dirty look. "Didn't you *just* eat two feet of sandwich?"

Heath's incredulous, hurt expression had Chase snorting with mirth. "That was like four hours ago. I'm a growing boy."

Brock rolled his eyes. "We grabbed Indian from a place Aaron recommended."

"And we picked up a bunch of Mediterranean chicken sandwiches from Paige's Bistro," Richelle said, pulling bundles of something that smelled delicious out of the bag. She glanced at Chase. "I was thinking ..."

Chase's brow lifted, and when he realized Richelle wanted to speak in private, he untangled his fingers from Stacey's and stood up, but not before pecking her on the top of the head.

He followed the tiny force of nature with the blonde pixie cut and intense amber eyes over to the living room. "What's going on?"

Richelle took a deep breath. "I've set up this program to help women who are in abusive relationships start over. Lawyers, counselors, moving companies, airlines, new identities and jobs if needed. The works."

His brows pinched. What was she getting at? "These are just kids though."

She nodded, her expression severe but also filled with genuine concern. "That's right. They're *just* kids. Innocent children. I think we need to set up a bit of a triage situation here at the hotel. Leave me here with Stacey. I've got a friend—Tessa—who is a child trauma therapist. She's agreed to come by tonight. Paige is going to bring more food. I've also called Colton's wife, who works for a massive clothing store, and she's going to hook us up with clothes for the kids. Mark Herron, Emmett Strong, Riley McMillan and Will Colson are doctors, and they've all agreed to come and help with the children as well. Who knows, you guys might need some patching up, too."

Holy shit. She'd organized everything. Right down to getting the children clothes and having a trauma therapist on site.

"You don't think taking them to the hospital is the best course of action?" he asked, liking her plan better than just carting the children off to the hospital, where they'd be treated by an endless stream of different faces and undoubtedly left alone or assigned to an overworked and underpaid social worker.

"I do if their injuries are enough that the doctors say they need to go to the hospital. If they say we need to move the kids, then we move them. I've also got a cop on my speed dial. So we'll call Isaac, too."

Even though his sister-in-law was a cop, Chase still had issues with the po-po. Ever since Peru and the way the cops there had treated him, he held a bit of a grudge against those who claimed to serve and protect. The shit on the news about cops lately and the way they were treating certain people—shooting first and making excuses later—didn't sit right with him, either.

Not all cops were bad, but the bad ones made you wary of the rest.

"You've thought of everything," he said, unable to keep the corner of his mouth from lifting into a lopsided smile.

Richelle nodded and plopped her hands on her slim hips. "I have. Once we determine who the children are, we can start making calls to reconnect them with their families. I've spoken with Skyler McAllister—Rob's wife—and she has agreed to fly the parents here and home with their children on her family's airline for free."

Chase's eyes widened. "Jesus, is there anything you *haven't* thought of?"

She struck him as the type of woman who came out of the womb telling the doctors what to do.

Richelle took a step closer and lowered her voice. "I've done some research into child trafficking, and the chances of these children having been violated already is low. They'll be dirty, hungry and possibly sick, but rarely do the handlers touch the merchandise. The buyers are paying big money for ..." Her throat moved on a swallow, and her complexion paled. "*Innocence*," she finally said. "Once they're shipped to where they're going, they'll be *trained*, but not beforehand. But we can't rule that out. We may need a female doctor if some of the children are girls and get triggered by one of the male doctors touching them."

Chase fought back his own shudder. "Impervious specializes in little boys, but you're right. Do you know any female doctors?"

She shook her head. "No, but Mark's going to call a colleague."

He nodded curtly and placed his hand on Richelle's shoulder for a brief moment. He normally wasn't big on touching, but this seemed to warrant a physical reaction to all the amazing things Richelle had organized. "Thank you. You've done an incredible job in a short amount of time."

"Already had the connections, just needed to make the calls."

"I appreciate you coming to stay with Stacey. She'll need someone to keep her calm and company, and since you've been through this, I'm glad it's you."

Richelle's lips pinned together, and her hawk-like eyes turned extra fierce. "Neither of us should have to have gone through this." She brought her voice down again. "Do me a favor." Her brows lifted. So did Chase's in interest. "Mercy is for those who deserve it. And these fuckers don't. Got it?"

God help any person who rubbed Richelle LaRue the wrong way. Yeesh.

But he understood where she was coming from and whole-heartedly agreed.

He nodded again and cleared his throat. "Prisons are too crowded as it is."

Her sly smile and a finger tap to the side of her nose were all that he got before she walked away to go sit beside Stacey.

Stacey smiled when Richelle sat next to her, the two women chatting animatedly as they picked at the buffet spread of food.

Heath was chowing down on a gluttonously stacked plate while everyone else had either found a place to sit or was standing with the plate in their hand and chatting.

It was kind of crazy when you thought about it all.

Here they all were, minus Liam, Richelle and Stacey, all men preparing to go into battle—in essence. Getting ready to take down the bad guys and save the children. Right now, they were all just ordinary dudes eating dinner, when in a few short hours, they'd be armed to the teeth and raiding a child trafficking ring.

This kind of shit never got easier.

Chase became better at it the more he did it, but mentally— emotionally—it never got easier. As hard as he tried to prepare himself for what he was about to see, there was no way to truly do it.

He'd rather see a thousand dead corpses of grown-ass men than one hurt and abused child. He'd go down fighting, to the death, to save a kid—and it didn't matter if it was Connor or someone else's child. He'd give up his life—and knew any of the men in that room would, too—to save any one of those kids.

And the more he thought about it, the more he'd dug into Impervious's reign of terror, the more he realized they weren't dealing with some two-bit hack out to make a couple of bucks. They were dealing with a man who had power, money and backing. Impervious would be guarded. The children would be guarded, and people would most likely get hurt.

He might get hurt.

Taking a deep breath, he strolled up behind Stacey and squeezed her shoulders with both hands. She broke off her heads- together, hush-hush conversation with Richelle and glanced up at him, worry streaking across her features. "Everything okay? Did you get new information about Connor?"

He shook his head. "No. Plan is still the same as before." He reached for her hand, and she stood up, allowing him to lead her to her bedroom. He shut the door, but not before catching Rex's eye. His brother quickly glanced away, but he'd seen enough to know that although they *said* things were okay between them, it would still take some time.

"What's going on?" Stacey asked, stepping over to the bedside table and turning on the lamp so there was more light in the room.

Everything was most definitely not all right. Her son was missing, and he and six other men were preparing to go into battle. He still needed to figure out a way to keep Liam from getting stuck in the crossfire.

She reached for his hand and stepped into his space, bringing the scent of her shampoo and her own fresh, feminine scent. "You're scaring me, Chase."

He shook his head and squeezed her hand. "It's going to be dangerous tonight."

Her eyes widened. "Like *how* dangerous?"

"Impervious is well equipped. He's been running this operation for a while. He's got means. He's going to be protected, and those men will be armed."

Stacey's chest began to move up and down quicker, and he could see the cogs spinning in her mind. "You think they could threaten to harm the children? To harm Connor?"

That was definitely a possibility—sacrifice one to get away with the rest—but that wasn't where he was going.

"I just need you to try to prepare yourself for what is to come next. Granted, Connor hasn't been gone that long, but still. He could be in rough shape if he struggled or tried to fight them."

Her gasp was like a thousand wasp stings to his heart. She covered her mouth with her hand, and her eyes became damp.

Fuck, maybe he shouldn't have said anything.

But then, he wanted her to be prepared. He wanted to be honest with her.

He was still keeping so many secrets, if he *could* be honest with Stacey, he wanted to be.

Drawing her into his body, he wrapped his arms around her, quieting the trembles that had suddenly begun to saw away at her frayed nerves. "I'm sorry. I shouldn't have said anything."

Even with her cheek pressed against his chest, he felt her shake her head. "I need to know. He's my baby. I need to be prepared to help him with whatever he's going to need." A harsh sob shook them both, and she fisted his shirt tightly. "I can't lose him, Chase. I've already lost so much. I can't lose him. He's my everything."

Chase rubbed her back and made gentle, hopefully comforting shushing sounds.

"He doesn't deserve this. He's a good kid. A happy kid. What if they've stolen all that happiness from him? Taken away his childhood simply by taking away his ability to trust people or not worry every minute of every day about being snatched?"

That was a real possibility.

Connor was a tremendous kid, but even the brightest of stars could have their light extinguished with enough force.

He just hoped that they were going to get him in time before all his light was lost to the darkness.

CHAPTER EIGHTEEN

He waited until they were outside the hotel and getting their gear on before he told the rest of them what he'd uncovered about Impervious.

"Not against a little maim and torture when it comes to these types," Aaron said, cracking his knuckles before wrapping them in black boxer's tape. He'd declined any kind of heavy artillery, saying he would never touch a gun again after what happened to his sister.

Chase would have to ask Heath or maybe Colton for more details later.

But Aaron had knives hidden all over him, along with zip ties, tear gas and—in Chase's opinion—the most terrifying thing of all: a long, thin, nearly invisible strip of wire with two wooden toggle pieces on either end. It was called a garrote, and Chase didn't need to ask what that was for. He knew.

Impervious, or Creed, had not only a child and human trafficking ring where he collected, stole and kidnapped children, only to sell them to perverts both foreign and domestic, but he also ran an enormous prostitution ring down in Oregon—made up mostly of underage runaways—and he had ties to other houses of depravity and pedophilia in Nevada and California. According to Chase's research, Creed was wanted in six states for human trafficking, assault with a deadly weapon on several of his working girls, and it was also rumored that he took part in black-market organ trafficking as well. That if his prostitutes weren't bringing in enough money, he killed them, harvested their organs and sold them on the street for top dollar to dying and desperate people.

The guy was beyond disgusting.

The more he told the team about Creed, the darker the men's faces grew.

Even Heath, who often reminded Chase of a happy puppy with floppy ears and an endless appetite, had grown quiet, and his demeanor had shifted. It usually shifted slightly when they were getting ready for the job, but Heath rarely stopped cracking jokes, even when he had his game face on.

He wasn't cracking any now.

A storm had begun to brew inside Chase's little brother. And when Heath brought the thunder, watch the fuck out. Thor and his mighty hammer had nothing on Heath Hart.

"Best guess is he's going to have the kids at Velour. They've got a garage-like thing in the back. Not insulated or anything, but if they've kept the kids at the motel, they're going to bring them to Velour tonight. Less eyes on them. Less of a chance of being caught. That's our best bet. That's where we need to put our team of three," Colton said.

Chase nodded. "Colton, Aaron and I will go to Velour and wait in the shadows while Liam does his pedo thing."

Liam, decked out in a light checkered shirt a size or two too big and a worn light denim jacket, looked pretty normal to Chase. But then there was no "stereotypical" pedophile. So he needed to look like an average Joe. He finished off the look with mussed hair, dirty khakis and a gross, thin, lip-hugging mustache. Richelle had done a pretty good job styling her husband for his first undercover job.

"Brock and Rob can go scope out the motel while Rex and Heath check out the lounge," Chase said, appreciating the nods all around and no challenge from the rest of the alphas—particularly his big brother. He knew it was a struggle for Brock to not take charge, but he appreciated that he was being given the opportunity to run point on this.

"Same plan as before. We'll stash two vehicles between the lounge and the motel, so those two teams can be backup for each other. If you come up empty, head here," he pointed to Velour on the map," because that means we'll need the backup."

Heads bobbed, and necks were cracked. It was only February and fucking freezing out, so they would need to be extra vigilant and not let their bodies get cold as they waited. They also couldn't let their warm breath expose their locations.

It was amazing the things you noticed when it was cold, dark and silent, particularly if you were trained to notice. And something told him Dakota Creed hadn't hired two-bit thugs off the street to protect his operation.

He checked his phone for the time.

Twenty to twelve.

They needed to get moving.

All eight of them stood in a circle, but nobody said anything.

Chase wasn't a religious person, and neither were his brothers. He didn't know if the other guys prayed to anybody specific, but he allowed those who needed it the opportunity to get centered, focused and to turn on *that* part of their brain.

If they mentally chatted with a deity, that was their business. Life was too fucking short to judge someone for who they believed in, Santa, Jesus or otherwise.

After about a minute, he cleared his throat. "All right, everyone. You know the plan."

"Hit like thunder, disappear like smoke," Colton said.

Everyone nodded, and they all climbed into their vehicles.

Aaron drove, as he knew where he was going.

Rex drove the other vehicle and Rob the last vehicle.

"Do we *have* money?" Colton asked. "That way we at least look legit."

"Ten Gs," Liam said from the far back of the Escalade. "I'd like to get it back, but it's no skin off my teeth if I don't."

"You'll get it back," Chase said, matter-of-fact.

They rode the rest of the way in silence.

At first, he had dismissed the idea of bringing doctors to the hotel, but when Richelle brought up the other children—because there would be others—he realized it was a good idea. They would bring the kids to the hospital if they needed to, but he hoped they wouldn't need to. They would also call the cops when they needed to, but he hoped they *really* didn't fucking need to.

Cops made things messy.

Eventually, of course, they'd have to involve the cops.

Chase just preferred to delay that call as long as possible.

But Brock was the Seattle PD's point of contact and he was keeping them as informed as they needed to be.

Much like he and his brothers used to when they worked black ops, they had special privileges when they went on raids and took down the bad guys that those who wore badges couldn't seem to find. And as long as Chase and his brothers were transparent with their intentions, the authorities tended to look the other way as long as the job was done and the mess cleaned up.

Cops just seemed to operate on their own timeline, and at a speed that did not work for Chase—too many doughnuts maybe?

But Chase acted quick. He struck while the iron was hot.

Maybe that's why you ended up in a Peruvian prison for six months? Acted before thinking.

That was neither here nor there. He did what he thought was right at the time. And everything ended up working out in the long run anyway.

After another five minutes, Aaron pulled the SUV over to the curb and turned off the lights. "One block to the left," he said, taking great care to hide their vehicle in the shadow of a warehouse and beneath a blown-out streetlight.

Chase swallowed, nodded and opened his door from the shotgun seat.

Colton and Liam met him and Aaron on the sidewalk, and Aaron handed Liam the keys. "You know where to park?"

Liam nodded. The man did not look confident at all. He looked like he was close to shitting himself.

Nerves were good—as long as you didn't have too many. He only hoped Liam had just the right amount.

Liam took the keys and headed to the driver's side. "How long should I give you guys before I drive over there?"

"Two minutes," Chase whispered. Aaron and Colton were already on the move, sticking to the shadows. He waited for Liam to get into the vehicle and close the door before he and the other two men disappeared around a corner.

They were silent as they moved.

They'd all done this enough times over the course of their careers that they knew the drill. Slide in undetected. Rain terror. Take out the threat. Extract the innocents. Convene at the muster point.

Earlier in the day, Brock and Rex had gone into the strip club at the front of Velour and decided there wasn't anywhere for Impervious to hide the kids in there. Aaron and Colton said the same thing about the inside of the sketchy speakeasy. But that decrepit old garage at the back was the perfect place to hide a bunch of terrified children. Particularly in a van with gags in their mouths.

As they made their way toward the back of the building, Chase kept his ears peeled for the sound of kids. So far, everything had been dead quiet, save for a couple of vehicles and one homeless man coughing like he had a chicken bone stuck in his throat.

The mud was thick, and there were deep potholes turned into puddles riddling the gravel road that led to the back of Velour, where the garage was. They stopped just before the building and ducked around the back of a large oak.

Using only his fingers and eyes, Chase gave the other two men instructions to break off and surround the building.

They nodded, and that's when they heard the Escalade pull up.

Aaron and Colton disappeared into the dark, and Chase did the same, but he made sure to keep Liam in his sight at all times.

Liam flashed his lights twice and honked once.

Chase held his breath.

Nothing.

He checked his phone. It was two minutes to twelve.

A thick wad of dread lodged itself in his throat. What if Connor wasn't here? What if Creed brought other children for Liam to pick from but Connor wasn't in that bunch? They couldn't just walk away from these kids knowing their fate. But then if they did go in to save them and Connor wasn't there, they'd shown their hand, and the chances of getting Connor back were slim to none.

Also, what if Creed and the children weren't even here? What if they were at the lounge or the motel and this was an ambush? He knew the other men could hold their own, but they were only teams of two, and who knew how many men Creed had on his payroll?

A thick fog had rolled in around ten o'clock, making it difficult to see more than ten feet in front. He shivered when a chilly breeze whipped around him, making him glad he had his knit cap and gloves on. If your muscles and head were cold, it made it more difficult to fight. Though fighting always warmed him up. He'd just be a little stiff in the beginning.

He'd ducked behind a big commercial-size garbage can and knew that Colton was waiting on the other side near the big arbutus tree and Aaron was around the back looking for another way in and out. They said there was a back door when they scoped the place out earlier, but it didn't look like it'd been used in years. Aaron's job was to kill the power, so he needed to find a way in and get to the electrical panel.

Chase was about to glance at his phone again when the sound of a heavy door being dragged open pulled his attention away.

Liam left his lights on but opened the truck door. "You Impervious?" he called out.

Nothing.

Shit, Chase had a bad feeling about this.

Something didn't feel right.

"Yo, Impervious, you there?" Liam beckoned. "I'm here, man. Not late, just like you said."

Deliberate, slow footsteps on gravel echoed around the foggy alleyway. Chase snuck closer and wedged his face between a gap between the garbage can and the side of the building to get a better view.

"Mr. Chimbo." Chase wasn't sure what he was expecting when it came to Dakota Creed, but the nasally voice wasn't it. There was no depth or grit to his tone. He sounded almost like a pre-pubescent teen.

Liam walked around to the front of the Escalade, a duffle bag in his hand, which he lifted in the air. "Got what you wanted. You got what I want?"

More gravel crunching, but this time it wasn't just one set of footsteps. It was several. He tuned in. Along with Creed's footsteps it sounded like there were three others walking with him.

Chase couldn't hear the awkward shuffling or whimpers of children though.

Where the fuck were the kids?

Where the fuck was Connor?

Two big men in black flanked Creed, and another man, not much bigger than Chase, but big enough, with a thick neck, gray knit hat and a black leather jacket, approached Liam. It was the same guy from the surveillance video. The one that had helped abduct Connor.

He would be the first to die.

"You won't mind if my associate pats you down? Can never be too cautious about these things. Need to make sure you're not wearing a wire or carrying a weapon," Creed said, remaining in the shadows and out of view.

Liam set the duffle bag down on the ground and spread his arms and legs so he looked like a starfish. "Pat away. Not carrying anything. Besides maybe a ..." He lifted his chin and bobbed his brows. "Just tell your man to be careful between my legs, if you know what I'm saying."

The thick-necked stooge gave Liam a thorough pat-down before turning back to Creed and giving one curt nod.

"Check the bag," Creed ordered.

Liam lifted the bag off the ground and held it out for the thick-necked goon. The guy unzipped it and ruffled through the stacks of bills, undoubtedly looking for a weapon, tracking device or recording device.

He wouldn't find any of that.

Chase knew that Creed wasn't an idiot. He'd managed to evade getting caught up until now, which meant he covered his ass and paid handsomely for others to cover his ass as well.

All that was in the duffle bag was cold, hard cash. They needed Liam to come across as legit as possible.

The thick-necked goon zipped the duffle bag back up, turned toward Creed and nodded again.

More gravel crunched, and Dakota Creed, aka Impervious, stepped into the beam of the Escalade's headlights. He was slim, with long black hair past his shoulders, and everything he wore was black. He wasn't very tall either. Maybe five feet six. Chase could snap the guy in two over his thigh—and he would. "Can never be too careful," Creed said, reaching out and offering Liam his hand.

Liam wore gloves, but he shook Dakota's hand. "Totally understand. Need to be careful myself." He bit his lip. "Truth be told, I've never done this." Liam swallowed. He seemed to have just the right amount of nerves to make it believable. "I mean, I've *done* things. But only with *dolls* I know. And I had to move. I want one of my own, you know?" He cleared his throat and let his brown eyes dart around the alley a bit. But he was keeping an eagerness about him that Creed seemed to be buying. Fuck, Chase was buying it. If he didn't know better, he'd believe Liam was a sex offender pervert.

"Everyone has their preferences. And I'm making a fortune providing people like yourself *with* those preferences. Come." Creed jerked his head and turned around, heading back into the large garage.

Liam picked up the duffle bag, swallowed again and slowly followed.

Lights came on inside the garage, and Chase moved silently around the garbage bin to look inside.

It was fairly empty aside for a black Mercedes-Benz Sprinter van.

Creed's minion opened the sliding door of the van, and all Chase saw was Liam's back go ramrod straight.

The kids—Connor—were in there. They had to be.

Out of the corner of his eye, Chase saw five other men, all heavily armed, standing around the interior perimeter of the garage. That meant there were the same amount or more around the exterior between the strip club, the speakeasy and the garage. He needed to move before he was caught, before this whole operation went up in flames and they lost not only Connor but all the other children as well.

Like a panther stalking his prey, he ducked out from behind the garbage bin and crouch-shuffled along the outside wall of the garage. Brambles and leafless vines caught in his jacket and pant legs, but he quietly untangled himself.

He hated that he didn't have a view of things anymore.

But he could still hear them. The garage—because it was empty —was acting almost like a cave, and voices echoed.

"Wow, how to choose," Liam said. "All the same price?"

Aaron, Colton, Rob and Liam had all studied pictures of Connor extensively before they left, so they would know which child was Connor if presented with several little boys around the same age.

"I have a thing for blonds," Liam said, which was their code word to indicate that they'd found him. "What do you say, kid? You want to come play with me? Do you want a new Daddy?"

Chase suppressed the rise of bile in his throat. He hoped Connor didn't have an aversion to Liam after this. The poor kid needed to know Liam was just acting to save him.

Yeah, the more he thought about it, the more necessary a trauma therapist was going to be for these kids.

Now that they knew Connor was there, he needed to wait for the next cue. Pulling his night vision goggles over his eyes, he waited for Aaron to get to the breaker box so he could kill all the lights and power.

Should be any minute now.

Come on, Aaron. If Liam stalls anymore, Impervious will start getting suspicious and could call the whole thing off.

He held his breath.

Any minute now. Any minute.

The crack of a twig behind him had him jerking around just in time to see a man behind him with a gun.

Chase shot first. Double-tap, center mass. The man went down. Thank God he'd remembered to put the silencer on his gun.

The lights went out in the garage, causing hollering and chaos to transform the once-quiet night into a night of mayhem.

More shots fired inside the garage.

Creed's guys didn't have silencers.

Men hollered.

Punches were being thrown.

The van door slammed.

Chase leapt up from his spot and darted around to the opening of the garage. He saw Aaron in the middle of hand-to-hand combat with two men.

Colton had knocked one man out and was fighting off another one.

Chase spun around the garage, looking for Liam. He wasn't one of the four bodies on the ground.

Maybe he was in the van with the kids.

That would be smart.

Chase ran to the van door. He needed to see Connor with his own eyes.

With his 9mm out and ready, he slid open the sliding door. Eight sets of terrified eyes and tear-stained dirty little faces stared back at him. The van stunk. All the children were gagged and had most likely soiled themselves. He scanned the kids, and relief flooded him like a gulp of fresh air after holding your breath until your lungs burned. There was Connor.

His eyes lit up when he recognized Chase, and he struggled against his bonds.

"It's okay, little man," Chase said gently. "We're going to get you out of here." He glanced at all the other kids. "All of you. We're the good guys."

More shots were fired, and he heard a bullet whiz past the open door.

The driver's door opened, and Chase prepared himself to knock whoever it was out, but when he recognized Liam, he relaxed and nodded. "Get them the fuck out of here." He looked back at the kids. "He's a good guy, too, okay? He's with us. He's not going to hurt you. Nobody is going to hurt you."

Liam nodded and started the van. Thankfully, it appeared that Creed or whoever had left the keys in the ignition.

Now that he knew Liam was going to get the kids out of there and to the muster point, he needed to find the fuckers that took Connor from the parking lot. He needed to find Creed, and he needed to end him.

More gunshots rang out, gravel crunched and punches were thrown as he watched through his night-vision goggles as Colton and Aaron continued to fight.

More and more of Creed's men were coming out of the woodwork.

They were heavily outnumbered.

Police sirens echoed in the distance.

Cops would be here shortly. No doubt somebody in the area called after hearing all the gunfire.

The sound of many people running drew closer. More of Creed's men? Police? SWAT?

Rex appeared first, gun out, goggles on. He nodded at Chase before heading into the thick of battle, taking out two guys with his gun in less than a second.

Brock, Rob and Heath were on his tail, jumping into the mix and swinging fists.

Chase needed to find Creed. That was his number-one priority, now that Liam was going to get the kids to safety.

He scanned the garage looking for Creed. For another exit. He dodged one of Creed's guys coming at him and took him to the ground, clotheslining him in the throat with his arm. He stomped on his face for good measure, then put a bullet in his head to make damn sure he wasn't getting back up.

Liam hadn't been able to drive away yet, since there wasn't any room. Men were fighting all around the van.

Chase went to the front of the van, hoping to clear a path, when he saw headlights flash in the alleyway.

Creed.

An engine revved, and he sprinted out of the garage, prepared to run down the fucking car, shoot out its tires or jump on the hood and punch his way through the windshield if he had to.

Creed was not leaving here unless it was in a body bag with Chase's handprints around his neck.

He slowed his roll and crouched down behind a shrub, waiting for the car to pull out of wherever Creed had it stashed. There was only one way out, and that was forward. The speakeasy and garage were at the dead end of the alley.

Gravel spun and the engine revved. Now was his chance.

The car came into view. He aimed his gun at the front tire, squeezed the trigger, but a hard slam to the side of the head had him crumpling to the ground before he could shoot, and the world went black just as Creed's car sped away, throwing up rocks and hitting Chase in the face.

CHAPTER NINETEEN

STACEY PACED the length of the hotel suite, wringing her fingers and biting her lip.

The suite was not empty. Not by a long shot.

Richelle sat on the couch chatting quietly with Tessa, the trauma therapist, while Mark Herron, Will Colson, Riley McMillan and Emmett Strong all sat at the dining table, their medical bags on the kitchen counter. They'd set up triage stations in Heath and Stacey's bedrooms.

A gentle hand on Stacey's shoulder made her stop. It was Pasha Young, or Dr. Pasha Young, as she should be called. The female doctor Mark called to assist with the children if some of them were girls and uncomfortable being examined by a male.

She held a mug of tea in her other hand and offered it to Stacey, her gentle golden-brown eyes holding a level of sympathy and kindness Stacey appreciated. "I've never been good at waiting," she said, her smile small but sweet. "Even at thirty-two, I'm still a painfully impatient person."

Stacey took a sip of the tea. It was chamomile. This was Pasha's nice way of telling Stacey to calm down. The woman, with caramel-colored, dark-blonde-streaked hair pulled up into a pony-tail, tilted her head toward Stacey's room, encouraging her to follow.

With nothing better to do than wear a rut in the carpet, Stacey followed.

"We won't sit on the bed, but the chairs will do," Pasha said, taking the seat farthest from the dresser.

Stacey took the chair beside the dresser and cradled the tea in both hands. "I just feel so helpless. All these men are risking their lives to bring back my child, and here I am"—her laugh was brittle —"drinking tea."

"Your job comes next. The hard part comes next," Pasha said, leaning forward and resting her left hand on Stacey's knee.

"Connor is going to need you more than ever," Pasha went on. "To help him sort out his feelings, his fears, answer the tough questions. It's going to be a long, hard road for all of you. So if you're only waiting right now, that's okay. You're doing your part and will *do* your part when the time comes."

"Do you have children?" Stacey asked.

The woman shook her head. "No. But I want them. I want lots of them. I love kids. It's why I went into pediatrics. I also come from a huge family, so I want a huge family."

"Are you married or with someone?" Stacey needed to distract herself from her own thoughts, and interviewing the friendly doctor seemed the best option right now. She hadn't noticed a ring on the woman's finger. But in this day and age, that didn't mean much.

Pasha smiled, but there was an intense sadness behind her eyes that made Stacey instantly sad. "I was engaged, but he ended things just before Christmas. He said he couldn't see himself growing old with me." The last few words came out with a hard, bitter bite that even Stacey felt.

She placed her hand over Pasha's. "I'm sorry. But at least you didn't have kids with him. I had kids with my lowlife ex. Who is now dead." Pasha's eyes widened. "But not by my hand," Stacey quickly said. "He married me while he was still married to another woman. Led a double life and then died in a car accident. Freya—the other wife—and I learned about each other after his death. We're actually friends now."

"Out of the ashes you rose," Pasha said, the gold in her eyes twinkling. "Like a phoenix."

Stacey couldn't stop the obnoxious snort and laugh that bubbled up from her chest. "I've never been compared to a phoenix, but sure."

Richelle appeared at the door, her amber eyes wide. "Liam just called. They're downstairs and bringing the children up."

Stacey's shattered heart began to ache in her chest as she bolted up from the chair, sending her tea to the floor in a splash. She took one look at it. "Oh shit."

"It's fine," Pasha said, touching her arm. "I'll clean it up. Go prepare yourself."

Stacey just glanced back at Pasha but didn't say anything. She followed Richelle out to the suite, where the other doctors and Tessa were standing and seemed to be mentally preparing themselves. Mercedes had sent a bunch of clothing, which was in a couple of boxes by the balcony sliding-glass doors. Food was in the kitchen for the kids, as well as water and electrolytes. Even though Connor had only been gone for a day, they didn't know how long the other children had been away from their families.

Richelle's hand on her shoulder impeded her from running to the door and opening it to greet them in the hallway. Tessa had already told her to remain calm, that these children would be scared and wouldn't necessarily know that this new group of adults wasn't going to hurt them.

The doorknob wobbled, and she held her breath.

"I'll get it," Richelle said, beelining it for the door and holding it open.

Aaron—his face cut, bruised and bloody—was first in, a small, dirty child in his arms. This kid wore red shoes and blue pants. It wasn't Connor. The little boy had his arms wrapped tight around Aaron's neck, and his eyes were closed, but not from sleep. He was squeezing them shut out of fear.

"It's okay, buddy," Aaron said, taking the little boy over to the couch, where Pasha was crouched down waiting. "This here is Dr. Young, and she's going to help you, okay? You're safe now. Nobody is going to hurt you."

Next in was Colton. He had a child in his arms as well. Relief swamped her at the same time the tears exploded from her eyes like a geyser when she recognized those camo pants and the blond hair. Connor's face was dirty, but his blue eyes were wide, and when he saw her, he flung himself from Colton's arms at her, crying out, "Mama!"

She caught him and held on probably too tight, but she didn't care.

"Oh, my baby. My sweet, sweet baby," she said through the sobs as she kissed every inch of his face and pushed the hair out of his eyes to get a better look at him. "You're safe now. Nobody is going to hurt you. Nobody is going to take you away from me again. We've got you." He clung to her like a baby gorilla, his fingers digging in tight to the back of her neck. He could draw blood and she wouldn't care. He was back in her arms and in one piece, and that was all that mattered.

A rough-looking Rob walked in carrying one little boy in his arms and another by the hand. They had filthy faces and terror in their eyes. The doctors went to them and led them to the bedrooms.

Liam came in, and he held a little boy of about seven by the hand.

Heath and Brock were next. They each held a little girl in their arms. These tiny things were probably no more than three—if that. Were they even potty-trained?

Pasha saw that there were little girls here and passed her patient off to Emmett, who took over bandaging up the boy's elbows, which were bloody.

Heath and Brock took the little girls to Stacey's room, and Tessa and Pasha followed.

Sitting on one of the dining-room chairs, Stacey kept her arms wrapped tightly around Connor and murmured into his ear how much she loved him, all the while keeping an eye on the open door.

Rex was next—a big bloody cut on his bald head—and he held a little boy roughly Connor's age in his arms. Will Colson guided them to the couch across from the one Emmett was working at.

Stacey continued to stare at the door.

Where was Chase?

She counted all the men and all the children.

Chase had not ducked in without her seeing.

He was not here.

Where the hell was he?

Rex stepped toward her, followed by Heath and Brock, their faces tight, stony and dark. Heath glanced at his feet, Rex's nostrils flared, and Brock looked close to breaking a lamp or putting his fist through a wall.

"Where's ..." Stacey's eyes darted frantically between Aaron, Colton and Rob.

They were all watching her and the remaining three Hart brothers.

"Where's Chase?" she asked, her voice cracking. She stood up and adjusted Connor in her arms, giving the men her best stare-down. "Where is Chase?"

Heath's throat moved. "They have him."

"Who?" Just when she thought she was over the sick feeling of fear in her stomach, it emerged again to the point where she thought she might puke.

"They had a lot of security," Rex murmured. "When the lounge and motel teams realized the kids weren't there, we got to the speakeasy as fast as we could. But they took Chase out when he went after Creed. We did what we went there to do, and that was get the kids out."

Her posture went limp, as if all her bones had dissolved away, leaving only her skin to make due with standing. "But you can't just *leave* him," she practically screamed, causing several of the children to look at her with their own level of fear. "What are you all still doing here? Go back and get him."

"We don't know if he's alive," Heath said, clearing his throat, pain in his dark blue eyes when he finally lifted his head. "He wasn't at the muster point, isn't answering his phone. I saw him out of the corner of my eye rush out of the garage, but then he was gone."

Stacey began to shake. Her body had turned to ice and her legs to jelly. She dropped back into the chair because she had no other choice and hugged Connor even tighter. Her gaze lifted to Brock's face. "You don't think he sacrificed himself, do you?"

Aaron shook his head. "It didn't go down like that. I think he was ambushed from behind, didn't see it coming. It was dark and foggy out there, and when we killed the power, it was like fighting ghosts."

Her mind raced, heart beat wildly in her chest. "But you need to go back and get him. You can't leave your brother behind. We know what those monsters are capable of. You can't just—"

A knock at the door had her gasping.

Chase!

Nearly elbowing Richelle in the boob, and with Connor still in her arms, she sprinted for the door. But when she opened it, Chase was not on the other side.

A man with dark red hair, muscles for days and piercing blue eyes stood with his hands in the pockets of his gray sweatpants. "Hi. I'm Isaac. Liam and Richelle called me."

Richelle was at the door behind her and welcomed him in. "Thanks for coming, Isaac. I know it's your day off, but we need some help."

Isaac's eyes widened as he walked into the hotel suite and took in what was happening. He cleared his throat and fixed Liam and Richelle with a concerned and borderline pissed-off expression. "What is going on here?"

Richelle went on to explain the situation to Isaac, which only caused the man's eyes to widen, then his brows to narrow and finally his mouth to open and give him a sexy codfish look. "You guys can't go all *vigilante*," Isaac said, his head shaking. "I have to call this in."

Liam approached Isaac. "We know that, man."

"Brock's been communicating with the authorities and higher ups all along. Seattle PD is aware of the situation." Richelle said. "We called you because you're a cop, and we know you'll know how to get these kids back to their parents."

"You called me because I'm a friend and think I'll hesitate before I cuff you all and haul you in for going all vigilante." Isaac said, his hackles still slightly raised.

Liam sighed. "We want to work with the authorities, particularly now that we got the kids back. Hand this job over to the law. But time was of the essence, and we had to do what we had to do."

"Yeah, but now you've got a missing Canadian civilian," Isaac said, pulling his phone out of his pocket. "I'm glad the kids are safe, but fuck, guys, come on."

Tessa was busy handing out food and water to the children while the doctors continued to check them out.

"No serious injuries on the kids I examined," Will said, his throaty rumble nearly as dark as his skin.

"Mine, either," Riley said.

"My kid is complaining of a sore ear, and I took a look and think it's a mild ear infection," Emmett said. "I can write a scrip for some antibiotics."

Pasha and Mark joined them.

"Little guy I looked at seems fine," Mark said. "Scared, but no injuries. I asked if they'd been touched inappropriately, and they said no."

Pasha's nostrils flared, and she removed her latex gloves. "One of the little girls is fine. But the other one is deaf, so I don't know how to ask her the right questions. Anybody know any sign language?"

Mark lifted a hand, but Heath stepped forward. "I do."

Pasha's gaze landed on Heath and instantly turned avid. "Come with me, then."

Mark knelt down next to Stacey and pulled on new gloves. "Mind if I give him a little checkup?"

She brushed the hair off Connor's face. "Can the nice doctor take a look at you? You can stay on Mummy's lap the whole time."

"You know what, I have a little boy, too," Mark said, gently pushing Connor's pant legs up so he could check out his knees. "He's a little older than you though. He's in grade two. His name is Gabe, and his favorite color is red. What's your favorite color?"

"Orange, right, buddy?" Stacey said, finding it nearly impossible to fake being happy, even though she had her little boy back.

Connor watched with intense interest as Mark gently gave him a thorough checkup. He asked him some questions, and thankfully, Connor shook his head to all the ones that would have made Stacey go ballistic.

Once Mark finished, Connor snuggled deeper against Stacey. He still hadn't said anything besides that first *Mama*, which made her worry if he was going to become mute from trauma.

Rex, Brock, Aaron, Colton and Rob were all huddled in the

kitchen murmuring while Sergeant Fox yammered away on his phone by the door to the hallway.

"I'm hungry, Mama," Connor said, lifting his head from her chest and gazing up at her with those gorgeous blue eyes.

Oh, thank God he spoke.

"What can I get you?" Tessa said, coming right over with a cooler bag full of food. "I have cheese sandwiches, PB&J, chicken and cheese, apple slices, orange slices, bananas, and these super yummy granola bars that look like they have chunks of chocolate in them."

Connor's eyes lit up at the mention of chocolate, and he nodded.

Smiling, Tessa handed him the already unwrapped granola bar, and he dove in like a savage, getting crumbs all over Stacey. Tessa set a juice box next to Stacey. "Try to get him to drink that. The kids are pretty dehydrated, so we need to make sure they get some electrolytes."

Stacey nodded and reached for the juice box, pushing the straw through the foil-covered hole behind Connor's back.

"Where's Chase?" Connor asked, chewing and spewing more crumbs.

Stacey swallowed and handed her son the juice box. "He was there with all the other superheroes. He just had to stay behind for a little bit. But they'll go get him soon."

"I didn't like those men," he said, wrapping his lips around the straw she offered him. "Or that lady. They were all mean. Kept making me sleep when I didn't wanna."

Oh God, Stacey was going to lose it soon.

She could feel herself beginning to hyperventilate.

A big, warm hand landed on her shoulder, and she glanced behind her to find Rex. He looked as fractured as she felt. His face was longer, his midnight-blue eyes haunted. "Easy, Mama," he said softly. "You're doing great."

She rested her hand on his as a tear sprinted down her cheek, and she hiccupped a sob she couldn't fight.

Isaac stowed his phone in his pocket and approached them. "Need to know what happened," he said, having seemed to calm down a bit. "So one man is left behind?"

Stacey gasped. Even though it wasn't new news, she still hated hearing that Chase had been left behind.

What happened to "No man left behind"? Wasn't that the motto with these military buffs?

Rex nodded and made a noise in this throat. "My brother, Chase. He was running point. We got all the kids out of the Sprinter van, took out just over half of Creed's goons, though Creed got away."

Isaac blew out a breath and shoved the fingers of one hand into his hair. "Okay, I've got a social worker coming, as well as two other police officers—female. We need to find out who these children are and get them back to their families."

"My wife's family owns an airline, and we've already offered to fly the parents and children wherever they need to go. We can fly the parents here to pick up their children," Rob said. "No cost, no problem. Got helicopters at our disposal, too." His attention was pulled away when his phone buzzed in his pocket. He put it to his ear and said, "Barney, where are you?" before walking away.

"Well-organized operation you have here," Isaac said almost sarcastically.

"I know you're pissed, but you're not wrong," Richelle said, looking proud.

Isaac only gave her a brow lift before settling his expression into a neutral one again. "Not happy with you guys going rogue."

"Nobody—besides Chase—got hurt who didn't deserve to get hurt," Aaron said. "And we're going to get Chase back."

"You're mostly pissed because you can't join us 'cause of your badge." Colton elbowed Isaac playfully, though even his smile seemed forced. Obviously, everyone knew each other, based on the level of familiarity among them all.

Another big extended family, kind of like the Harts.

The atmosphere in the suite was thick and tense. Nobody spoke much, and jokes were at a minimum and fell flat. They were all struggling with Chase being in the hands of the enemy.

Isaac's rancor having pretty much disappeared, his shoulders slumped slightly, and he pushed both hands into his pockets. "Really sorry what happened to one of your men."

"I'd know if he was dead," Rex said, his face tight. "I'd feel it. He's not. They have him."

"We just need to figure out where," Aaron said.

"What about getting your tech guy back on the dark web and reconnecting with Impervious?" Isaac suggested. "Offer a trade. Cash for Chase, and then we set up another sting at the exchange. Get SWAT and Seattle PD involved."

"Only one problem with that," Brock said, his gravelly bass causing a hush to fall about the room.

Isaac regarded the bigger-than-life Hart family patriarch with a skeptical brow lift. "And what's that?"

"Chase *is* our tech guy."

CHAPTER TWENTY

CHASE HUGGED his knees to his chest and scooted his back harder against the concrete wall of the cell.

Sure, he was cornering himself, but at least this way nobody could sneak up on him.

He was outnumbered.

At least fifteen sets of brown eyes, all curious, all wary, all *interested,* watched him with intensity. Waiting for him to let his guard down, to close his eyes and give in to sleep so they could pounce.

He'd taken out one guy already. Bashed his head into the wall when he came at Chase with a shiv.

But that didn't seem to send enough of a warning to the rest of them. It'd only incited them.

The floor was filthy.

He was filthy.

A mix of body odor, shit, piss and puke mingled on the thick, unmoving air. His gut burned with the need for food. He had a headache from lack of water, and his tongue felt like a dry sponge. He couldn't remember the last time he'd pissed.

Weren't they at least going to move him to gen pop? Why were they keeping him in the holding cell with all the petty degenerates?

He was arrested on drug charges. Surely that meant hard time?

His eyelids were heavy. He hadn't slept in days.

Even when the rest of them slept, he didn't.

He couldn't.

If he slept, they'd come for him.

He'd done what was right, taking the blame for Piper.

She was innocent in all of this, just like he was.

But she was a woman, a Canadian, and the chances of her surviving a Peruvian prison were a hell of a lot slimmer than his. So he'd done what he knew he had to do. He took her place. Sent her off with Derrick and Heath while the authorities hauled him away, charged him with drug trafficking, obstruction of justice, and then his Spanish got a little rusty after that.

Either way, they'd had him going away for a long time if they got their say about things.

His eyelids dropped, but he quickly threw them open. Over half the men in the cell were watching him. Waiting for him to slip up and nod off.

He was just so fucking tired.

His mind was starting to play tricks on him, too. He kept thinking he heard Heath out the window yelling his name. But that wouldn't make any sense.

Heath wouldn't be stupid enough to get this close to the prison.

Heath needed to get Piper and Derrick to safety and then get home.

Chase was a lost cause.

He would die here. He just knew it.

Maybe he should just let sleep come and they could kill him while he slept. Perhaps he wouldn't feel anything.

Or he could go up and punch the second biggest guy in there—

since he was the first—punch him out and let the rest of them dogpile on top of him. Shiv him and end it quick.

That was always an option, too.

His eyelids dropped again and stayed down.

Sleep was so enticing.

Maybe he could shut out the world for just five minutes. A little "power nap," as his mother liked to call her three o'clock coffee and siesta.

"I'm just having a power nap, boys. Leave me be for fifteen minutes, then I'll be right as rain and can help you with your homework."

Fuck, he missed his mum.

He missed his brothers, too.

His body began to relax as he dreamt of their last family dinner, right before he and Heath headed down to Peru for their latest job. They were to keep tabs on a new drug-trafficking ring. A street drug laced with a fatal amount of Fentanyl was killing a lot of backpackers and tourists. He and Heath were being sent down there to find the source and shut it down.

Their mother had pulled out all the stops for the dinner. A big barbecue in the backyard with her famous dry-rubbed ribeye steak, baked potato, salad and probably half a dozen other sides.

Joy Hart knew her boys liked to eat, so she always made sure there was enough food on the table to feed a football team, as well as send every member home with a container of leftovers.

He'd been so hellbent on keeping his eyes open and staying awake that he forgot how good it felt to close them and think of his family. To think of happier times.

Bony fingers gripped his ankles, causing his eyes to flash open just as he was tugged forward and his head made a hard smack on the concrete.

Five men stood over him. All of their faces dark and angry.

He was too out of it to understand their Spanish. Heath was the better linguist. Chase was the tech guy.

The one who held his ankles made to flip him over onto his belly. He kicked and thrashed, swiped at ankles and tossed his head back and forth, hoping to catch a limb or finger between his teeth.

But he was outnumbered.

Five on one.

And he was a weak one at that. He hadn't eaten or had anything to drink in days.

They got him onto his belly and hauled him up to his feet, each of them taking a limb. A bench was cleared and they tossed him over it, his ribs colliding with the unforgiving wood and knocking the wind out of him.

They went for his pants.

No.

He managed to get one arm free and took a swipe at the man closest to him. He made contact with the guy's knee and sent him to the ground with a painful cry.

A quick smack across the face had Chase seeing stars, and a ringing formed in his ears. He tasted blood.

They tried again for his pants and managed to get them down halfway on his ass cheeks. He fought them with everything he had.

He didn't want to die.

He didn't want to go out like this.

Sure, when the delirium set in, he thought he would be better off dead, but now that death stared him in the face, he knew he wasn't ready for it.

He had more things he wanted to do.

He wanted a wife.

He wanted children.

He wanted a family.

He wanted to live.

———

He'd been in and out of consciousness for a while now.

Dreams, all of them bad and from another time in his life, spun through his mind like an old movie reel on hyperdrive.

Peru.

Prison.

He'd rallied the last ounce of strength he had, fought for his life in that hellhole as four men pinned him down and another one prepared to "claim" him.

He broke free, killed two of the men by snapping their necks, and put another two in the hospital. One would never walk again. The other would be blind for life.

They'd thrown him into solitary confinement after that.

A six-by-six cell with no window. No light. No bed.

Just a toilet, a sink and one meal a day.

For four fucking months.

With nothing but the voices in his head and the monsters in the dark to keep him company.

With a groan, Chase tried to roll over, but he couldn't.

Where was he?

Not back in the Peruvian prison.

No.

His brothers had busted him out of there.

But he wasn't at home, either.

He tried to move again, but pain shot through him from various parts of his body. His shoulders. His ankles. His wrists. His head.

He was also fucking freezing.

And naked.

Another attempt to move had him seeing stars, but he pushed past the pain and opened his eyes. A small shuffle and he saw that his ankles were bound together with zip ties.

They were too tight, and the skin around them was raw and bloody.

The same was probably true for his fingers, but he couldn't see them since his hands were bound behind him. But he was losing feeling in his fingers, and if he moved his hands even an inch, raw flesh was scraped and agony swamped him.

But that was nothing compared with the agony in his shoulder. They'd dislocated it for sure, binding his arms so aggressively behind his back.

The pain was almost enough to make him puke.

When he came to after taking a coldcock to the head, he couldn't see a damn thing. It was pitch black, he was naked, and everything in his body was turning to ice.

He knew he was bleeding. He could smell it. The scent of blood—along with a lot of other disgusting smells—hung metallic and fresh in the dank air.

"Hey!" Chase called out into the darkness, his throat raw and voice scratchy. He was lying on his side on the cold concrete ground. The room was pitch-black, but he knew it was a room.

He could feel the walls around him.

Feel them moving closer.

His muscles were beginning to freeze solid, and he shivered like dry ice had been poured down his throat.

Where was he?

What happened?

Then, like a flash, it all came back to him.

Creed.

Impervious.

They'd found the kids, found Connor, and their backup had arrived. But he went after Creed and was hit in the head from behind.

Fuck.

Then he woke up here—wherever he was—naked, cold and bound.

Did they get the children to safety?

Did they have them bound and naked somewhere, too? What about his brothers and the other guys?

He'd had a bad feeling about the whole thing from the moment they got to the garage behind the speakeasy, and he was right. The whole fucking operation was probably botched. He should have let Brock run point on it. Chase was obviously not cut out for the leadership role. He was a grunt. The tech guy, that was it.

Ignoring the pain in his left shoulder, he slowly wriggled along the floor like a fish out of water enough to find a wall. He pushed and squirmed so much, tears sprang from his eyes from the pain, but he did it anyway and eventually managed to prop himself up to sitting.

Not that it did much good.

His ass was still on the cold concrete, not to mention his balls. His dick had probably all but retreated back inside him, thinking this was the end.

If it wasn't for the freezing cold and the seizing up of his muscles, he might be able to get out of the zip ties around his wrists. He'd done it before. But last time, he was being held by a bunch of Somali pirates, so he was sweating his ass off in the heat and used his sweat like grease to help him slide out of the restraints.

He wasn't sweating now.

Nope.

His body was hanging on to every last bit of precious moisture it could to try to keep his organs from shutting down. If he sweat, he'd only catch hypothermia faster. He needed to remain calm and not freak out.

Easier said than fucking done.

He was in the dark.

He hated the dark.

He was in a small space.

He hated small spaces.

Neither of those things, the dark or the small space, was helping with his rapidly beating heart or the direction his mind was headed.

Monsters lurked in the dark, and they were particularly fond of small, shadowy spaces—which was exactly where Chase feared he was.

Much like the dark and closing-in walls, the cold was beginning to fuck with him, too. Playing games with his thoughts.

Using his back and feet, he pushed back against the wall and awkwardly, painfully climbed his way to standing. He needed to figure out where he was. Find a door, a window, a shard of light.

"Hey!" he called out again, moving along the wall with his back to it, feeling with the last shred of working nerves in his fingertips for something, anything to give him an indication of where he might be. "You're a fucking coward, Creed," he called, hoping to goad the sadistic bastard into showing his face. "Dealing in children. And now you won't even show me your fucking face. Won't even face me like a man."

The cold air burned his lungs as he hollered and moved around the room, his feet feeling like they were on fire from how goddamn cold they were.

Noise somewhere across the room had him trying to run, but his ankles were bound, so he almost lost his footing and face-planted into the floor. He managed to catch himself and just fell face-first into the other wall, groaning in pain as his cheek smashed into the bricks. There was no time to give in to the pain, though. He would freeze to death if he didn't move, if he didn't figure a way out of there.

Moving his cheek along the freezing concrete at a slow and awkward shuffle, he found what appeared to be a metal door. That's where the sounds were coming from.

Pressing his ear against it, he heard voices. They were too quiet and muffled to understand, but he could pick out about three different people speaking. His eyes were beginning to adjust to the room, but that didn't mean it still wasn't dark as hell. However, a small, barely discernible sliver of light filtered through next to the door where the jamb was starting to warp. He got down on the ground next to the light and used it to study his feet and ankles. Both were covered in blood from where the zip ties dug into his flesh. He couldn't see his hands, but they were as raw as his ankles, so chances are, he was bleeding there, too.

"Creed!" he practically screamed, kicking the door. "Face me like a man, you sadistic sack of shit. If you're going to kill me, I suggest you just fucking do it!"

The door opened a moment later, the light from the outside making him squint and hide his face so his pupils could dilate in a more natural way.

"Chase Hart, one of the four Harty Boys. Vigilantes for justice. Security and surveillance." Creed's nasally voice was just a touch deeper now but still not something Chase would associate with an adult man in his late thirties. "However did you get tangled up in this?"

"You took ... a child I love," Chase said, now back on his ass on the ground, staring up at the figure in the doorway. "You took children. You're pathetic. A loser."

Creed clucked his tongue. "And you just cost me a lot of money with your little sting operation."

Chase spat, though he was reluctant to give up any moisture from inside his body. But he was glad when he watched the wad of saliva land on Creed's black wingtip.

"I know a lot of people in a lot of places, Mr. Hart. A lot of people with a lot of *preferences*. And although I don't generally deal in adults of your"—he wiggled his finger and pointed at Chase —"size, I do have clients who prefer your type."

"If the children are safe, that's all that matters."

"We'll see if you're still thinking that after being whipped, flogged and sodomized with a broom handle for days and weeks on end." He chuckled and stepped forward, bringing his face into the light.

Not that Chase was into any of those vampire movies, but Jesus Christ, did Creed ever look like a fucking vampire. Pasty as fuck, long black hair hanging stringy around his face, dark circles beneath dark eyes and lips so red you'd think he'd just been drinking blood.

Who the fuck knows—maybe he was? The guy seemed to have no limits or scruples. The guy didn't have a fucking soul.

Creed approached Chase and glared down at him. "You picked the wrong person to mess with, Mr. Hart. I'm going to make sure your life—what little is left of it—is more excruciating and miserable than you can ever imagine."

Chase swung his legs and knocked Creed in the ankles, sending the vampire to the ground in a grunt and a heap.

Creed growled, surged to his feet, and glaring like he was preparing for murder, he wiped the back of his hand over a cut on his lips.

There wasn't much Chase could do when Creed started kicking him in the stomach, nothing besides curl up in a ball and protect his cock and balls.

Creed screamed like a wild, murderous beast, the toe of his wingtip making contact over and over again with Chase's ribs, his gut, his head, his chest. He changed positions and started kicking him in the back, nailing his kidneys with the pointed toe of his shoes. And because Chase's arms were around his back, Creed eventually did get a couple of good blows between his legs, which only caused Chase to vomit, groan and feel like he was going to pass out again—which eventually, thank God, he did.

When he finally came to, he was still on the ground in the cold, dark room. His hands remained bound, his ankles, too. His entire body ached from the top of his head to the bottom of his feet. He was bleeding more, too. Probably internally, as well. He did a quick survey of his body parts and figured he had at least two, possibly three cracked ribs.

The only upside to any of it was that he was bleeding more and could use the blood around his wrists as a lubricant to help peel off the zip ties.

The pain of the rough plastic digging into his fresh wounds was enough to make him see stars, and he vomited again—though that could have been from his obvious concussion or internal bleeding. It was really anybody's guess at this point.

The cold had his fingers seizing up as the bonds cut off his circulation the more he got them over his hands. He thought about giving up a few times, when he couldn't feel his fingers and his dislocated shoulder started to throb and the shakes and shivers got to be too much. But it was either wait in here for Creed or one of his lackeys to come back and cart him off to become some monster's torture slave, or he did what he could to survive until he did everything.

It was just like back in the Peruvian prison. He would do everything he could to stay alive. That way if he did die, he'd leave the Earth knowing he fought the whole way out, that he hadn't given up. He was a fighter, and now, more than ever, he had something—someone—to fight to get back to.

He'd lost all feeling in his fingers, and they kept slipping as he worked the zip tie over his left hand with his right. Folding his thumb and pinky inward to the center of his palm, he inched the tie over. He was making headway; it all just hurt like a motherfucker and was taking forever. How much longer before he lost all feeling in his entire right hand and couldn't do anything?

Folding his ring and index finger beneath the middle finger, he tried to make his hand as narrow as possible to slip the tie over. It budged, but just barely.

With his numb right-hand fingers, he gathered some blood from his left wrist and smothered it on the tie as best he could. It was all awkward as fuck, and his shoulders cried out in agony, but he had to ignore all of that and focus on getting the zip ties off. Then he could worry about a dislocated shoulder or losing a finger.

He was born with ten. If he lost one, it wouldn't be the end of the world.

He'd popped dislocations back into place on his own before. He could do it again.

But, like everything in life: one thing at a time.

The blood seemed to help, and the zip tie finally, at long last, slipped off his left hand.

"Thank fuck," he breathed, pulling it off his right hand as well.

He wiggled his fingers and twirled his wrists around to get the circulation flowing again.

Then he went to work on his ankles and removing the zip tie.

It wasn't easy, but he knew how to get out of them. Using friction from the tie that was around his wrists and after about fifteen minutes of intense struggling and rubbing the ties against each other, he was sweaty and shivering, but the zip tie snapped.

Now that he had his limbs free, he could do a better job of figuring a way out of that hellhole. He couldn't see much, and the darkness only made the space feel smaller. His fears, along with the intense cold and mounting pain, were seriously starting to fuck with his head.

A skitter of what could only be rodent feet had him whipping around, his fists up and ready in fighting position.

What are you going to do? Punch a rat?

Now his mind was really starting to go.

Something tickled his big toe, and he kicked hard, hearing a squeak and a *thwack* against the wall, followed by a *splat* to the ground.

He'd dealt with rats, mice, cockroaches and lice in Peru, but it wasn't like he was immune to that shit now. They still fucking disturbed the hell out him. He'd been eaten alive for days on end by the baby cockroaches who liked to bite him while he slept. Mosquitoes were bad, too, since the prison they had him in was close to a dried-up creek bed, and when they finally moved him to gen pop, his cell window had no glass pane to protect them from the outside elements and pests. He was lucky he didn't catch malaria or dengue fever.

Running his hands along the wall, he searched for something— anything—to help him figure out where he was. A crevice in the bricks, a small door. Or something he could use as a weapon. He really didn't want to resort to throwing a dead rat at whoever opened that door next, but he would if he had to.

His feet, although better now that they were no longer bound, still ached from the intense cold of the floor. If he didn't know any better, he'd say he was in some kind of cold storage. Perhaps a cellar of some sort for the speakeasy or lounge.

But then the scent of fish had him thinking maybe he was somewhere in a shipyard or a cannery.

He hoped to God the children hadn't been kept in here. Not for a minute.

He was a grown-ass man. He could take this.

But a kid?

This would fuck up a kid for life.

Noises at the door had him pausing.

He pressed his ear to the crack where the sliver of light was and turned on his military hearing, focusing on the nuances, the lifts and drops of tone, the upward inflections that indicated a question. The different pauses, timbres and lilts. From the sounds of it, at least one of the three people on the other side of the door had a bit of a Southern accent. They spoke softer, slower and emphasized different syllables than the other two people.

It was a thick door, and they were deliberately keeping their voices low, so he couldn't hear much, but he heard enough to know that they were getting ready to move him. There were only three of them out there. Creed and two others.

He might be able to take them.

He could take Creed no problem. Now that the fight was fair and he wasn't bound like a hog on the way to slaughter.

But he was weak and injured. So even with Creed being a weakling, the other two men probably had combat training and weight to them. They might prove to be too much.

"Open it," he heard Creed order, his nasally tone easy to pick out between the other two.

Chase backed up, found the dead rat lying on the ground and picked it up.

When the door opened, using his nondominant arm because the other shoulder was dislocated, he did his best to aim true and tossed the rat at the shadowy figure on the threshold.

Square in the face.

Fuck, yes.

Creed cried out in anger and disgust.

"Fuck," the vampire man shrieked.

But Chase didn't have a chance to charge the distracted Creed before he was hit in the chest with something that resembled two bee stingers and was brought to the ground in a heap of agony and convulsions as they used the Taser pulse on him.

Creed came to stand over his trembling body. "You don't think we have cameras in here, Mr. Hart?"

No, he didn't think about that. But now he wished he had.

CHAPTER TWENTY-ONE

TIME CEASED to exist now that he was in total darkness. They'd moved him like he figured they would, stuck something in his neck, too—probably the same shit they gave Stacey. He was bound again, this time tighter, and they had a dirty old rag or something wrapped around his head and lodged in his mouth to act like a gag.

He ran his tongue over the fabric and fought the urge to vomit from how horrible it tasted: moldy, metallic and vaguely of fish.

He was on his side, his arms back behind him, tied much tighter than before, to the point where he couldn't feel his fingers any longer. His ankles were strapped together, too, the plastic cord digging into the raw, bleeding flesh.

He was still naked. Still freezing.

Groaning, he tried to roll over in an attempt to ease the agony in his shoulders and ribs, but he couldn't. His hands hit wood, his feet hit wood, and when he lurched up his torso, his head bonked wood.

What the fuck?

Panic engulfed him and not just from the intense cold. He began to shake.

He was in a box.

A coffin.

They had him in a box, in the dark, and by the sounds of things —seagulls and traffic noises—outside.

"Help!" he tried to scream over the gag, but his words came out garbled and his throat hurt from the cold. His heart raced and thoughts began to twist.

He tossed and flailed his body as best he could, to little avail. He was in the fetal position, and stretching out was impossible. The box was shorter than he was. His eyes darted frantically around the small, dark space. Even though the gag smelled horrible, the wood around him did not.

The wood beneath him was rough and unfinished pine, and he was pretty sure he felt a sliver embed itself in his ass cheek as he moved and tried to bang his hands against the side of the box. He kicked, thrashed and smashed his head into the side, but after all that effort, he barely made a noise decent enough to rise above all the other sounds outside.

What time was it?

Where was he?

If he concentrated hard and blocked out everything else, including the pounding pulse in his ears and his ragged breaths, he could hear the faint sound of water lapping and boat motors.

Had they knocked him out for so long, he was already on some freighter bound for foreign sadists?

A loud, fierce gust of wind carried his cries away as he shivered from the mounting cold.

This was how he died. Either from hypothermia or some heartless bastard torturing him. But either way, this—soon—was how he died.

He kind of hoped it was from hypothermia and when he arrived wherever they were sending him, his would-be new master opened up the box to find Chase dead. That couldn't bode well for Creed, right?

Eyes closed, eyes open, it didn't really matter.

He saw nothing.

Whatever box they had him in, although rough and still holding that fresh-cut wood scent, it was sealed up tight. Not tight enough to block out the cold, but tight enough to prevent light from filtering in.

Then again, maybe it was still dark outside. Maybe Creed hadn't held him for as long as he thought and it was only four in the morning?

Or maybe it was the next night or the following week and Creed had held him for a hell of a lot longer? He had no idea how long he'd been unconscious.

His stomach grumbled, and his mouth was desperate for water. It would also appear that he had pissed himself at some point because the scent of urine in the box was strong and competed with the scent of cut pine.

His body shook like he was still being hit with the Taser, and he felt himself beginning to drift off into a quiet sleep.

Sleep sounded like a good idea.

He could dream of warmer places, like back in bed with Stacey, wrapped up in her arms, with her softness and the little noises she made when he brought her to climax. Her nails on his back, lips on his neck.

She was perfect, and he wanted to be with her.

He wanted to share his life with her and her children.

But it seemed that whenever something good started to happen —like the first time they had sex—his body had this weird security system that started to go off at all the wrong times. His wiring was seriously faulty—he had prison to thank for that. But Stacey, she was light and lovely, all things good, and he was dark and broken, messy.

He'd killed.

Sure, nobody he'd killed hadn't deserved it plus a thousand more deaths, but he was a damaged man nonetheless.

Was he even a man? He couldn't have children. Would never have children of his own. Stacey deserved more than what he could give her.

How could he chase away the monsters in the dark for Connor and Thea when he himself was afraid of them? He couldn't tell them monsters didn't exist because he knew damn well that they did. They might not be *real* in the physical sense, but the mind is a powerful tool. He understood what it meant to see and feel things so fully that denying their existence felt more like a lie than claiming that they were real.

His breathing and heart rate were escalating, and he was beginning to hyperventilate through his nose, the noise of his breaths now competing with the thundering pulse in his ears.

And the voice started talking.

He hadn't heard it in a while.

But it was a voice he would recognize anywhere.

Stacey doesn't deserve you.

The kids—Connor and Thea—don't deserve you.

You're not husband or father material.

You're sterile for a reason.

You're not a good man.

You're not a man at all.

Your family is better off without you.

You should have died in that prison.

Rex belongs with Stacey.

Rex will give her what she needs.

She doesn't love you.

Nobody loves you.

The voice in his head grew louder, the tone getting more and more nasty. His demon—if that's what you wanted to call it—had the voice of Gollum from *Lord of the Rings*, sinister and almost snakelike.

Your death would make everyone's life easier.

Welcome death.

Embrace death.

Your end is everyone else's new beginning.

You're too broken to be a good father and husband.

You're not fit to be a father.

You're not fit to be loved.

Nobody is looking for you.

Nobody wants you.

Everything that happens to you is deserved.

You're not a good person.

You're a killer.

He was streaming in and out of consciousness now. The voice in his head brought him back just enough to fuck with him before he dropped into another pit of darkness and quiet.

Stacey belongs with Rex.

Rex can give her a family and more children.

Rex isn't afraid of the dark.

Stacey deserves Rex.

You deserve nothing.

Off in the distance, noises, like men fighting and yelling, gunshots and hand-to-hand combat, filtered around him like a fuzzy din. But he wasn't sure if all that was his imagination toying with him or real sounds outside.

A big explosion nearby shook his box, and he whimpered in fear.

He tried to grunt, to moan and kick, but his limbs weren't cooperating in the cold and lack of circulation.

Quiet, the demon hissed.

A long, low groan broke past the gag as he shifted and pain shot through his broken ribs and shoulder. A pain so powerful it felt like fireworks going off inside his head and all over his body. He felt another blackout coming on and welcomed it.

At least in sleep, he wouldn't feel the cold.

At least in sleep, he wouldn't feel the pain.

He was on his way out, moving toward the calm, when the noises around him grew louder and his box began to move.

"Gotta get him out," one male voice said with panic.

"He can't be in small spaces," a voice he recognized as Heath's said.

"Need a fucking crowbar," Brock said, his voice just as recognizable.

"Here."

The box started to move again, and he could hear the whinge and groan of the lid being pried open. They'd probably nailed it closed or something, so there was absolutely no way for him to escape.

"Chase, we're getting you out, bro. Just gotta give us a minute, okay?" Heath said, his voice sounding louder and closer to Chase's feet.

"Is that the only fucking airhole?" a voice he didn't recognize asked.

"Motherfuckers," said another guy that sounded like Colton.

More squeaking and groaning and then suddenly a rush of cool air and dim light from an orange street lamp down the way.

A bright flashlight was shone into his eyes and he squinted and groaned from the pain of something so bright hitting him in the retinas.

"Get that out of his face," Heath ordered.

The light disappeared.

The breeze sweeping across his skin had him shivering uncontrollably. His body started to shake. He was going into shock.

"Jesus Christ," Brock breathed out.

"Holy fuck," Heath said.

"He's going into shock," Colton said.

Rex came into view. Terror and worry filled his eyes. He rested a hand on Chase's shoulder. "You're okay. We've got you."

————

"THEY HAVE to know how impossible this is," Stacey said to Dr. Pasha as they waited in one of the Escalades a block or so away from the shipping yard where the men had all gone to get Chase.

How they figured out that's where he was, was beyond her. Isaac had made some calls and, instead of suiting up in his cop uniform, had joined the team with Rex, Heath, Brock, Aaron, Colton and Rob. Rob's friend Barnes Wark was also in the area and joined the team on their rescue mission. There were eight of them going in, risking their lives to save one man.

The least she could do was sit tight and wait for them.

Pasha gave her a sympathetic smile. "They know. But it is what it is. He's going to need you, so now's the time to prepare yourself."

It'd grown dark again, with night settling in. They'd spent all day tending to the children, calling their parents and working with the authorities and social workers. All of the children were being reconnected with their families. Some of the kids were from as far east as Wyoming, but the majority of them were from the area.

Connor was the only Canadian though.

Her son seemed to be doing okay, and he'd grown attached to Dr. Mark, so when Mark offered to stay with Connor while Stacey went to be with Chase, and Connor was okay with it, she kissed her child a thousand times, said she'd be back and then left with the rescue crew.

Mark was texting her every ten minutes with updates, which she appreciated immensely.

"You think he's going to be okay?" she asked Pasha, staring out the window of the back passenger seat.

"I think he's going to need all of us," she said gently.

Just then a person sprinted past the vehicle, glancing behind themselves. It was a woman. Panic filled her dark eyes, and her light blonde hair and black coat trailed behind her like a cape.

Stacey would recognize that woman anywhere.

Her face was burned into Stacey's brain for eternity.

Before she could think twice—or rationally—about what she was doing, she flung the door open, bailed out and started to run.

"Hey!" she called, gaining ground on the woman from the dollar store. All her running with Emma had paid off, and she had her pre-children stamina back. Too bad she didn't have her pre-children body back, too.

The woman glanced behind her, and her eyes went wide when she recognized Stacey. She picked up the pace and her running became more erratic, more desperate.

Stacey picked up the pace, too.

The woman turned the corner. Stacey was right on her heels now. She could hear the woman's ragged breathing and the grunts and groans of her discomfort.

Stacey was just getting started. This bitch didn't know discomfort, not by a long shot.

Ignoring the cold air searing her lungs, she engaged her mama-bear strength, pushed harder to run faster, caught up with the woman and took her to the ground.

The blonde let out a shriek as Stacey spun her around, sat on top of her and started to essentially scratch out her eyes.

"You stole my baby!" Stacey wailed, batting away the woman's hands as she tried to protect her face. "You took my son, you bitch!"

The claws were out. She had the scent of blood.

Protect her cubs.

Protect her mate.

And this woman—this villainous monster from the deepest pits of hell, this waste of skin cretin—had messed with Stacey's cub and mate.

And she would pay.

Just like at The Rage Room, all of Stacey's fears and her anger, her resentment and frustration came out. She was screaming, growling and grunting with each punch as her hair flew everywhere and she made sure this woman would never forget the kind of pain she'd caused.

An excruciating throb emerged in her knuckles when her fist connected with the woman's face, but that was a mere blip on her radar. The adrenaline coursing through her, the need to avenge and take the eye for the eye, quickly masked the pain.

It barely registered with her when hands came up from behind, slid beneath her arms and she was being lifted off the woman. Her fists kept flying.

"Easy now." Heath's deep timbre beside her ear brought her out of her bloodlust fog. "I think she knows you're mad. Time to let her live and not raise your kids from prison."

She blinked a few times and looked up. Colton was next to the woman, assessing Stacey's damage. Heath had Stacey. Aaron was there, too, along with Isaac and the man she'd been introduced to briefly as Barnes Wark, a friend and fellow SEAL of Aaron, Rob and Colton.

"Where's Chase?" she asked, shaking Heath off her and whipping around to face him. "Did you guys get him?"

Heath nodded, but worry clouded his midnight-blue eyes. Deep lines fit for an elephant seemed to have emerged overnight between his brows. "We did, yeah, but—"

She didn't bother to listen and took off back toward the Escalade. She realized she hadn't really run that far in order to catch up with the woman from the dollar store, and she was back at the SUV in no time.

The back hatch was open, and Pasha was there, her own worry lines deeper than her thirty-two years would suggest.

"Chase!" Stacey cried, elbowing her way past Rex, Brock and Rob to get a look at him. Her gasp morphed into a harsh, gut-wracking sob when she saw him, and instinct had her turning away.

Bloody, bruised, naked, shivering.

His ankles and wrists were both covered in blood and had fresh wounds. His face and chest were riddled with bruises and cuts, too.

Heath emerged beside her, and he took her in his arms, her face hitting his hard chest as she started to cry.

"I've popped his shoulder back into place," Pasha said, "but we need to get him to the hospital. He has hypothermia and is very close to going into shock. Plus, I want to check for internal bleeding and look at those ribs. I can tell right now at least three are probably broken." Stacey glanced away from Heath's chest. They had heaped blankets on Chase, along with one of those foil-looking warmth-retaining blankets, but even so, Chase continued to shiver.

Pasha pulled the blankets up over Chase more and tucked them around his filthy bare feet.

"I'm coming with you to the hospital," Stacey said, glancing up at Rex and Brock, who both looked like they couldn't decide whether to cry, kill or puke. She felt very similar.

"No!" Chase called out, though it fled his lips as more of a groan. "Go away. Get her out of here."

"He's delirious," Pasha said quietly. "Been in and out of consciousness since they got him out of the box."

The box? What box?

"Stacey should be with Rex. He's the better man. He can give her what I can't," Chase mumbled.

Stacey rushed to his side and ran her fingers over the only spot on him that wasn't filthy, bruised or crusted in blood—his temple. She bent her head. "I'm not going anywhere, Hart. You're stuck with me."

His arm came out from beneath the blanket, and he shoved her away. "I don't love you. Can't give you the family you deserve. The life you deserve. Choose Rex! Fucking go! Get out of here! GO!"

Just when she thought her heart was in repair mode, he went and hit it with a tire iron, causing it to shatter like one of those vases at The Rage Room. She took a step back. Her shoulders slumped, and a chill wracked her. The adrenaline was leaving her system.

"He needs fluids and medical treatment," Pasha said. "We'll get him to the hospital and call you from there. I'm sure this is all just the delirium and shock. He doesn't mean it." With a nod at Brock, she went about closing up her medical bag and making sure Chase was comfortable.

Rex pulled her aside with a gentle hand to her elbow. "He's in a bad state right now." But even Rex looked worried, so his words of comfort fell short.

She tightened her coat around her body as a chilly wind whipped her hair into a frenzy and cruised across the back of her neck. "They had him in a box?"

Rex's mouth grew tight, and he nodded. "Yeah."

Hot tears sprang from her eyes and slid down her cheeks.

"Give him some time. Let us take him to the hospital, and then I'll call you with an update. You go back to the hotel with Aaron, Rob and Barnes. Isaac has called the police and is going to handle that side of things. You need to go be with your son."

She knew he was right. She also knew she didn't want to abandon Chase.

He's not being abandoned. His brothers will be with him.

Rex touched her shoulder, the deep bags beneath his eyes looking almost purple from the bright orange glow of the street lamp. "I'll call you with an update as soon as I can."

Aaron appeared beside them. "Cops and paramedics have been called for the woman and those left breathing on the dock."

"Impervious?" Stacey asked, hoping to God that he met the kind of fate reserved for scum like him.

Rex's face was suddenly like a rocky mask. "He got away."

Again.

Her heart sank. "No."

"We'll get him," Heath said, his face just as stony as Rex's. "I will make it my life's mission."

Aaron glanced at her. "Ready to go back to the hotel?" Rob, Colton and Barnes had already climbed into the second Escalade.

Heath and Brock were in the driver and shotgun seats of the Escalade. Dr. Pasha double-checked Chase and smiled at Stacey before climbing into the passenger seat in the back.

Stacey, with tears now falling down her face at a volume she struggled to comprehend, gazed up at Rex. "I can't lose him. *We* can't lose him."

They both knew that Chase would survive physically. Even though she'd been a dermatology nurse for over eight years before having children, she'd gone through nursing school just like everyone else. She could tell he'd have some aches and pains and need time for his body to heal. But it *would* heal. He would get better.

At least physically.

She didn't have to say the rest for Rex to understand what she meant, though—that Chase's body might return to working order with only a few white scars as reminders, but it was his mind that they were at risk of losing.

And even though Chase Hart was the strongest, bravest man she knew, he wasn't invincible.

Everyone had their breaking point.

She just hoped to God this wasn't his.

CHAPTER TWENTY-TWO

"WHO WOULD DO SUCH A THING?" Stacey kept murmuring in the back seat of the Escalade as Aaron drove them back through the quiet, foggy streets of Seattle toward the hotel.

"Soulless, sadistic fuckers, that's who," Colton said from the front seat. "I'm glad we got a lot of Creed's stooges, but I'm fucking pissed we didn't get Creed himself."

"Like a motherfucking Bond villain, that guy," Barnes said. He was sharing the back seat with Stacey.

"He was just in shock, right? He'll snap out of it. The cold, the small space, the dark, it was all just messing with his head, but he'll get better. He just needs to get warm, feel safe." She twisted the elastic cord at the bottom of her raincoat around her index finger until it turned purple. That had been the color of a lot of Chase's bruises. Deep, dark purple. Even his eye was black and bloodshot.

The men in the vehicle were silent. She caught Aaron's concerned gaze in the rearview mirror, but he quickly averted it when he saw her looking at him.

"Focus on your kid right now," Colton said after a few minutes of traveling in silence. "We all came here for Connor, to get him back, and we did that. Focus on him. He's going to need his mother fully. You can't let your concern for Chase distract you from your little boy. He needs you."

Aaron's head bobbed, as did Barnes's.

"He's got his brothers there for him. You be who your son needs," Aaron said. "Chase will pull through."

Yeah, she knew he'd pull through physically, but mentally was a whole other question.

They pulled up to the hotel, and Stacey climbed out. Barnes got out with her, as he was apparently staying there while in town.

"We're just going to go park the Escalade in the back where Rob told us to, then we'll head home." Aaron glanced at Barnes, who stood next to Stacey. "Let me know if you need anything and how Chase is doing. Will follow up once I've had some sleep."

Barnes nodded. "Will do."

Colton waved at Stacey, Aaron nodded, and then they were gone.

Stacey turned to head into the hotel lobby, and Barnes pivoted to join her. They approached the elevator in silence, got into it in silence, and it wasn't until they were nearly halfway up to her floor that the man with the steely gray eyes and heavily salt-and-peppered hair decided to speak again. "He's going to need everyone. Including you. Including your kids. The more people he has around him that love him and accept him for what he's ... *lacking*, for lack of a better term, the easier it will be for him to accept himself again."

Stacey's brows scrunched as she watched the elevator buttons climb.

Barnes lifted up one pant leg enough to reveal a metal rod going into his left shoe. "Came back from a mission—one with Aaron and Colton—missing a body part."

"I'm sorry," she said, feeling the tears threatening to spill again.

Barnes shook his head. "Don't be sorry. I'm not. Would I like my leg? Sure. But legs don't make a man. I function just fine without it."

"But how was your mind when all of this happened?" The elevator doors opened, and she stepped out, Barnes right behind her. "I'm not worried about Chase's body so much as I am his mind. He was already fragile, and now ..."

"Oh, my head was super fucked up," Barnes said bluntly. "I developed a pill problem for a bit afterward. Pushed everyone I loved away—including the woman I loved."

"And did she stick by your side and help you get through the dark, never-ending tunnel?" They walked down the hallway, dropping their voices low so as to not wake sleeping guests. They were outside her door in no time.

He shook his head again. "No. She didn't. Which only made it all worse. It took my brothers in arms—Colton and Aaron and even Rob—to knock some sense into me. Even when I told them to fuck off, after I called the cops on them for trespassing, they would not leave me until I realized I wasn't just a write-off. I was somebody other people cared about. I was somebody other people wanted to live. He's going to push you away. You saw him in a very vulnerable state. He's going to have a hard time looking you in the eye. He's going to feel like he failed you and Connor."

"But he didn't. I have my son back. He didn't fail. He won. *We* won."

"That's not how he's going to see it. Creed got away, and Chase wasn't the man to bring Connor back to you. In his mind, he failed. And because he got caught and was tortured and held captive, he sees himself as an even bigger failure. It's going to take a lot of work and patience and a thick skin on your part to get through this. He might tell you he hates you, that he hates your kids and that he doesn't want you. But you need to know that none of that is true." Barnes rested a hand on her shoulder and squeezed at the same time a small smile creased his handsome face. He really was a nice man to look at.

"Connor is my first priority."

"And so he should be. But if you want Chase in your life, you're going to need to fight for him to be there." He nodded at the door handle and waited for her to flash her key card and open the door. "I'm just two doors down that way," he said, pointing to the left. "If you need anything, just knock." He squeezed her shoulder one more time before heading to his room.

Stacey thanked him and stepped into her hotel room, where sleepy-looking smiles from Tessa and Richelle greeted her.

"All the kids are asleep," Tessa said with a yawn and a stretch. "We've got Connor in your bed, the girls are in Heath's bed, and then Skyler got us more hotel rooms for the rest of the kids. Mark, Emmett, Riley and Will are the designated adults in those rooms, as the kids trusted them and put up a bit of a stink with the social workers until the doctors were allowed to stay with them. The guys were more than happy to just crash on the couches if it meant the kids felt safe. Parents are all set to arrive tomorrow."

"Thank you," Stacey said, finally feeling the harsh adrenaline crash and struggling to keep her eyes open. She just needed to cuddle up around her little boy and smell his head until she fell asleep.

"How's Chase?" Richelle stood up and yawned, her eyes tired, expression concerned.

"They're taking him to the hospital now," Stacey said, the memory of Chase's injuries coming back to her in a flood. Hot tears burned behind her eyes, and her throat felt tight. "They had him in a box smaller than an average coffin. No insulation. Harsh wood. And he was—" A rough sob got lodged in her throat. "He was bound and naked. God, he looked so bad." Her lips trembled, and the tears fell down her cheeks.

Tessa's hand flew up to her mouth, and she gasped. "Oh my God."

"He had bruises and broken ribs. His eye ... oh God, his beautiful eyes."

Richelle rushed forward and caught Stacey just before she collapsed to the floor. Richelle sat down and gently brought Stacey with her, letting Stacey crumple against her and cry.

She cried and she cried and she cried as the tiny woman rubbed her back and made soothing *shushing* noises.

"He's got a team of people rooting for him," Tessa said. "He's not alone. He's with his brothers, and he's going to get the best possible care at the hospital. Then I'll make some recommendations for counselors in Victoria, and hopefully we can get him the help he needs."

Stacey wasn't sure that was going to be enough.

She also knew it was too soon to tell, but based on Rex's expression, on the concern on each of the other Hart brothers' faces, she knew they were worried about him. They knew more of what they were dealing with. If Rex was scared, that had to mean something really bad, right?

Richelle's phone buzzed in her pocket, and she adjusted herself on the floor with Stacey enough to answer it. "It's Heath," she said, glancing up at Tessa.

She put the phone on speaker mode, and Stacey sat up, wiping the tears from her cheeks.

"Got you on speakerphone, Heath," Richelle said. "What's up?"

"They're rushing him into surgery," Heath said, his voice sounding hollow and tired. "Some pretty bad internal bleeding. Worried about one of his kidneys. Pasha got his ankles and wrists all cleaned and bandaged up on the drive to the hospital, but he's got three broken ribs, dislocated shoulder, and then there's all the internal bleeding. They're thinking his spleen may need to go and possibly a kidney."

"Dear God," Tessa whispered, her hand back over her mouth while tears spilled from her blue eyes.

"How you doing, Stace?" Heath asked.

"Worried," she croaked.

"Kids are all asleep after a big dinner of mac 'n' cheese and the new Pixar movie," Richelle said. "You guys need anything?"

"We'll be okay," Heath said, though they could tell he was yawning. "Slept in way worse places. A hospital waiting room is like a five-star hotel compared to some rat-infested hovels I've gotten shuteye in."

Tessa, Stacey and Richelle exchanged grim expressions.

"You'll keep us updated on him?" Richelle asked. "Like as soon as you get an update, you'll update us."

"You know it," Heath said. "But you ladies get some sleep. It's been a hard day for all of us."

"Send Chase our love," Tessa said.

Heath grunted. "Will do. And hey, Stace?"

Stacey wiped more tears away and blubbered a half-assed, "Yeah?"

"Don't take what Chase said to heart, okay? He loves you. He loves those kids. He's just in a bad place right now, but we'll get him back."

Her throat was still tight and she was chomping down hard on the inside of her cheek to keep herself from losing it completely.

"Stace?" Heath probed.

"Gotcha," she said with an exaggerated nod even though he couldn't see her. "Thanks, Heath."

"Talk soon." Then he ended the call.

Tessa frowned. "Chase said some pretty mean stuff?"

Stacey nodded. "He was hurting. I know he didn't mean it."

"Doesn't mean it still doesn't sting, though," Richelle said, standing up and then offering Stacey a hand to help her up, too.

"If he was how you said he was," Tessa started, "naked, bound and beaten, he's going to be angry that you saw him in such a vulnerable and compromised position. His ego—along with a lot of other parts of him—will be severely bruised."

Stacey's head hurt. Her heart, too. "That's what Barnes said."

Richelle's eyes went wide, and she nodded. "Men who are normally marshmallows can turn into monsters when their egos get bruised."

They all went over to the couches and sat down. The women had a teapot on the coffee table and mugs that were still half-full. Without even asking, Richelle topped both she and Tessa up and then poured the third mug for Stacey.

A stiff drink would have been better, but she'd settle for tea.

"And as a Harty Boy, he's used to being the protector," Tessa said, curling her legs under her and cradling her steaming mug with both hands before blowing on it. "And there's not a lot of protecting he can do in his current state, and that's bound to make him feel like he's left you and the kids vulnerable."

"Yeah, but he left us for months. He was our bodyguard during the whole Petralia fiasco, where my late husband's other wife and I were being threatened by a Greek crime family because our husband was an undercover cop who had infiltrated their organization and run off with a bunch of their money." Stacey blew on her own tea before taking a sip. The too-hot water was a welcome burn on her tongue as she took in the other women's bulging eyes of surprise.

"*Other* wife?" Richelle asked slowly.

Stacey nodded and pointed at herself. "Looking at a sister-wife.

Not by choice though. Ted was living a double ... or triple ... possibly quadruple life. But he's dead, so ... karma."

Richelle and Tessa nodded.

"Gonna need more on that story another day," Richelle said, taking a sip of her tea.

"For another day and one with alcohol," Stacey replied. "But as I was saying. Chase was our bodyguard. Then, when the Petralias were taken down and I thought things between us were starting to heat up, we had one night together and he vanished."

"Ouch," Tessa said, sucking in air between her teeth. "Just like *poof*, gone?"

Stacey exhaled. "Basically. He came back briefly, but he saw Rex hugging me—without a shirt on, I might add—then, like an assuming jerk egomaniac, he thought I'd chosen his brother over him, so he took a six-month job down in Georgia. He wasn't doing much *protecting* us from down there."

"Because he figured his brother was doing that," Tessa said, tucking a strand of her long, curly blonde hair behind her ear.

"Men can be so dumb," Richelle said with an exaggerated eye roll.

"Dumb as soup," Tessa confirmed.

Richelle's lips pursed and her head shook. "I like soup. Don't knock soup."

Stacey and Tessa both smiled and snorted.

"But you guys seemed better now, no?" Richelle asked. "I mean, I was picking up on some serious sexual tension. You explained that you're not with Rex. That you were never with Rex." She cupped her hand around her mouth. "*Were* you with Rex?"

Stacey shook her head. "He opened that door, but I closed it."

Richelle set her mug down on a side table. "And you and Chase?"

"We got back together last week. I stormed his apartment, told him I was mad at him for leaving. We hashed it all out, and then he spent every night at our house for dinner after that. He never slept over, but we've had sex." She closed her eyes briefly before lifting her head toward the ceiling. "God, I don't even know what day it is. It feels like so much longer than just a few days that we've been in this hotel, that Connor was gone and Chase was gone. It felt like my baby was gone for months."

"Trauma messes with your head and all concept of time," Tessa said gently. "Just because *you* weren't the one taken doesn't mean you can't suffer from PTSD, too. You were stuck in the neck with a needle, left unconscious in your car, and your son was abducted with the intention of selling him. That's like a parent's worst nightmare."

Richelle's head bobbed in agreement. "I've lived it. It is."

Exhaling, Stacey glanced out the window into the black sky. It was still foggy, and they were so high up that unless she walked close to the window, she could barely see any lights. Their reflections were nearly clear as a mirror in the enormous picture windows, and she could tell, even from where she sat, that she looked like shit. Turning back to the women, she nibbled her lip before speaking. "But things are still rocky. He's got secrets. A lot of them. From jobs gone bad—or maybe they went well, but they were still hard on him. I don't know. And he won't talk to me about it."

"Men suck at communication," Tessa said with an affirmative nod.

Stacey wholeheartedly agreed. "He said we had to sleep out here, and with the blinds open and light on. Said he couldn't stay in the bedroom."

Tessa's head nodded slowly. "Anything else?"

Stacey shook her head. "No, but ..." Her eyes narrowed. "The first time we had sex, we didn't have any condoms, so we pulled out instead. But then I made a comment about having to buy condoms for next time, and he got this really weird look on his face. It was only for a moment, but it was like this ... I dunno how to describe it. Almost like an intense sadness when I said I wasn't ready to have any more kids, so we needed to buy condoms. But then like a flash it was gone, and he just nodded and agreed with me."

Richelle tapped her finger to her lip. "Interesting."

"Well, I can tell you right now, I bet you he's claustrophobic," Tessa said. "Not able to stay in the bedroom, needs the windows open and the light on. That all makes sense. What's his apartment like?"

"It's a loft. It's not big, but it's spacious and all one room besides the bathroom. He also has floor-to-ceiling windows, which he keeps open all the time.

"And his bathroom?" Tessa probed.

Stacey pressed her lips together. "Why does that matter?"

Tessa shrugged. "Humor me."

"Average size, I guess. About the size of the one here."

"Shower curtain? Shower door? Opaque? Transparent?

"Transparent. Why?"

Tessa's lips formed a thin, grim line, and she regarded Stacey with a worrisome look. "I mean, I can't *actually* diagnose him since I haven't spoken to him, but I'd say he suffers from severe claustro-phobia. And if they had him in a box ..."

Stacey gasped and covered her face with her hand. "Oh God."

"Yeah, that's not good," Richelle said softly.

"But it *is* something he can work on," Tessa offered, though the lack of sparkle in her eyes and the remaining grim expression on her face said that even if Chase wanted to work on his claustro-phobia and whatever other demons haunted him, it was going to be a long, tough slog no matter what.

"Man's got a lot of demons," Richelle said. "But what he doesn't seem to realize is that we all do, but by not allowing them to rule you is how you conquer them."

"Amen," Tessa agreed.

Stacey glanced back out the window. "Yeah, he's got a lot of demons."

She only hoped that when the bruises faded and his ribs healed, he would trust her enough to help him face those demons and not cast her aside like she was just another monster out to hurt him.

CHAPTER TWENTY-THREE

STACEY COULDN'T BELIEVE that it was only Monday when she arrived home with Connor, late that evening. She'd swung by Joy's, of course, to pick up Thea—the baby hadn't even let Stacey into the house completely before she was pulling on her shirt to nurse.

"Hungry little monkey," Joy said, the worry lines around her eyes and mouth extra deep. Joy looked how Stacey felt—lost and helpless. "But she was so good. Slept and ate well. Krista pumped a bit and brought it over, which was helpful when Thea would get a little fussy before naptime."

Stacey smiled as she cradled her daughter in her lap and held Thea's hand, gazing into her baby's enormous blue eyes. "I'll have to thank her," she said quietly.

"It's what family does for each other," Joy said. "You're family, dear."

It was a struggle to keep the corners of her mouth up. All thoughts led back to Chase. "Any news?" she asked, lifting her head. Connor had snuggled right in next to Stacey, unwilling to let her out of his sight, let alone stop touching her, and he was quietly looking at a Paw Patrol board book.

Joy shook her head. "Not since the last time they called, which was this morning." Diesel was happily snoring at her feet. Every so often the dog would fart or start to whimper and kick his feet, dreaming of chasing rabbits or birds no doubt.

"I'm glad his surgery went well and they were able to salvage his kidney."

Thea popped off and went to sit up, though she wasn't finished. She just wanted to switch sides. Stacey helped her daughter pivot and waited for Thea to re-latch.

"Yeah, I'm glad, too." Joy glanced at Connor thoughtfully for a moment before turning her attention back to Stacey. "Have you two talked at all about ... *anything?* I know you were spending a lot of time together last week. Rekindled the fire. But has he opened up?"

Stacey shook her head. "No. And I wish he would. I wouldn't judge him. Not for anything. I know he's a good man. A wonderful man. And I want to be with him, faults and all." She swept a rogue tear off her cheekbone and swallowed. She'd done so much crying in the past several days, she was surprised she had any tears left.

Joy's expression was kind. "Give him time, dear. He'll come around."

"Did Brock tell you anything about what happened to him, though?" Just like Joy wouldn't divulge her son's secrets, Stacey wasn't sure how much the Hart brothers told their mother about their missions. Particularly the ones that landed them in dangerous and life-threatening situations.

"Just that he was hurt really badly in a mission gone sideways." Joy's chin quivered and her pout deepened. She cleared her throat, glanced at the fireplace and discreetly wiped a tear away. "Sometimes I think I want to know what really happens, what they go through, but then I think I'm better off staying in the dark. He told me a bit about what happened to him in Lima in that prison, and I tell you, I had a hard time sleeping for some time after that.

Knowing what one of my babies went through, the way he suffered." Her eyes filled with water, which caused her to reach for a tissue from the side table.

Stacey sat up straighter, much to the protestations of Thea. "In Lima? What happened to Chase in Lima? He was in prison?"

Joy's head shook tightly. "Never mind. Not my story."

"Joy ..." Stacey warned. "What happened to him?"

Joy's gaze bounced from Connor to Thea. "It's too late, and you're much too tired to be driving home with grandbabies in the back seat. Chase's old room is ready. Thea's been staying in the Pack 'n Play in there. You can stay in there." She stood up.

Stacey lifted her brow at the woman who had essentially adopted her as one of her own. "We'll put them to bed, and then you're going to tell me."

Joy let out a deep exhale through her nose, her gaze laser-focused on Stacey for a moment. Then she shook herself free, tossed on a big, fake smile and held her hand out for Connor. "Come on, angel. Let Nana Joy help you into bed."

Connor nodded. He was having a hard time keeping his eyes open. He allowed Joy to lead him down the hallway. Mercedes had sent over clothes of various sizes for the children, so Connor was wearing a dark blue and dark green pair of long-sleeved pajamas, and they had bright yellow diggers and dump trucks on them.

Thea's eyes were starting to droop, and she was now cupping Stacey's breast like it was a bottle. The baby popped off a moment later, and when Stacey lifted Thea's arm to do the satiated and asleep test, it fell like cold spaghetti. The baby was out.

She tucked her breast back into her shirt and stood up, carrying her daughter down the hallway to where she could hear Joy and Connor murmuring.

She would stay here tonight. It did make sense.

But it also made her feel better knowing that Joy was just down the hallway, so if Connor needed extra attention, Joy could look after Thea.

Connor was already asleep in the big queen-size bed, and Joy was just adjusting the blankets on him.

Stacey laid Thea down in the Pack 'n Play, and her daughter immediately flipped over to her belly on her knees and stuck her butt in the air.

Stacey would join Connor in the bed later, not only because she didn't want to mess up any of the other guest beds in Joy's house but also because the thought of being away from either of her kids right now, even if it was just across the hall, made her insides twist to the point of nausea.

She kissed both kids more times than she could count before following Joy back out to the living room.

"They're still my babies," Joy said, though it came out more like a croak as she took a seat in the chair she was in before.

Stacey sat back down on the couch. Diesel was now in his dog bed by the hearth. He popped one eye open slightly and watched her sit down, but once he knew where everyone was, he went back to snoring.

Joy cleared her throat. "Even though they're twice my size, grown men and have probably done some very *questionable* things, all for the greater good, they'll always be my babies." Her eyes focused toward the end of the hallway for a moment. "Just like these two will always be your babies. Even when they're all grown up and off to college or with families of their own. You will never forget what it felt like the moment they were placed in your arms for the first time or how your heart doubled in size the first time they said *Mama*."

Well, that was all true.

She could still remember the day Connor said *Mama* for the first time. She'd burst into tears of joy, picked him up, spun him around and kissed him until he was pushing her away so he could get back to his blocks.

It would probably be the same when Thea finally said *Mama* for the first time, too.

"I love him," Stacey finally said. "It might not make sense, given how we started, all our time apart—"

"Love doesn't always have to make sense," Joy said, glancing at a picture of Chase's late father on the mantle. "In fact, it rarely does, which is part of what makes it so magical."

What she felt when she was with Chase certainly seemed nothing short of magical. The man was a damaged soul, a tight-lipped wonder with an enormous grumpy side. And yet, when she thought of her future, of growing old with someone and raising her children, the only image she could conjure was one of her and Chase.

He made her feel safe and beautiful. And he loved her children, and they loved him. After Ted died, she didn't think she would ever be able to trust men again. But Chase proved to her that she could. Until he took off without a word, that is.

But they'd buried that hatchet and were moving past it.

He wasn't like Ted. He didn't have a second family and a second life.

He had a troubled past and secrets that bogged down his soul and tortured his dreams. But through it all, he was a good man. An honest man.

She wanted to be his soft place to land. For him to come home to her and the kids, rest his head on her chest and be vulnerable, allow her to get in and see the darker side of him. Help him find the light again and hold his hand and his heart as he fought his demons. She wanted to fight alongside him. As a good partner should.

"You two have a lot to sort out before you can start making all the big plans and ideas that are swirling around in that head of yours," Joy said, her small smile coy and knowing.

"Get out of my head, you witch," Stacey said with a laugh.

Joy merely chuckled, but then her expression tightened again. "He went to prison in Peru to save someone else. Someone who they all knew wouldn't survive in prison. He was in there six months before the boys got him out."

Stacey stayed quiet.

"I aged ten years at least during those six months. Knowing my son had been put away for a crime he didn't commit. For a crime not even the person he was protecting committed. The conditions were terrible. He was in solitary a lot. Then there was an outbreak of the mumps, and he got it. Got an infection from it, which—" Joy wiped beneath her eyes and reached for a tissue from the side table next to her chair.

Which what?

"Which what?" Stacey gently probed.

Joy blotted at her eyes and beneath her nose. "I shouldn't say any more. It's really not my story to tell. I feel like I'm betraying him with this little bit that I am saying."

"Is he sterile?" Stacey asked. She was a nurse, after all. And although the mumps were rare now, since most people got the vaccination as a child, and sometimes boosters again as adults, it was still possible. Particularly in developing countries. And although the probability of the mumps causing infertility was rare, if paired with an infection ...

Joy's lips were so tightly pinned, they were turning white.

"He's sterile, isn't he?"

"I've tried to tell him that it doesn't make him any less of a man. That fathering children doesn't necessarily mean you can't *be* a father." Fresh tears sprang into the woman's blue eyes, and she dabbed at them with the tissue. "But you didn't hear it from me." She glanced away and shook her head. "He's so troubled." She blinked a few times and hiccupped. "But he's a *good* man. And he deserves to be loved by a *good* woman. He deserves a family, and you and the kids are that. I know it. You know it. And I know he wants it. He's just ..."

"Got a lot to work through before he feels worthy of it," Stacey finished, her heart heavy, throat thick and eyes burning.

Joy nodded. "A lot."

The unspoken question hung in the air. *Was Stacey willing to tough it out and wait for Chase to work through it all? Or had she been through enough of her own chaos that she was going to cut him loose and focus on her kids?*

She'd be as dishonest as her dead husband if she said the thought hadn't crossed her mind. Because she and the kids *had* been through a lot. Connor was kidnapped, for Christ's sake. And it would be a hell of a lot easier to just walk away from Chase and let him figure himself out.

But then, she'd never had an easy life.

And she knew what it felt like for people to give up on you. And she didn't have any issues as a child, and yet her parents had given up on her anyway. She wasn't what they wanted, so she became just another mouth to feed.

She wouldn't give up on Chase.

He was worth sticking around for. He was worth waiting for. Worth fighting for.

"If I'm being honest," Joy said, pulling Stacey from her wandering thoughts, "I need you here tonight, too. I don't like being alone when one of my boys is hurt."

"I love your son, and I'm not going to give up on him. I'm here for you, Joy. I'm here for Chase. I'm here for the whole family."

"Because you *are* family. You're a Hart. Those kids are Harts. And whether my son figures himself out or not, we're not letting go of you."

Stacey smiled through the pain that squeezed her chest. Easier said than done, unfortunately. She'd love nothing more than to be a Hart, but if Chase rejected her and the kids, she didn't think she could continue to come around. It would be too hard. Too hard on all of them.

"Whatever you need, honey, just ask. No request is too big or too small. This is a scary time for all of us." Joy's lips twisted, and it seemed like she was fighting a pout. Her chin wobbled again as fresh tears sprang into her eyes.

Stacey stood up from the couch and went over to Joy in the chair. She knelt in front of the woman and opened her arms. Joy didn't resist for a moment—she was a hugger—and wrapped her arms tight around Stacey.

"I don't care what happens between you and that buffoon son of mine, you're my daughter," Joy said between sobs that were so fierce for her tiny stature, they shook Stacey as well. "You're a Hart."

Now Stacey's eyes were damp. She half chuckled, half sobbed as she held on tight to the woman she'd come to love like a mother over the past several months.

They sat there in the living room, wrapped up in a hug for a while, until their tears had ebbed and a sense of calm had settled over both of them. Joy was the first to break the embrace, wiping her fingers beneath her eyes and smiling brightly. "How does French toast sound for breakfast?"

Stacey used her sleeve to wipe her own eyes and grinned. "French toast sounds perfect."

"CAN I have another piece of toast?" Connor asked the following morning at the breakfast table.

"Absolutely, my hungry little man," Joy said, stabbing a piece of French toast from the stack and lifting it over to Connor's plate. Then she went about cutting it up into bite-size pieces.

Thea was also enjoying the French toast and had nearly

finished two slices on her own. However, Diesel the shark was circling beneath her seat, so who knows how much the baby actually eaten, since she seemed to be dropping her hand over the side of her highchair and awful lot.

Although plagued with worry, Stacey slept rather well. Connor had snuggled in tight to her when she finally joined him in the bed, and Thea woke sometime around 5 a.m. claiming starvation and in desperate need of sustenance. But then she fell back asleep after only a couple of minutes of nursing, and Stacey felt threads of warm contentment worm through her as she drifted back off to sleep with both her babies in her arms.

They all slept in until nearly eight thirty, until the smell of French toast and coffee had them all rising from the bed like zombies and staggering down the hallway.

Stacey took a sip of her coffee and glanced out the window at the gloomy, rainy Tuesday morning. February was not a pretty month, even for Victoria. Though the lack of knee-high snow was a nice change of pace from Edmonton.

As happy and well-rested as Stacey felt and Joy seemed, there was still an overhanging fog of worry that seemed to have settled over the house like a thick smoke. They hadn't heard anything from Rex, Heath or Brock since earlier last night.

And of course, that meant their imaginations were going wild.

Were they not hearing anything because there was nothing to report and Chase was healing nicely? Or were they not hearing anything because they were afraid to call and tell them Chase had taken a turn for the worse?

After the last several months of Stacey's life, her mind immediately went to the absolute worst-case scenario. It was better to think the worst and be relieved than think the best and be brutally disappointed or heartbroken.

She glanced at Joy's cell phone on the edge of the table. Hers was over by her purse in the living room.

"Nothing yet," Joy said, popping a purple grape into her mouth. "And believe you me, I'll be giving each and every one of those boys a piece of my mind for not keeping us better informed." She shook her head. "Bunch of evasive buggers. They get that from their father, I'll tell you that."

And as if they knew their mother was preparing to rip them a new one, Joy's phone lit up and Brock's face appeared on the screen.

"About damn time," Joy said before answering the call and putting it on speakerphone. "Not happy about being kept in the dark for this long, Brock Lionel Hart," Joy said, planting her hands on her hips and staring at her phone like it was a video call and not just a voice call.

Brock grunted uncomfortably. "Nothing to report."

"BS and you know it," Joy said, her hackles up. "What's the latest?"

"He's stable. Doing well as can be expected. They ended up having to sedate him during the MRI because of the confined space."

Joy's ire disappeared and she closed her eyes, her hand covering her mouth.

"Got him on morphine for the pain now. There's always at least one of us in the room with him," Brock went on.

"How soon until he can be airlifted here to the hospital?" Joy asked, her blue eyes having grown watery.

"At least a week," Brock said. "Want to make sure there's no infection or new bleeding."

"And what are you guys doing while you wait for him?" Joy asked. Her temper was beginning to rise again, Stacey could see it. This woman knew her sons, and even though Stacey had only known the Harts for less than a year, she knew them well enough to know that not one of the four men were capable of sitting around idly and waiting. Broken brother or not.

Brock cleared his throat. "Doesn't matter."

"The hell it doesn't," Joy said, snatching her phone off the table, turning the speaker mode off and getting up from the table. "Now you listen to me, Brock Lionel Hart, you get your brother—*all* of your brothers home in one piece, you hear me? You got Connor back. You rescued all the other children. Now get home." She wandered into the kitchen, but Stacey could still hear her.

"Nana Joy mad at Uncle Brock?" Connor asked, his cheeks all puffy, making him look like a chipmunk prepping for winter.

"No, honey, she's just making sure he takes care of Chase, that's all." Stacey ran her hand over the back of her son's head.

"Leave that shit for the cops and the feds," Joy went on. "Stop this vigilante BS and get back to your wife and children."

Stacey could practically see the steam rising up from Joy's ears.

"You might not listen to me, but I'll call your wife if I have to," Joy threatened, which made Stacey snort a laugh. Her snort instigated Connor to snort. Then Thea snorted, which only set both her and Connor off in a fit of belly giggles.

Joy growled.

Connor growled.

Thea growled.

Stacey rolled her eyes.

Eventually, Joy rejoined them at the table, her complexion flushed, eyes fierce. "That stubborn buffoon," she muttered, stabbing another piece of French toast.

"Are they going after Creed?" Stacey asked, glancing up from her plate.

Joy was viciously cutting into her squishy toast like it was a piece of overcooked steak. "They're looking for him, yes. Haven't come up with anything, but they—Heath mostly—say they won't stop looking for him until they find him." She shoved a piece of toast into her mouth. "I just want them to come home safe and in one piece." But then she glanced at Connor, and her anger seemed to deflate. "I also don't want anything bad to happen to anybody else's sweet, precious babies, so I understand why they're not ready to quit looking. But it just makes a mother worry, you know?"

Stacey nodded.

"Bunch of stubborn buffoons if you ask me."

"Yeah, but they're our stubborn buffoons," Stacey said, reaching over and grabbing Joy's hand and giving it a gentle squeeze atop the table.

Joy's eyes lit up. "They are, aren't they?"

"And we love them dearly."

CHAPTER TWENTY-FOUR

"FUCKING WATCH IT," Brock barked at Heath as they all unloaded Chase and his wheelchair from the airplane after ten days spent in the Seattle hospital. Skyler and Rob were kind enough to offer them all a flight home to Victoria once the doctors cleared Chase for travel.

"His legs aren't broken," Heath said, after accidentally bashing Chase's knee into the doorjamb of the airplane.

"They will be with the way you steer that fucking thing," Brock grumbled.

Chase stood up from the wheelchair. "I can walk." He slowly, gingerly, painfully, descended the stairs from the airplane, gripping the handrail until his knuckles ached.

He loved where he lived, but the airport was damn small. So small that there was no jet bridge from the aircraft to the gate. The plane parked on the runway, and they rolled a staircase to the door for passengers to load and unload.

He reached the tarmac and stopped. He needed to catch his breath.

Grumbles and heavy footsteps behind him had him moving out of the way.

Heath plopped the wheelchair down beside Chase. "Here you go."

Reluctantly, Chase sat back down and allowed his younger brother to push him to the doors.

Rex and Brock were behind them with all their bags.

They went through customs and immigration, and he had to say, as much as the lack of a jet bridge was an irritation, the lack of a line at the customs and immigration desks was welcome. Score one for a tiny airport.

"You know they're waiting for us, right?" Brock murmured, sidling up next to Chase.

That's what he was afraid of.

He didn't want Stacey, his mother or the children to see him looking the way he did. Which was like he'd just endured the beat-down of the century—which he had.

The doctors had deemed him "out of the woods," but he still had a long road of recovery ahead.

Frustration and dread coiled around his insides like a molten snake, and his heart began to beat wildly. He did not want them to see him like this.

He did not want them to see him, period.

He'd failed Connor.

He'd failed Stacey.

He'd failed them all.

He deserved every ache, pain and scar Creed inflicted on him because he'd forgotten the most important rule of battle: Watch your own six. He'd been so hell-bent on rescuing Connor, he'd neglected to watch his back and had nearly compromised the entire operation. Then they stupidly came back for him, risking their lives a second time.

And Creed was still at large.

Brock gently squeezed his shoulder. "You ready?"

No.

The double doors slid open, and they were greeted by giant handmade *Welcome Home* signs scribbled on by Connor and Zoe, as well as smiles larger than life and eyes full of tears.

Stacey had Thea in the baby carrier on her front, facing outward. The baby's legs and arms were flailing wildly. Connor held Stacey's hand, but when he saw Chase, his eyes lit up and he kept trying to pull from Stacey's grasp.

She said something to him, her brows knitting together, but he simply gave her the same look of irritation back and tugged again. It took Chase's mother taking Connor's hand and slowly leading him toward Chase for the little boy to calm down.

"Chase!" Connor cried when he was not five feet away. "You're back. You saved me." Well, if that didn't fucking gut Chase like a bayonet to the abdomen.

Connor went to lunge at Chase for a hug, his arms stretched out, but Chase's mother pulled him back. "We can't, honey. Chase is hurt, remember. I don't know if he can handle a wiggle-bum like you climbing all over him."

Connor's pout was just another stab to the chest.

"It's okay, little man," Chase said, gently reaching for Connor. "Your hugs have special powers, right?"

Connor's expression made the whole airport terminal brighter. "Yeah, they do. They fix all kinds of things. Booboos, owies, hurt feelings. My hugs are awesome." He climbed up into Chase's lap with the help of Chase and Joy, then he wrapped his arms around Chase's neck and squeezed. Chase hugged him back with his one good arm, ignoring the pain in his ribs and shoulders and just letting the little boy's superpowers heal him.

They actually kind of did. When Connor finally let go, Chase did feel better.

But it was a temporary relief because as soon as he let his gaze drift to Stacey, the ache in his chest quadrupled in size.

Connor spun around in his lap but left one arm looped around Chase's neck. "Are your legs okay, Chase?"

He was still distracted by Stacey and the way she was watching him, but he nodded and gave Connor the attention he deserved. "Yeah, little man." He tilted his chin toward his shoulder in a sling. "I just have a few other owies, so the doctors don't want me to do too much, and that includes walking."

"Owies you got saving me from the bad man and lady?"

Jesus, kid, way to rip my heart right out of my chest.

"That's enough, honey," Joy said, helping Connor out of Chase's lap. She leaned toward Chase and gave him a gentle embrace, her blue eyes glassy. He could hear his mother sniffling and her body shaking as she held on to him. "Don't you give me a scare like that ever again, Chase Marvin Hart. Or so help me God."

He chuckled. His parents, in their brilliance, had given each one of their sons a middle name that corresponded with the musician they were listening to while the baby was conceived.

Brock was Brock Lionel, for Lionel Richie; Chase was Chase Marvin for Marvin Gaye; Rex was Rex Barry after Barry White; and poor little Heath was Heath Leppard, because his father said the sexiest song in the world was "Pour Some Sugar On Me" and when it came on, he couldn't resist their mother.

As gross as it was to think about his parents doing anything besides holding hands, and in Chase's mind the last time they did anything more than hold hands was when Heath was conceived, it did warm his heart to know how much his parents had loved each other. Theirs was the kind of marriage that love songs were written about.

"I lived, Mum," he said next to her ear when she refused to let go of him. "Still kicking."

She finally pulled away and regarded him with a look he only used to see as a kid when their mother was on the phone and Chase and his brothers thought that was an ideal time to get up to mischief. If they got too carried away, Joy Hart would rip her slipper off her foot and throw it at them, not caring who she hit.

"Don't look at me like that," he said with a wince.

His mother's eyes widened, and concern replaced her ire. "You're in pain."

"I'll be fine, just a few broken ribs and some bruises."

She swatted his arm. "Don't dumb down your injuries for me, you buffoon. I'm your mother."

He rolled his eyes.

She swatted him again. "Don't roll your eyes at me, either."

That pulled a smile from him.

"Uncle Chase," Zoe said, timidly approaching him as he allowed Heath to wheel him closer to the rest of the group. He held out his hand for her, and Zoe climbed up into his lap. Her red curls were in pigtails on either side of her head, and she wore a puffy, navy winter jacket with tiny pink cats on it. She hugged him much the same way Connor had. "We missed you," she said, pressing her lips to his cheek. But instead of kissing him, she blew a big raspberry.

He laughed and tickled her until she giggled. "I missed you, too." His gaze fell to Stacey, even though in all honesty, he'd kept her in his line of vision the entire time. He also hoped she knew he wasn't telling just Zoe that he missed her.

Stacey's lips pursed, and he watched her nostrils flare as she drew in a deep breath through her nose.

"Well, let's get Uncle Chase home so he can rest," Heath said. He started to wheel Chase toward the doors to the parking lot, but Chase shook his head and asked his brother to stop.

"I want to walk," he said, knowing he would probably be exhausted and in pain by the time he reached the vehicles. But he also hated how weak and needy he felt having his baby brother push him around in a wheelchair like he was some geriatric man in a nursing home.

With a grunt and a groan he did a shit job of stifling, he pushed to his feet. His mother was by his side immediately, wrapping her arm around his waist. "Such a buffoon," she muttered, but she knew better than to challenge him on his decision.

She'd save her chastising for later.

Everyone kept pace with him as they exited the building. Brock now had Zoe on his hip while Rex and Heath acted as mules and brought along all their bags.

Once the children and bags were all loaded into the vehicles, Chase gave his brothers and mother a curt nod, which meant they could pile into the trucks and leave.

Heath's vehicle had been brought to the airport, so his brother was going to give Chase a ride home. He told the rest they could leave, and they did.

Stacey had put her kids in her SUV and was hanging around the back hatch, eyeing him warily.

He approached her at a slow, groan-inducing shuffle. He also couldn't stop his hand from shooting out and resting against the back hatch of her Santa Fe for support. His other arm was in a sling to support his dislocated shoulder.

"Listen," he started, "about what I said last week. When they got me out of the—"

She shook her head, cutting him off. "It's okay. You were delirious. In pain, in shock. Had hypothermia. I know you didn't mean it." Her hands trembled as she reached for his hand.

But he tugged it away, shaking his head. "I did though."

No, you didn't, you idiot. You fucking love this woman.

Her eyes went wide. "What?"

"You belong with someone better, Stacey. With someone whole. Someone who isn't so fucked up." Every word felt pulled from him like they were stuck at the back of his throat by superglue, and when he ripped them free and spoke, he ripped out flesh, as well.

But it needed to be said. He wasn't a well man. He wasn't healthy. His demons had demons. He couldn't be in small spaces. He couldn't sleep with the lights off. Fuck, he couldn't even have children if he wanted to. He was a broken, lost soul, and after everything life had thrown at Stacey so far, she didn't deserve for his problems to become hers. She didn't deserve to be saddled with a man like him and the heap of baggage that accompanied him.

She deserved happiness and love, rainbows and sunshine all day long for the rest of her days. She'd seen enough heartache and trauma to last a lifetime, to darken even the brightest of days. And she didn't deserve the constant cloud that followed him around like an FBI tail.

Her head began to shake, and tears formed in her beautiful brown eyes. "No. You don't know what you're saying. Is this about you being sterile?"

His eyes went wide. "Who told you—"

Her gaze narrowed. "I might be blonde, but I'm not an idiot. I put the pieces together. Did some digging."

"Apparently."

"But I don't care about that. I don't want any more children. And my children can be *our* children. They love you. I love you. And you love us. That's what makes a family. Love. Not blood. And we can work through the claustrophobia and other things. I can sleep with the lights on. I can buy one of those sleep masks. We can get a place with a huge bedroom and floor to ceiling windows without any blinds. I'm willing to compromise, to do what it takes to make this work."

Jesus, she'd really done some digging. He'd have to have a *chat* with his mother later.

"Please, Chase."

His throat had grown increasingly tight, and the next words

came out as a frog-like croak. "I'm fucking broken. I was beaten bloody. Bound naked and gagged like some fucking pig. They put me in a box the size of a child's coffin and intended to sell me overseas to some sadist with a fetish. I can't bring that into your world. Into your house."

"We can work through it," she said. "We can take it slow. Get you the help you need." The tremble of her lips had his fists bunching at his sides. He wanted to grab her and kiss her so fucking badly. But he knew it wasn't fair. Not to her, not to the kids.

He was too fucked up to be a family man. To be a husband and a father.

Connor, Thea and Stacey didn't deserve his mess.

She reached for him again, gasped and recoiled when he stepped away with his head shaking. "I'm not right, Stacey. You need to be with someone like Rex. Someone who's not fucked in the head."

"I'm not some whore that can bounce around from man to man like it's no big deal," she said, the anger in her eyes replacing the sadness.

Good. He would prefer to know she hated him than to think of her crying and pining over him. Her anger would push her to get over him quicker.

"Why are you doing this?" The tears were beginning to tumble again.

Fuck.

He needed to get away from her before his willpower crumbled, before his heart took the reins and made him grab her and kiss her and tell her he didn't mean a damn word.

Because he fucking didn't.

He was just trying to do what was best for Stacey and her kids.

Her lower jaw jutted out and shook, causing her breath to release in a rattled staccato. Thick puffs rose up and disappeared into the drizzly February sky. "You don't mean this."

He needed to get away from her now.

His shoulder lifted. "Go home. Be with your kids. Let me clean up my mess on my own. It's not your job." He turned to go, hating himself more than he'd ever hated anyone in his life, because those sobs that echoed around the parking lot were caused by him.

He heard her stomp, open her door and slam it shut.

He climbed into the passenger seat of Heath's truck, wincing and groaning from the pain and difficulty, since his brother liked his truck to be obnoxiously high.

"Everything okay?" Heath asked, starting up the engine.

Chase closed the door and watched through Heath's side window as Stacey backed out of her parking stall and sped away.

Heath backed out of his parking stall, too. "You meeting up with her later?"

Chase shook his head and watched the world go by outside his window. "No. I ended it."

Out of the corner of his eye, he saw a flurry of blond hair and knew that Heath had whipped his head around so fast, a weaker person would have severe whiplash. "You did what?"

Chase ground his molars together. "I'm too fucked up."

Heath made a noise in his throat that sounded like a half scoff, half gargle. "Mum's right. You are a buffoon."

CHAPTER TWENTY-FIVE

"I'm sure he'll come around," Emma said later that week as she and Stacey were out for their weekly evening run. It was colder than usual, and their breath created a heavy white mist as they panted their way up the hill.

She'd been nervous as hell leaving the kids with James for the hour they were going to go running. But like the calm, cool and collected man that he was, James showed her his state-of-the-art security system, set it after they left and told her that you can't bubble-wrap your children, as much as we would all like to, and that the kids would be fine while their mother took an hour to clear her head.

He'd been one hundred percent right, of course.

The run was exactly what she needed.

"I know Chase, and he's a stoic man, a proud man—all the Hart brothers are. He just hates that you've seen him in such a broken and vulnerable state. But once his bruises and bumps heal and he's back in beefy protector mode, he'll see how he acted and come crawling back." Emma rested her hand on Stacey's arm to get her to stop. They'd reached the top of their big hill, and like Stacey, Emma seemed to need a breather.

A metallic taste filled Stacey's mouth from the overexertion. "I just hate that he doesn't think I can handle his issues. Why can't he see that it's better to lean on someone and work through your problems together than shoulder the entire burden alone?" She lifted her arms above her head and wandered around in a circle to let the freezing night air fill her lungs.

"Because he's a man and he's communication-inept, even though he was raised by a mother who probably made them sit in a circle and pass the sharing and talking stick around."

That made Stacey snort. She could totally see Joy pulling something like that on her sons when they were younger. *"Share your feelings, or I won't feed you."*

"I waited five months for him. And I'm still pissed about that. He just made assumptions and then dicked off. No *see you later, thanks for the fuck*, nothing. Is he going to dick off again for months on end, come back and ask for forgiveness and think the kids and I will just take him back? I can't do this wishy-washy BS to the kids. It's hard enough on me, let alone them." Taking a deep breath, Stacey glanced up at the starry sky, hoping the heavens or universe had something wise to bestow.

The night was quiet. So were the heavens and universe.

"Then don't wait for him. Why does he get to call the shots on *your* life? You need to just focus on your kids and not be actively looking for romance." Leave it to Emma to shoot straight. "Don't be trolling the apps for some strange." She elbowed Stacey with a big grin, and they started running again.

"I've never in my life *trolled for some strange*." She was smiling, though, and that elevated her heart, because since Chase walked away from her in that parking lot, her heart had felt like a damn anvil in her chest.

"How's Connor doing?" Emma asked, changing the subject.

"Good, I think. The children's trauma counselor was by today, and she'll be back on Friday. But he's doing all right, all things considered. He wants to sleep in my bed, but at least he's sleeping soundly, talking and eating. Those were some of our initial concerns. We know he's going to need to be monitored and that trauma from this could come out later on. We just need to be ready for it."

"And Thea?"

Stacey scoffed. "The boob is back, so she's totally fine."

Emma's giggle was breathy and choppy as they started up another hill. "Babies are a lot like men. They really only need the basic necessities."

"Too true."

"And for a lot of men, the boob *is* one of the basic necessities of life."

They continued on with their run until Stacey's lungs burned from the cold air and she thought her cheeks might get frostbite. But it was a run she needed. It was time alone in her head that she needed. And as she and Emma grew more exhausted as they headed back toward Emma's house, they didn't talk as much and Stacey was able to think about things.

Not that she hadn't been thinking about things since before Chase got home, but Emma's comment about men only needing the basic necessities struck a chord with her, and by the time they arrived back to Emma's, she knew what she had to do.

"Your friend Steve is a Realtor, right?" she asked Emma as she helped Connor get his shoes on in James and Emma's foyer.

Emma nodded. "Yeah, why? You looking to finally buy?"

"I think so, yeah."

James leaned against the wall of his entryway. "Going to miss you as a tenant."

Stacey smiled and tightened the strap on Thea's car seat. "Yeah, but I think it's time we put down some roots. I have the life insurance from Ted's estate and some money saved up. I think we can do it."

Both Emma and James nodded.

"Let me know if you need me to come take a look at the house or call my building inspector," James said. "Whatever you need, just ask."

With her hand on the doorknob, she nodded at two of her best friends and offered them probably the biggest smile she'd made since the whole ordeal began. "I really love you guys. And thank you."

"Get those babies home and call me tomorrow," Emma said, stepping forward and helping Stacey get the kids out the door.

Stacey nodded and escorted her brood to the driveway. "I will."

She was just getting Connor strapped into his car seat when her phone in her purse buzzed. It was James, and he was texting her Steve's number.

Excellent. Tomorrow, she would begin the hunt.

The hunt for their future.

————

It was nearly four weeks that Chase had been home, and even though he was healing physically, mentally he was a fucking mess.

And it wasn't the dreams or claustrophobia that were fucking with him. It was his heart that had him angry at the world.

His heart was furious with him.

He hated himself for what he'd done, even though he knew it was the right thing to do. For all of them.

The selfless thing to do, was to let her and the kids go, not get them tangled up with his problems. Keep them from being introduced to his demons.

Nobody needed to meet those fuckers. Nobody.

But since Heath dropped him off at his apartment, he'd been a fucking wreck.

His mother had come by on several occasions, always bringing food, and each time her worry lines appeared deeper than the time before. She'd also sent each of his brothers to check up on him, as well as Krista and James and Emma Shaw.

But he gave everyone the brush-off. He let them into his place, told them he was eating, sleeping and doing his physio exercises for his shoulder but that he just wanted to heal in peace. He also promised his mother that under no circumstances would he kill himself. That's not to say he hadn't thought about it once or twice when the monsters in his head grew extra loud and nasty.

But he'd witnessed firsthand what his father's death had done to their mother and wasn't about to do that to her again. Plus, if he was dead, how would they ever track down Dakota Creed and bestow upon him the justice he so rightfully deserved?

But he needed to get better before he started hunting the devil again.

His body needed to heal.

Thankfully, it was spring now.

The cherry blossoms in Victoria always bloomed earlier than anywhere else Chase had ever been, and the streets below his apartment looked like they were covered in pink confetti. The sun also beat into his living-room window without relent, and he could hear birds chirping on the tree outside.

Thank God for warmer weather and longer days. He wasn't somebody who usually complained about much, but he wasn't a big fan of the winter and knew his level of depression was greatly increased by the gloomy weather.

It was a Wednesday afternoon in late March, and he was busy working on his shoulder exercises when his phone on the coffee table started to buzz.

Since he'd left Stacey standing there in that airport parking lot, he hadn't heard a word from her. His brothers and mother dropped snippets of information here and there, but after a while, they got the hint that it was more like rubbing salt in the wound telling him about her than it was helpful.

But now she was calling him.

He debated answering it.

Debated ripping off that scab—it was still so fucking fresh.

But he was unable to let it get past the fifth ring before he lunged for the phone, which only caused his shoulder to scream at him in pain.

"Hello?" He massaged his angry joint with his free hand. He'd be paying for that later.

"I'm going to text you an address, and I would appreciate it if you could meet me there in an hour." Then she hung up, and sure enough, his phone vibrated and an address out around Prospect Lake popped up. It wasn't too far from Brock and Krista's place either.

Damn it, as much as he didn't want to see her, she also hadn't given him much of an opportunity to decline. And even though he told himself that it would be easier if she hated him, deep down that was the last fucking thing he wanted.

Grumbling, he finished his exercises, googled the address on his phone and then headed down to the parking garage. It was about a twenty-minute drive to the address during midday, mid-week traffic. Another glance at Google said the address was right on the lake. It was also right next to his friends Derrick and Piper's house.

What was going on?

Only one way to find out.

With his gut in knots and pulse racing, he climbed into his truck, pulled out of his parking garage and headed to the address. His brain rioted. He wanted to see Stacey in the worst way, but he also knew that it was just going to be torture because he'd scorned her and pushed her away. No way would she still want him after how he'd treated her.

So why was she asking him to meet her next door to Piper and Derrick's?

None of this made sense. But then again, he couldn't remember the last time the world had made any sense to him. Maybe their last family Christmas before his father died? That was over twenty years ago. So things in life hadn't made a lick of sense in twenty years?

Yeah, that seemed about right, actually.

His mother was widowed way too early in life. Then she was forced to raise four young sons on her own. How did that make any sense?

His dad had been a cop and died when a drunk driver crashed into his car. How did that make any sense?

Then, as he grew up, he saw what kind of shambles the world was falling into. The hardships his family faced, how the man who hit and killed their father was released from prison after a short sentence, free to go on and live his life with his wife and children.

When innocent people suffered and the bad guys got away with murder—and worse—it made him realize the world was never meant to make sense.

And that it never would.

So he stopped trying to figure it out. He put his head down and went to college, got a computer science degree, then he enrolled in the naval reserves, worked his way up and joined Joint Task Force 2. He worked for years saving and protecting those who needed help the most. He fought for his country and tried to rid the world of the bad guys intent on hurting. And he'd done a lot of that.

But through it all, things continued not to make sense.

Children, innocents, families thrown into the crossfire of gang wars. Kidnapped and tortured by drug lords and arms dealers. Churches and schools bombed in retaliation to something those injured or killed had no part in. Children ripped from their families and sold on the black market like bags of heroin. None of it made any fucking sense.

And yet the closer he got to the address on Prospect Lake, the more his nerves calmed and things in his mind started to fall into place.

The address was an empty lot. So he parked on the weed-riddled gravel and got out. Stacey's SUV was already there.

Thankfully, it was a nice day with fluffy white clouds in the sky and a warm sun overhead. The wind still held the icy bite of early spring, but he could feel the tendrils of summer working their magic, and the scent of freshly blossomed flowers eased the last of his jumpy nerves.

Gravel crunched under his shoes as he made his way deeper onto the property and down a gentle slope toward the water. She had her back to him, but he knew she knew he was there, and when she finally spun around, it was like a bolt of lightning straight to his chest. She was so goddamn beautiful.

Her smile was big and bright, and the way the sun shone in her eyes, they appeared to glow gold more than anything else.

"What do you think?" she asked, spreading her arms wide.

He shook his head, not understanding what she meant at all. "What do you mean?"

"I'm thinking four bedrooms. We can make one the office, put in a giant rec room downstairs for the kids. Floor to ceiling windows, of course, because why would we obstruct this view? We'll have our room overlooking the lake, as well, put a wall of windows in there, too. A big deck off the living room and kitchen, and then we can put a dock off the beach for kayaks and stuff." Her arms were waving around, and she was pointing. "I've talked to James, and he figures once we get all the necessary permits, we can probably break ground by mid-May or early June. We can get chickens, maybe some ducks. I've always wanted a pet pig—not for food, of course." She shuddered. "Can you imagine turning Penelope Hammerstein into bacon?"

She was about to start speaking again, but he grabbed her shoulders and shook her gently. "What are you talking about?"

"I bought the property, and I'm going to build us a house."

His brows pinched together so tight, a mild headache formed on his forehead. "What?"

She shook herself free from his grasp and walked toward the water, glancing over the glass-calm lake. "I realized something recently."

He joined her, and they stood side by side, watching as a couple of ducks paddled lazily from one bunch of reeds to another. "And what have you realized?"

"That you don't get to call the shots on my life. That *men* don't get to call the shots on my life." She spun to face him. "You're a simple creature, Chase Hart. All men are. You're like babies in a lot of ways."

He resisted the urge to roll his eyes.

"Roll those eyes all you want. It's true and you know it. You're content with the basic necessities of life. But *your* basic necessities are a little different than most. You require wide-open spaces, light, patience and purpose. Those are your basic necessities."

He was quiet.

She wasn't wrong.

He just hadn't had anybody serve him a dose of cold, hard facts like that before.

She waved her hand dismissively. "Sure, you need food, water, air and a roof over your head. But those are what you need to *survive*. Your necessities are different. And I think everyone's necessities vary. They are what we need to get through to the next day. To make us the most bare-bones functional version of ourselves."

He'd never thought of it this way, but the more she spoke, the more it made sense. "What are your necessities?"

"My children. A sense of purpose. A sense of safety. And going to bed each night knowing that I gave the day and all the problems that came with it the very best of myself." The way she looked up at him so earnestly had him falling in line with her way of thinking almost immediately. "You might have pushed me away, Chase *Marvin* Hart, but like I said, you don't get to call the shots on *my* life. You're not my bodyguard anymore. You are the man that I love. The man that my children love, and ... the man that loves us. We are your family, and we will stand beside you and hold your hand through every obstacle, every setback. We will fight your demons right along with you. We will vanquish them together." She stepped forward and took his hands in hers. "I don't want to be a part of the Hart family unless you're the reason we belong. You can't fight for us right now because you're too busy fighting for yourself—so until you're better, I'm going to fight for us. For what we know is meant to be. You don't get to call it quits on us. Not without me agreeing to it, too. And I don't. So you're stuck with me. Deal with it."

He hung his head and stared at her navy tennis shoes, his throat raw. "I'm so broken, Stace. I can't—"

She growled and stomped her foot. "Stop saying that. You're not *broken*. You were lost. You cracked a couple of ribs. You were kidnapped, held hostage, thrown in prison, beaten. But when I look at the man standing in front of me, I don't see somebody who is broken. I see somebody who is so damn strong, it amazes me. I see a man who doesn't realize just how strong he is, and rather than harnessing that strength and building on it—*re*building on it—with the love and support of those around him, he only sees the small, fractured pieces of himself and focuses on those." She shook his hands until he glanced up at her. "You need to step back from the mirror. You're too close. You're only seeing the small, scuffed parts of yourself but not all of you. Step back and see what I see. See the whole man. The strong man. The worthy man."

The worthy man.

He sure as hell didn't feel worthy. Not of Stacey. Not of her love. Not of everything she was offering him.

"You *are* worthy of my love," she continued. "And you have it. So you can push me away again and again and again, but I'm not going anywhere. Just like you fought for my child, I'm fighting for you—for us—and I won't stop until you see yourself the same way that I see you."

He'd been clenching his back teeth together so tight, he had to work his jaw side to side a couple of times to release the tension. But when he did that, the emotions, the love, the acceptance came barreling in, and he felt the backs of his eyes begin to burn.

Even though he knew his mother and brothers would step in front of a moving train or a bullet for him, it meant something different to hear how hard he was loved by a woman. That a woman like Stacey could love him for everything that he was and, even more importantly, everything that he wasn't.

That he was a man worth fighting for, a man worth battling demons for.

"It's okay to cry," she said, the tears breaking free from her eyes and sliding down her cheeks. "You're no less of a man for showing your emotions. It's okay to ask for help. To say you're struggling and to take a step back and take care of yourself. You don't always have to be the one with answers or the one doing the protecting." She wiped a tear from her cheek and smiled. "If there is anything this past year has taught me, it's that I don't *need* a man. I can make it on my own with my children just fine. And we will all be okay. But I don't *want* to make it on my own. I want to share all this love we have—Connor, Thea and myself—with someone who we know loves us back. He's just too stubborn, blind and buffoon-like to admit it."

His lip twitched. "Buffoon-like?"

"Your mother has me on the word *buffoon*. It's very fitting for a lot of situations. Particularly when it comes to the Hart men."

He snorted, and one side of his mouth lifted up. "I'm a lot of work, Stace. A lot."

She shrugged. "I know."

"I'll have good days and bad days."

"Don't we all?"

"Yeah, but my bad days aren't like everyone else's bad days. They can get *really* bad."

"And we'll get through them together. We'll make a plan so when you feel a bad day coming on, we turn to the plan. So everyone feels safe and considered."

So everyone feels safe.

Did she think he would hurt the kids if his demons got to be too bad?

"I will never, ever, ever hurt you or the children. You have my word on that. That's not what happens when the darkness closes in. I don't get violent. I swear."

She shrugged again, and this time the shrug was accompanied by a smile. "I know. I've known that since day one. I trust you completely, Chase. It's not my safety or the kids' safety I'm worried about. It's yours. You need to feel safe enough to be yourself, to feel your feelings and deal with your issues. We will be that safe space for you. Let me be your soft place to land, just like you're mine."

"You're sure you want me?" How he got this fucking lucky, to find a woman like Stacey, he would never understand in a million years. But then again, not much in the world made sense, so maybe it was okay that he didn't understand why Stacey loved him. But she did, and that was all that really mattered.

"I'm one hundred percent sure," she said, stepping into his space and wrapping her arms around his waist. "But I need something from you first. Before we can move forward."

If he had it in his power to give to her, he'd bring her the damn moon. "Anything."

"I need an apology."

Yeah, he owed her about a thousand of those.

Bowing his head, he looked deep into the gentle brown of her eyes. "I'm sorry. I'm sorry for leaving months ago and not calling. I'm sorry for assuming you were with my brother and not just asking. I'm sorry for the things I said when I was delirious and for the things I said in the airport parking lot. I meant none of it. I have loved you since the moment Connor came out of your bedroom wielding your dildo around in the air like a sword and your cheeks turned the color of a cherry. And I will love you and those children for as long as I live."

She was blushing. "And you're sorry for taking so damn long to realize that we're stronger together than apart," she added, regarding him with a challenging look.

"I'm especially sorry for that," he said, feeling all the tension he'd held on to for far too long lift off his shoulders and get carried away with the gentle zephyr.

"No more pushing me away. If you need some space, just say so. I'm a big girl, and after the year I've had, asking for a little space won't offend me."

Jesus Christ, as strong as Stacey said he was, as much as he could take out the bad guys with a swift kick or a right hook, Stacey Saunders was by far the strongest person he had ever fucking met. She stared straight into his eyes, knowing exactly what she wanted, and for some crazy reason, that was him.

"No more pushing you away," he finally said. "Never again."

She nodded. "Good. Now that we've got that settled, I hear you know and have saved the life once or twice of our new neighbors."

And as if on cue, Derrick, Piper and their one-year-old daughter, Holly, were making their way through the tall grass that divided their property with what was apparently now Chase and Stacey's property.

They'd work out the finances later. He'd pay her for half of the lot and building costs. He knew she had money from Ted's life insurance policy—the one good thing that man had done for his family was take out over a million-dollar policy on himself—but if this was going to be *their* home, then he wanted to have a financial stake in it, as well.

"There goes the neighborhood," Derrick said, all grins. His stormy gray eyes danced as he balanced a flaxen-haired Holly on his hip, the little girl sucking furiously on her thumb while clutching a stuffed bunny. He reached out and took Chase's hand, giving it a firm shake. "Nice to see you again, my friend. It's been far too long."

"Agreed." Chase smiled and gave Holly a gentler smile before turning to Piper. She lunged right at him and hugged him hard. "I'll kick your ass next time you leave for months on end without telling us." Then she swatted his good shoulder.

"I'll remember that," he said letting go of Piper and looping an arm around Stacey's waist. "Though I don't think I'll be going away for any long periods of time anymore. Got a lot to do and a lot of people who need me here." He glanced down at a now beaming Stacey. She had the kind of smile that made everyone else smile, too.

"I'm Derrick, and this is Piper and our daughter, Holly," Derrick said, offering Stacey his hand.

"Nice to meet you guys," Stacey said. "Hope you don't mind that we bought the lot beside yours."

"Couldn't ask for better neighbors," Piper said. She was a blonde-haired, blue-eyed beauty who Chase had helped in Peru. Through a series of circumstances, they'd become entangled, Piper, Chase and Derrick. Piper was framed for smuggling drugs, and the Peruvian authorities wanted to take her to prison. But Chase gave himself up as the mule instead and went in her place. As much as he had endured, as much as he was still going through, whenever he saw his friends and their perfect, happy family, he knew it had all been worth it.

And now, he was going to have a perfect, happy family of his own.

Derrick and Piper had only recently moved back to Canada, as they were teaching abroad for a few years, but they bought their house on the lake the moment they decided to make Victoria their home. Chase had stared longingly at the empty lot beside theirs, hoping it would one day come up for sale.

Apparently, it had.

"Where are your kids?" Piper asked, taking Holly from Derrick and setting her down on the ground. The little girl took off into the grass at an awkward toddle.

"They're with Chase's mum," Stacey said.

Chase's arm around her tightened. "She needed to knock some sense into me, and that's best done without the children around."

Stacey was back to grinning up at him, her eyes sparkling, face radiant.

"I didn't even know this lot was for sale," Derrick said.

"It wasn't," Stacey said, lifting a shoulder. "But I know a Realtor who has some magical powers, and he tracked down the land owners, told them there was an interested buyer, and I made them an offer they couldn't refuse."

"Sounds like a cement shoes kind of deal," Piper said with a chuckle.

Stacey shook her head. "Not at all. I knew you guys lived here after talking to Heath, and the moment I saw the lot, I fell in love and knew I wanted to raise my family here. It's such a beautiful location, and I hear the schools in the area are great. Particularly that Montessori school out on West Saanich Road."

"That's where we have Holly registered," Piper said.

"Well, welcome to the neighborhood," Derrick said. "We're glad to know the new neighbors aren't going to be jerks or steal my Weedwacker."

"I'll bring it back with a full tank of gas," Chase said, his heart and soul feeling light but also full. He took in a deep breath and filled his lungs with fresh air. He could already see himself out in a canoe on the lake or sitting under the stars in the backyard with the kids during the summer. Wide open spaces. There was plenty of that out here. And all those windows and the love and understanding of a good woman. What more could he ask for out of life?

And like the last remaining pieces of a puzzle, the pieces that had fallen to the floor and been swept under the couch for months only to be found during a good, thorough spring cleaning, everything finally started to click into place.

He was a man who had the love of a good woman.

Not being able to have children didn't make him any less of a man.

He had children.

He had two beautiful kids who would grow up calling him *Dad*. He would walk Thea down the aisle at her wedding, help Connor pick out his first car, chaperone field trips and school dances, give his kids piggyback rides and teach them how to ride their bikes. He would be the best damn dad he could be because now he knew he deserved the life Stacey wanted to give him.

He deserved his family, and they deserved him.

And they all deserved a wonderful, happy life together.

Because they'd certainly fucking earned it.

EPILOGUE

Eighteen months later ...

STACEY ROLLED over to her side and opened her eyes. The enormous picture windows in their bedroom had the drapes pulled open completely—they were rarely closed since they looked right onto the lake—and the morning sun was high and hot, beating into their room.

It was going to be a beautiful, perfect July day, she just knew it.

The clock on her nightstand said it was only about six thirty, and when she tuned in to the house, there were no noises or warbles of children asking for Peppa Pig or Cheerios. Maybe her children were sleeping in.

It had been a late night for all of them last night.

It would undoubtedly be another late night tonight.

She was about to snuggle in deeper to her pillow and close her eyes for a few more minutes of lovely sleep when a big, warm hand gripped her around the waist and tugged backward. She let out a little squeal until an iron bar prodded her in the butt.

"Well, good morning to you, too," she said, giving her butt a little shimmy.

Chase growled behind her and nipped the shell of her ear. "It can be a great morning, if you get my drift." He thrust harder against her and with his free hand went to work on her pajama shorts. He only pulled them down far enough to access what he needed.

"Door's not locked," she said, relaxing and closing her eyes when he traced an erotic path across the top of her shoulders with his tongue.

"I can be quick and quiet if you can." The head of his cock pressed against her center, and she tilted her hips back to give him easier access.

He took that access and drove into her.

They both let out a moan and a sigh when he was seated inside her fully.

"Nothing better or harder than a morning chub," he said, gripping her breast from behind and starting to move inside her.

"Not going to argue with you there."

He was hitting all the right spots inside of her, making her body hum and getting her close quick, just like he promised.

The man was an insatiable beast. He could go for what seemed like hours if he wanted to, or if a quickie was necessary, he could give her a rapid but satisfying *wham, bam, thank you, ma'am* just as easily.

His quiet but manly grunts behind her only had Stacey getting to her own pinnacle faster. She pushed two fingers down between her legs and worked her clit with rough circles, every so often pushing her fingers farther between her legs to feel him sliding in and out of her, thick, wet, hard and veiny.

Bright lights began to flash behind her closed eyes, and her lower belly grew hot. Every time he twisted her nipple between his thumb and finger, her body would quiver and her pussy would squeeze.

"You close?" she asked.

"Anytime you're ready, babe." His teeth fell to the back of her shoulder, and he nipped, causing a zap of pain to shoot through her body and land firmly in her clit, morphing instantly into a beautiful, warm bloom of pleasure.

"Gonna come," she said with ragged breath. "Gonna—"

She couldn't even get that word out. She came before the word did, and then no words could come out at all. Her eyes squeezed shut, her body tensed and her back bowed. The wave of the orgasm crashed into her with full force, taking her for a ride.

Chase stilled behind her, opened his mouth wide and chomped down hard on her shoulder. She felt his cock pulsing as he shot his hot load into her pussy. His deep, baritone grunts heightened her own pleasure. Her fingers worked double-time on her clit. Her orgasm kept going, the first one rolling into a second, then, right as she could tell Chase was on the way down from his climax, she started to come down from hers as well.

They were so in sync.

But she liked to think they had been since day one. It just took him a bit longer to realize it.

When they'd both finished, Stacey slid out of bed and padded barefoot across the parquet flooring to the master bathroom. She peed, washed her hands and pulled her pajama shorts back up before returning to the bed. When she slid back under the covers, Chase pulled her back into being the little spoon. He had tugged on his boxers, and there was no longer a steel rod trying to turn her into a human shish kebab.

"You ready for today?" she asked, snuggling in deeper to his warmth and love.

He kissed her neck. "Absolutely, you?"

"It's wedding day!" Connor shouted, flinging their bedroom door open.

"It's wedding day!" Thea echoed.

Both children clambered onto Chase and Stacey's king-size bed and stood at the end of it.

"Why are you still in bed?" Connor asked, his blue eyes wide with panic. "We have so much to do before the wedding. So much to do."

"So much to do," Thea said, shaking her head, before getting down on her hands and knees and crawling until she was between Chase and Stacey. Chase was forced to let go of Stacey, and Stacey was forced to move out of the way and roll over.

"We were cuddling, you know," Stacey said, giving her daughter the stink eye.

"My turn cuddle Daddy," Thea said, lifting Chase's arm and wrapping it around her so she was now the little spoon. "You cuddle Connor."

"Such a daddy's girl," Stacey said, pretending to pout.

"No time for cuddling," Connor said. "We have chairs to set up, tables to decorate. I mean, Mum, you need to get your hair done, your makeup. You can't get married looking like that." He pointed to her and made a face.

"Looking like *what*?" Stacey asked her cheeky offspring.

"Freshly fucked," Chase mouthed with a big grin.

"Like you just woke up," Connor said exasperatedly.

"We have time, sweetheart." She opened her arm wide and encouraged Connor to slow down his runaway train of a brain and come lie down next to her. "It's a small wedding, just the family and a few friends. We have lots of time."

"Yeah, I know," Connor whined, but he slid under the covers and snuggled into her without complaint. "But I'm just really excited."

"We going to be a famiwee," Thea said with a nod.

"We already are a family," Chase said, kissing the top of Thea's head. "Just 'cause your mum and I are finally getting married doesn't make a difference. I'm still your dad, she's still your mom, and we all still love each other."

"Yeah, but a wedding makes it *official*," Connor said, his tone laden with authority.

There was extra significance to the day besides Chase and Stacey finally getting married. Today was also the day Chase's adoption of Connor and Thea was finally official. He would, after today, legally and completely be their father.

They were all going to change their names to Hart as well.

She held no emotional attachment to her maiden name of Saunders, especially considering her parents wanted jack-shit to do with her anyway, and no way was she going to saddle her children with Ted's last name, particularly since she refused to go by Gordon since the day she found out he was a two-timing wife collector.

"It's a big day for sure, little man," Chase said. "And I'm so glad you are going to be my best man."

"I'm Mommy's rice maid," Thea said, contorting her body enough that she could run her hand over Chase's bald head.

"Bridesmaid, honey," Stacey corrected.

Thea only nodded.

"Can we go watch Paw Patrol?" Connor asked, wriggling out of Stacey's arms and moving to sit toward the end of the bed.

Thea pried herself out of Chase's arms and went to sit next to her brother. "Yeah, Pawtrol, please. Cheerios, too."

"I can get the Cheerios for her," Connor said.

Chase yawned and nodded. "Go turn on the television, and I'll cast it from my phone. Just give it a minute."

Connor leapt off the bed and sprinted down the hallway to the stairs.

His thunderous *clomp clomp* echoed around the house.

"Turning it on!" he bellowed.

"Get up soon, okay, guys?" Thea said, sliding off the bed carefully and then heading off in the same direction as her brother.

Chase had his phone out, and he was getting ready to cast Paw Patrol to the living-room television.

"Think that will buy us fifteen more minutes of sleep?" Stacey asked, turning back onto her other side and snuggling into her spot as the little spoon once again.

He set his phone on his nightstand and wrapped his arms back around her. "Hopefully."

"Are you excited about today?" she asked, placing her hand over his hand and letting their fingers naturally lace together.

"I am. I'm excited to officially call you my wife. And to have those adoption papers signed and legit." His deep inhale of her hair made her smile. "Though I'd be just as happy without. You're already my wife in every way that matters, and those two are already my kids in every way that counts, too."

"I agree." Pieces of paper and pomp and circumstance were great, but in their hearts, in their souls and to the whole world, they were already everything that a family should be. People who loved each other unconditionally, for better or worse.

It hadn't taken long for her kids to start calling Chase *Dad*, and when Thea said "Dadda" before she said "Mama," that pretty much sealed the deal for all of them.

"I thought I'd lost my heart back in Lima," he said gruffly, his voice suddenly hoarse and strained.

She tried to turn in his arms to see if everything was okay, but he wouldn't let her. He held on tighter to her though, as if she might suddenly slip from the bed or vanish into thin air. His fingers dug into her flesh and his chin rested possessively on her shoulder.

She heard him swallow and take in a deep breath through his nose before he cleared his throat and started speaking again. "I thought I'd become so screwed up that nobody could love me or trust me again. That I was too broken and damaged to ever be good enough for someone to call their husband or father."

Tears behind her eyes burned just like the raw ache in the back of her throat. She tightened her hold on his hands. Both of them now were holding on to each other for dear life.

Her heartbeat picked up and her breath stuttered a moment. "But you found my heart, buried deep down, and you brought me back from the darkest depths of hell with your love, stubbornness and determination. You believed in me when I'd all but given up on myself, and for that, Stacey, I will be forever in your debt."

"No debt. You gave me back my son, have given our family a wonderful life, and restored my faith and trust in men. We're square."

She needed to look at him. To see him and only him as they spoke.

She loosened her own old on him and swatted his hand gently to release her, waiting until he let go and she could spin around to face him.

What she saw was the face of a changed man.

A found man.

The love she had for Chase ran so deep, so pure and true, she was overwhelmed and sobered by it every damn day. The man was a part of her. Every beat of her heart beat for Chase. He was in her marrow. An extension of her soul. They were one now, and today, getting married in front of their family and friends would only strengthen that bond.

She felt it every single dad, how hard he tried.

How much he loved their children and their life.

And she saw that love staring back at her now.

He was obsessed with her as she was with him.

Two addicts, unwilling to quit, because without their fix, they were nothing. Shells of their former selves.

Sure, she could live her life with her children, without a man or a husband, but she didn't want to. She wanted Chase and the family they had more than she'd ever wanted anything in the world.

She cupped his cheek and ran her thumb over his lips. "You're my heart, Chase Hart. My soul. My other half."

He grabbed her hand from his face and kissed her palm. "I love you, Stace. I love our family, and I can't wait to marry you today."

With hot tears of pure joy stinging her eyes, she smiled. "It's the first day of the rest of our life." Then she leaned in and pressed her lips against his. "And I happen to think it's going to be one hell of a great life."

————

FOR A DELETED SCENE FROM *LOST HART*
CLICK HERE whitleycox.com/bonus-material

TO GET BROCK AND KRISTA'S STORY
CLICK HERE mybook.to/hard_hart

SNEAK PEEK - TORN HART

Read on for a sneak peek of Chapter 1 from
Torn Hart
Book 3 in The Harty Boys series

CHAPTER 1 - TORN HART

Fuck, sweet and sour pork was goddamn delicious.

Rex's stomach grumbled, demanding to be filled.

Was there anything better than the smell of Chinese food wafting up from the back of your vehicle?

Rex didn't think so.

Well, maybe the smell of Chinese food wafting up from the back of your vehicle while a woman's head bobbed in your lap in the front seat.

But he only had one of those things currently, and his angry belly was winning out over his full balls and lonely dick.

Especially after a long fucking day at work—he'd been up since four and on the job by five—followed by an hour at the gym hitting the punching bag. He'd earned every damn carb that he intended to consume tonight—and then some.

Pussy would have to wait.

He'd also have to find some—not that it was hard.

With enough Chinese food to feed a family of six, and a six-pack of beer from a local microbrew in the back seat of his truck he was gearing up for satisfying evening alone.

It didn't matter if it was a Wednesday night, he was going to head up to his apartment, grab Diesel, and take him for a quick piss outside. After Diesel did his thing, they'd head back inside, he'd feed his dog, strip down, have a shower and nut one out. Then, finally, at long last he'd sit in his incredibly expensive recliner, put his feet up and eat a fuck-ton of chow mien and sweet and sour pork, drink his beer and watch a riveting documentary on the Discovery Channel while his dog snored and farted at his feet.

Was there a better plan out there?

There sure as fuck wasn't.

Unless of course while he did all of that, a beautiful woman's head bobbed in his lap.

Again, he'd have to settle for the Chow Mein and beer for now.

With his belly continuing to grumble like an angry bear woken up mid hibernation, he pulled his big, beefy black Chevy into his parking spot behind his apartment building and turned off the engine.

Thank fuck the weather was starting to get better.

Spring had arrived and with it, longer days, warmer weather and the heady and sweet scent of blossoms on the air.

Always on the alert, even when he wasn't on the job, he scanned the parking lot as he climbed out of his truck, slammed the door, then opened the back cab to grab his beer and dinner.

He'd been in his apartment for nearly two years, and so far, nothing weird or nefarious stood out to him. It was a decent neighborhood, not too far from the University of Victoria, and the building was only about five years old. The majority of his neighbors were students, but nobody was rude, loud or obnoxious. And the odd party he heard didn't affect his sleep at all.

He'd been to hell and back during his time with Joint Task Force 2 and the special operative team he and his brothers joined after their stint in the Canadian Navy. He could sleep on a concrete floor next to a mosquito infested swamp while ten other men farted and snorted around him.

If he was tired, he could sleep.

He tossed his coat over his arm, grabbed his gym duffle bag, and heaved the Chinese food and beer out of the back seat of his truck, his keys in his teeth as he struggled and juggled all his shit before finally getting to the lobby door. He'd done this over a hundred times—this exact same scenario, you'd think he'd have figured out a more productive and affective way to carry all his shit.

He was just checking his mail when the sound of sobs and sniffling drifted down the hall, followed by the sweetest smell of wild strawberries and summer sunshine.

He'd always had the nose of a blood hound.

As a kid he could usually guess what his mother was making for dinner, simply by how she smelled when she picked up him and his brothers from school.

He glanced up from where he was scrutinizing a misaddressed letter only to come face to face with a beautiful tear-stained cheeks and red-rimmed eyes.

She was stunning, tall and lithe, with feminine curves, long auburn hair that coiled down just past her shoulders and wide, deep set hazel eyes. Eyes that were filled with sadness as tears continued to fall. She looked up at him, her nose red while her cheeks held a rosy glow.

Rex had never met this woman, but he'd seen her around the building—only from a distance however. She liked to run on the weekends, and he liked to watch her leave. She pulled off Lulu Lemons like no woman he'd ever met.

He wasn't sure how he could fix her, but he really wanted to try. Those weren't just tears from a sad movie or seeing a three-legged dog on the side of the road. Those were tears of pain. Heartbreak. Devastation.

He instantly felt the need to protect and find out what or *who* made her cry and make them pay.

It was just how he and his brothers had been raised.

If someone was in trouble or needed help, you helped them. Simple as that.

And right now this woman looked like she needed help.

"Are you okay?" he asked.

She shook her head, her breath catching as she struggled for words. "N-no."

"Is...is there something I can do to help? Do you need me to beat up an ex-boyfriend or something?"

She snorted a small laugh and wiped the tears from her cheeks and beneath her eyes. "Unless you're willing to kick the shit out of a twenty-six-year-old, hundred and thirty-pound chick, I don't think your muscles are needed."

"Uh..." he scratched the back of his neck, "ex-girlfriend?"

"No," she sniffed loudly, "I was fired!" And then before he knew it, she flung herself at him, collapsing against his chest and wailing.

His hand gently fell to her back, her small body feeling like a child's in his giant palms. Then he found himself petting her back and shushing her like he did his nieces and nephews when they fell and hurt themselves. "It's okay," he hummed, "it'll be okay."

He shifted her under his arm, and with his free hand grabbed his dinner, coat, gym bag and lastly—and most importantly, his beer —and he ushered her toward the elevator.

"Which floor are you on?" He asked softly. She didn't say anything but hit the number three. They rode in silence, and then when the door opened, he figured she'd take off, leaving him to his Chinese and microbrew, but he suddenly found himself inside this stranger's apartment, watching her take off her shoes and then slump onto her couch, clutching tissues to her nose.

"You know I've *never* met a nice girl named Odette?" she

sneered. "Not that I've met a ton or anything, but the few I've come across have been the biggest bitches ever. The one I went to grade school with was a mean girl—even two years younger than me she was still just a little witch—and this cow was no different. I worked there for one month. Did EVERYTHING right, went in early, stayed late, bought my own supplies, took work home with me. I spent three hours of my own time at home sewing up the holes in the canvas parachute and the big stuffed alligator that sits in the reading corner. I never asked for money for doing it. Never even told them I did it. I just *did* it. I was an exemplary employee, and she waltz's in as the new manager, is there for less than a week and she fires me because she thinks I'm after her job."

Rex watched her reach into her purse and pull out a brown paper bag, the neck of a booze bottle sticking out. She took a swig, then made a face, only to take another sip before offering it up to him.

"No, thanks." He grimaced. "I have beer."

She shrugged. "More for me." She tipped the bottle up and took another drink. "Have you ever met a nice Odette?" She caught a rather dainty burp with the back of her hand before offering him a crooked, slightly embarrassed smile.

He snorted. "Can't say I've ever met one. But I did date an Odessa briefly. She dumped me."

"Why?" Another cute little burp, followed by a hiccup.

"Ah, you know, same old story...she complained that my penis was too big." He grinned wide, hoping his joke made her smile.

Her sweet little rosebud mouth hung open for the briefest of seconds before she shot him a skeptical look, hiccuped again and then burst out laughing.

Good. His joke did the trick.

He widened his smile. She had a really adorable laugh and at least for the moment he'd managed to take her mind off her problems. Little did she know that it was actually a true story. Odessa *had* dumped him because she said his cock was too big. If he remembered correctly, she'd called him Godzilla dick, said he nearly split her in half and then tossed him out of her apartment in nothing but his boxers and his work boots.

Good thing she hadn't tried to sleep with his brother Heath. He might be the baby of the family, but he was also the *biggest*. She'd probably chase him down the hallway—at a cowboy waddle—claiming he was part horse.

He snorted hard at that thought.

He lifted his shoulder. "So...uh, can't you just get another job? What did you do?"

She mimicked his shrug before taking another sip from her brown paper bag of secrecy. "I was working full-time at this daycare and loving it. I got the job mid-year because another teacher went on maternity leave. It was perfect. Monday to Friday, eight until five. Then they hired a new program manager. She's younger than me and doesn't have near the experience with kids that I do. I've been babysitting since I was thirteen, then I nannied and babysat all through college. I got my preschool teacher certification as soon as I finished my teaching degree, because I knew that I wanted to teach little kids. I'm also certified to teach Montessori and special needs kids.

"But preschools aren't open as long as daycares and the money isn't as good—unless you're at a full-day Montessori, or a Waldorf, or some fancy private preschool. And I applied to those, but they had no available positions—or they said I was over qualified and they couldn't afford me. So I found this job. It's the best of both worlds. A preschool in the morning, then daycare for the rest of the day. I still get to teach—sorry, I still *got* to teach, past tense and all since I was canned." She sighed. "Canned from the perfect job by the biggest bitch on the west coast."

"Did you try telling them this?"

"*Pfft*," she scoffed. "I was still within my three-month probation period. They could fire me for having a hangnail if they wanted to."

He looked around her apartment, unsure what to say next. Her place wasn't quite the carbon copy of his, but it was close. Small, but open concept. A big bedroom, small but homey living room and kitchen, new stainless appliances and cramped bathroom.

Or maybe everything just felt cramped and small to Rex, but to an average sized person it was all completely normal. She'd decorated her place in a very feminine way, with soft oranges and light blues, a white overstuffed leather couch faced the television with a slew of throw pillows on it, while paintings of seashells and flowers in black plastic frames hung behind the couch. He saw very few photo frames, or pictures of people, except for a small black and white photo of what he could only assume was her as little girl, maybe six or eight, at the beach with a woman who he would guess was her mother.

"So what's your name?" she slurred, appearing to be bored, or perhaps just too upset to want to continue talking about her job, or lack there of. "I've seen you around the building a bit, you have the big black truck and the Pitbull puppy, right?"

He nodded. "My name is Rex. What's your name?"

"Lydia." She yawned. "Rex, eh? Like T-Rex."

He rolled his eyes. "I suppose."

"Is it short for anything? Like Rexworth, Rexwell or Rexington ... Rexthalomew?"

"Rexthalomew?"

She shrugged again. "Rexly?"

He simply snorted and smiled, ignoring the grumble off his belly. Man, she was drunk. "It's not short for anything."

She shrugged again. "Do you have any siblings?"

"Three brothers."

"And do they all have weird names too?"

"I personally don't think Rex is weird, but no, they don't. We all have one syllable names, though. Brock, Chase, and Heath. And our dad was Zane, and our mother is Joy."

She made an interested pout. "And what's your last name?"

"Hart."

She rolled his name around on her little pink tongue like foreplay. "Rex Hart ... Rex Hart," she murmured, cocking her head to the side and giving him a once over. "I like it." He continued to watch her, wondering when the bottle of whatever spirit she'd chosen to numb the pain, was going to hit her like the freight train it inevitably was and send her rushing to the bathroom to go and vomit. She tipped back her booze bottle then frowned when she realized it was empty. She set it down on her coffee table and her eyes darted to his case of beer. "So ... *sexy* Rexy, how are you going to make me forget about my jobless woes?"

He searched her face for a moment.

His belly grumbled again.

He needed to go let Diesel out.

He needed to shower.

He needed to fucking eat.

His bald head was covered by a black knit cap, but he pulled it off and ran his hand over his bare scalp. "I'm not in the habit of taking advantage of drunk women," he said slowly, choosing his words carefully. "So I can offer you some dinner—got enough Chinese food here to feed a family of six—but as far as *sexy* Rexy goes, I'm afraid I'm going to have to say 'no'."

Her face fell. "How old are you?"

"Thirty-six. How old are you?'"

"Twenty-eight." She pursed her lips. "So you reject me but then you offer me food. What the fuck?" Her anger was building, and without thinking his gaze flitted to the door. She saw him and he watched heat and embarrassment creep up her neck and into her cheeks.

Rex took a deep breath. Despite his hunger, and how drunk this woman was, he could already tell she was a good person. Anyone who wanted to work with kids usually was. He'd already come up with a few ways that he might be able to help her. "What kind of qualifications do you have?"

"I told you. I have a degree in education and preschool teacher certification, and a Montessori teaching certification. I've also taken courses to work with children with special needs and kids who are on the autism spectrum. I have my first aid certificate, a clear criminal record and a clean driving record. Why? Do you have kids that need watching?" She took a hard swallow before standing up and heading to her kitchen where she ran the tap in the sink and filled a small tumbler of water.

"I don't have kids. But I know a lot of people who do and they are looking for childcare. It might not be completely full-time, but it will probably be close. Unless this is just you licking your wounds and allowing your ego to heal and you could go out and get another similar job tomorrow. Seems to me you're crazy-qualified and people would be champing at the bit to hire you."

Her eyes formed thin slits as she stood in her kitchen, her hip cocked against the counter as she sipped her water. "It's hard to get hired in March for anything school related. I lucked out with covering that maternity leave. And I was looking everywhere before I got that job. It's slim pickings. And I don't want to teach older kids." She huffed. "Even if I did, the on-call teacher list is a mile long and the school districts have put a moratorium on hiring new substitute teachers."

Well that was shitty.

His gaze drifted to the furball that had wandered into the living room from the bedroom. A calico cat with bright yellow eyes sauntered toward him and rubbed it's back up against his leg. His mind immediately flew to Diesel upstairs and he knew that he had to get to him and take him out for a walk. Poor guy was probably pacing the living room with a full bladder.

He made to stand up, but the intense look in her eyes had him pausing where he sat.

"I can't figure you out, Rex Hart. You turn me down for sex, then you offer me food and now you might have a job for me? What's your deal, dude?" Her words were only slightly slurred for someone who should be struggling to remain vertical if she'd consumed that entire mickey like he figured she had.

Relaxing his shoulders, he stood up, reached for his duffle bag, beer, coat and dinner. "I'm in unit four-eleven if you want to come up and have some dinner. I need to get my dog out first. But I'm more than happy to share my food with you."

She stumbled back into the living room and squinted at him. She was either on the verge of passing out or puking. And even though he normally found drunk chicks to be nearly as intolerable as two cats mating at midnight, Lydia was a cute drunk. "What's your angle ... *Rexly?*"

Rexly? Oh lord.

His head shook. "No angle. Just a nice guy. Give me twenty minutes. I need to get Diesel out and then have a shower. I was just at the gym."

Her eyes struggled to roam his body in a new way—a way of appreciation—but she finally smiled. "Maybe."

He was not one for head games. If she didn't come up then so be it. More food for him. But if she was going to come up for dinner, she needed to get there before he ate it all.

His stomach made another noise of impatience and desperation. If he didn't get something in it soon it was going to start consuming him from the inside out.

"Am I not pretty enough?"

Oh good lord.

This was one of the things he hated most about drunk chicks. The self-deprecation and melodrama.

However, Lydia was an unusual case. She wasn't drunk simply

to party, she was nursing a wound. She'd been fired out of the blue from a job she loved. She deserved to wallow for a night with whatever spirit was her vice, and he needed to cut her some slack.

"Lydia, you're fucking gorgeous and you know it. Let's not play that game. But you're also drunk as fuck, and I don't fuck drunk chicks." He paused for a moment. "Unless we're already together and it's a consensual thing, but you know what I mean. But I'm turning you down for sex because we just met, you're drunk off your cute little ass and you're sad. The only kind of man who would tap you in that state is not a man worth knowing. If we have sex, I want you sober and knowing what you're agreeing to. If I fuck you, it'll be until you're damn near cross-eyed, and forgive a guy for wanting the chick awake and aware for something like that." He headed to her door and rested his hand on the knob. "I'm upstairs in four-eleven if you're hungry for Chinese food and want to know more about the job."

He went to open the door, but her voice had him pausing again. "I know what I want," she slurred.

He highly doubted that

She tossed her feet up on to the couch and slid down into a horizontal position, her eyes closing like a vintage doll when her head hit the orangy-pink chequered throw pillow. His mother would probably call that color *coral*.

Turning the knob, he opened the door but glanced back into her apartment. "Well, if you still want it tomorrow when you're sober you know where to find me."

But she didn't reply. A low and very unlady-like snore rumbled up from the sad little drunk woman on the couch, while her cat hopped up and snuggled up next to her leg.

Rex took a deep breath, closed the door again and stepped back into Lydia's apartment. The glass she'd been drinking water from was empty on her counter, so he filled it again. Then he opened up a couple of kitchen cupboards until he found a bottle of Advil. He shook out two tablets and carried them and the water over to her coffee table.

Reaching for the baby blue knitted blanket off the back of her couch, he draped it over her, making sure not to disturb the cat. "I hardly know you," he whispered, "but I don't like how sad you are. I'd like to help."

IF YOU'VE ENJOYED THIS BOOK

If you've enjoyed this book, please consider leaving a review. It really does make a difference.
Thank you again.
Xoxo
Whitley Cox

ACKNOWLEDGMENTS

There are so many people to thank who help along the way. Publishing a book is definitely not a solo mission, that's for sure. First and foremost, my friend and editor Chris Kridler, you are a blessing, a gem and an all-around terrific person. Thank you for your honesty and hard work.

Thank you, to my critique groups gals, Danielle and Jillian. I love our meetups where we give honest feedback. You two are my bitch-sisters and I wouldn't give you up for anything. But I'd also like to double thank you, Danielle. You helped me brainstorm this book and get past my mental block. Without you, this book would not be done. Thank you.

Kathleen Lawless, for just being you and wonderful and always there for me.

Author Jeanne St. James, my alpha reader and sister from another mister, what would I do without you? You get an extra special thank you as well for your very brutal, but necessary feedback on this one. Your help was so needed. Thank you.

Tara from Fantasia Frog Designs, your covers are awesome. Thank you.

My street team, Whitley Cox's Fabulously Filthy Reviewers, you are all awesome and I feel so blessed to have found such wonderful fans.

The ladies of Vancouver Island Romance Authors, your support and insight have been incredibly helpful, and I'm so honored to be a part of a group of such talented writers.

Author Cora Seton, I love our walks, talks and heart-to-hearts, they mean so much to me.

Author Ember Leigh, my newest author bestie, I love our bitch fests—they keep me sane.

My parents, in-laws and brother, thank you for your unwavering support.

The Small Human and the Tiny Human, you are the beats and beasts of my heart, the reason I breathe and the reason I drink. I love you both to infinity and beyond.

And lastly, of course, the husband. You are my forever, my other half, the one who keeps me grounded and the only person I have honestly never grown sick of even when we did that six-month backpacking trip and spent every single day together. I never tired of you. Never needed a break. You are my person. I love you.

ALSO BY WHITLEY COX

Love, Passion and Power: Part 1

mybook.to/LPPPart1

The Dark and Damaged Hearts Series Book 1

Kendra and Justin

Love, Passion and Power: Part 2

mybook.to/LPPPart2

The Dark and Damaged Hearts Series Book 2

Kendra and Justin

Sex, Heat and Hunger: Part 1

mybook.to/SHHPart1

The Dark and Damaged Hearts Book 3

Emma and James

Sex, Heat and Hunger: Part 2

mybook.to/SHHPart2

The Dark and Damaged Hearts Book 4

Emma and James

Hot and Filthy: The Honeymoon

mybook.to/HotandFilthy

The Dark and Damaged Hearts Book 4.5

Emma and James

True, Deep and Forever: Part 1

mybook.to/TDFPart1

The Dark and Damaged Hearts Book 5

Amy and Garrett

True, Deep and Forever: Part 2

mybook.to/TDFPart2

The Dark and Damaged Hearts Book 6

Amy and Garrett

Hard, Fast and Madly: Part 1

mybook.to/HFMPart1

The Dark and Damaged Hearts Series Book 7

Freya and Jacob

Hard, Fast and Madly: Part 2

mybook.to/HFMPart2

The Dark and Damaged Hearts Series Book 8

Freya and Jacob

Quick & Dirty

mybook.to/quickandirty

Book 1, A Quick Billionaires Novel

Parker and Tate

Quick & Easy

mybook.to/quickeasy

Book 2, A Quick Billionaires Novella

Heather and Gavin

Quick & Reckless

mybook.to/quickandreckless

Book 3, A Quick Billionaires Novel

Silver and Warren

Quick & Dangerous

mybook.to/quickanddangerous

Book 4, A Quick Billionaires Novel

Skyler and Roberto

Hot Dad

mybook.to/hotdad

Harper and Sam

Lust Abroad

mybook.to/lustabroad

Piper and Derrick

Snowed In & Set Up

mybook.to/snowedinandsetup

Amber, Will, Juniper, Hunter, Rowen, Austin

Hard Hart

mybook.to/hard_hart

The Harty Boys, Book 1

Krista and Brock

Lost Hart

The Harty Boys, Book 2

mybook.to/newyearssingledad

The Single Dads of Seattle, Book 6

Zara and Emmett

Valentine's with the Single Dad

mybook.to/VWTSD

The Single Dads of Seattle, Book 7

Lowenna and Mason

Neighbours with the Single Dad

mybook.to/NWTSD

The Single Dads of Seattle, Book 8

Eva and Scott

Flirting with the Single Dad

mybook.to/Flirtingsingledad

The Single Dads of Seattle, Book 9

Tessa and Atlas

Falling for the Single Dad

mybook.to/fallingsingledad

The Single Dads of Seattle, Book 10

Liam and Richelle

Hot for Teacher

mybook.to/hotforteacher

The Single Moms of Seattle, Book 1

Celeste and Max

Hot for a Cop

mybook.to/hotforacop

The Single Moms of Seattle, Book 2

Lauren and Isaac

Hot for the Handyman

mybook.to/hotforthehandyman

The Single Moms of Seattle, Book 3

Bianca and Jack

Doctor Smug

mybook.to/doctorsmug

Daisy and Riley

Upcoming

Torn Hart

The Harty Boys, Book 3

mybook.to/torn_hart

Lydia and Rex

Dark Hart

The Harty Boys, Book 4

Pasha and Heath

Quick & Snowy

The Quick Billionaires, Book 5

Brier and Barnes

Raw, Fierce and Awakened: Part 1

The Dark and Damaged Hearts Series, Book 9

Jessica and Lewis

Raw, Fierce and Awakened: Part 2

The Dark and Damaged Hearts Series, Book 10

Jessica and Lewis

ABOUT THE AUTHOR

A Canadian West Coast baby born and raised, Whitley is married to her high school sweetheart, and together they have two beautiful daughters and a fluffy dog. She spends her days making food that gets thrown on the floor, vacuuming Cheerios out from under the couch and making sure that the dog food doesn't end up in the air conditioner. But when nap time comes, and it's not quite wine o'clock, Whitley sits down, avoids the pile of laundry on the couch, and writes.

A lover of all things decadent; wine, cheese, chocolate and spicy erotic romance, Whitley brings the humorous side of sex, the ridiculous side of relationships and the suspense of everyday life into her stories. With single dads, firefighters, Navy SEALs, mommy wars, body issues, threesomes, bondage and role-playing, Whitley's books have all the funny and fabulously filthy words you could hope for.

DON'T FORGET TO SUBSCRIBE TO MY NEWSLETTER

Be the first to hear about pre-orders, new releases, giveaways, 99 cent deals, and freebies!

Click here to Subscribe
http://eepurl.com/ckh5yT

YOU CAN ALSO FIND ME HERE

Website: WhitleyCox.com
Twitter: @WhitleyCoxBooks
Instagram: @CoxWhitley
Facebook Page: https://www.facebook.com/CoxWhitley/
Blog: https://whitleycox.blogspot.ca/
Multi-Author Blog: https://romancewritersbehavingbadly.
blogspot.com
Exclusive Facebook Reader Group: https://www.facebook.
com/groups/234716323653592/
Booksprout: https://booksprout.co/author/994/whitley-cox
Bookbub: https://www.bookbub.com/authors/whitley-cox

Subscribe to my newsletter here
http://eepurl.com/ckh5yT

JOIN MY STREET TEAM

WHITLEY COX'S CURIOUSLY KINKY REVIEWERS

Hear about giveaways, games, ARC opportunities, new releases, teasers, author news, character and plot development and more!

Facebook Street Team
Join NOW!